smc

Tales from Stool 17
The Nigel Logan Stories #2
Trouble in Tate's Hell

By Kirk S. Jockell

DEDICATION

For Barbara "Barbie" Everett

Had she not taken a seat at our table to interrupt our dinner at the Indian Pass Raw Bar, had she not introduced herself to spark up a lengthy conversation, had she not introduced us to her husband Randy, who in turn, took me under his wing and treated me as if we had been friends forever, our initial visit to The Forgotten Coast very well could have been just another great vacation. However, it turned into so much more: A new life with new friends and family.
Love you, sis.

When them storms come rolling in,
we don't break but we sure can bend.
It's in the sawgrass and the mud,
we got salt … Yeah, we got salt … in the blood.
--Brian Bowen, *Salt in the Blood*

CONTENTS

ACKNOWLEDGEMENTS

Port St. Joe and Florida's Forgotten Coast are real. The same can be said of my dear friend Brian Bowen. He is a talented troubadour entertaining folks up, down, and across the Forgotten Coast. He's back as a character getting caught up with the likes of Nigel, Red, and all the shenanigans which make up the Stool 17 episodes. In addition to BB, there is another entertainer mentioned, Sailor Larry. He is the quintessential coastal serenading sailor, navigating his boat up and down the coast looking to entertain a willing ear. Last I heard he found a fair wind that took him down the west coast of the sunshine state towards the Tampa-St. Pete area, but he very well could have pulled anchor by now and headed towards Key West. Who knows?

Also real, but used fictitiously, is Michael Allen and Oyster Radio, WOYS 100.5 FM out of Apalachicola. Michael is the owner, main DJ, News Director, and all around gofer of the operation. The station remains my favorite on the radio dial and is continually pumped through my speakers. When I'm away, it is streamed via my TuneIn radio app or from www.OysterRadio.com. I recommend you listen too. While real, all the above are used fictitiously throughout these episodes.

When I published the first book, I didn't know what to expect. It's tough being an Indie writer. When you are out here alone, void of all the resources available to traditional published authors, it means you have to work even harder to create, polish, and publish your project. A project you hope will be well received by its readers. That said, I would like to personally thank everyone that purchased and read the first book. The kind words and positive feedback I received from new readers has been nothing short of amazing. Please know that each of you have served as a special source of inspiration as I worked on book two and as I continue to pen book three. Again, thank you everyone.

KIRK S. JOCKELL

Writing the second book was still hard, but it's getting easier. *Practice makes improvement.* But like the first book, I didn't do it alone. Words cannot express how grateful I am for the never-ending encouragement of my dear friends and family. I'm grateful for my father, Ron Jockell, and buddy, Brian Bowen. Both provided eyes and helped identify little bumps along the way. Special thanks go to Jan Lee. She had the final look. Her edits and contributions paved the way for a much better reading experience. And my bride, Joy, again shouldered the duties and responsibilities as the first reader of all my shitty drafts. Pouring over every word multiple times is tough, especially when you are personally connected to the author and project. But her keen eye and perspective, as both an editor and a reader, has again proven invaluable. Love you, baby. We did it again.

Prologue

It was late. Heavy fog blanketed the roads. The plain white van eased through the city connecting the orbs of light generated by the street lamps. He angled the rearview mirror down to keep a close eye on the body. His eyes shifted to the mirror. It was still there, curled up in the back, tied up and gagged. He said to himself, "Wake up, dammit."

A young girl was crying in the passenger seat. She wailed, "What are you going to do? You can't do this!"

He heard her voice and checked the rearview. Then he looked over and sent a silent message. *Yes … Yes, I can.*

He drove on through the gray haze. The fog was thick enough to need the windshield wipers from time to time. He was cruising around, trying to be patient, waiting for his guest to join him.

He again checked the rearview mirror. This time the body was gone. He snapped his head around, and there, only inches away, was the face of his guest staring at him. The face said with a smile, "What do you plan to do?"

He stood on the brakes and the van slid on the moist pavement without a squeal. It came to rest in the middle of an intersection underneath a flashing traffic light. He looked down to the passenger side floorboard. The big thick social studies textbook was still resting there. He reached and picked it up, clasping his fingers around it tight as he opened the door and got out of the van. There wasn't another soul around. The streets and sidewalks were empty. Then she appeared again.

She was standing on the corner under a street lamp. The light pierced through the fog and created enough of a glow around her that he could see the ribbon in her hair. She was still crying and shaking her head. He walked to the back of the van. He looked at her as he grabbed the door handle and opened the back of the van.

The body was still there, still tied up, still gagged, and still unconscious. He looked over at the little girl on the sidewalk. She didn't say anything out loud, but, like once before, he read her lips, *No. Please, no.*

He gave her an innocent looking smile and spoke to her, repeating the only words he ever uttered to her, "Don't cry for me." And he squeezed the big text book and crawled up in the back of the van. As he reached out to grab and close the door, he saw his father standing at the back of the van. He had his hand on the open door.

His father asked, "Does he deserve this?"

He looked out at his father, nodded his head and said, "Yes, sir."

His father smiled back and said, "Well, you've done nothing wrong then." Nodding towards his hand he said, "Do you know how to use that thing?"

He looked down at the 9mm Beretta in his hand. He examined it. He twisted it back and forth with a smile. Then he pressed the barrel against the temple of his unconscious guest. He pulled back and cocked the hammer. He looked at his father and nodded. The van door slammed shut with a bang.

Nigel was gasping and panting when his eyes opened. He was looking up, eyes fixed on the ceiling fan. He turned his head to look at the alarm clock. It was 0225 in the morning. He turned his head the other way. Candice was there, asleep. He turned back to the ceiling and remained still, waiting for his breathing to regulate. He closed his eyes and tried to relax.

It's been quite awhile since he last had the dream. For the most part, it was all the same: always the van, always the little girl, always his father. But there was something different this time. Then he remembered. It was the book, the textbook.

Nigel kissed Candice on the head and got out of bed. He went into the spare bedroom and pulled out an old seabag from the closet, stood it up on the floor. It was full of an assortment of items. He was pulling stuff out and digging around with his hand. Then his fingers found a corner. He worked his fingers around an edge and got a grip. He pulled and worked it out and around until it was free of the bag. He still had it.

It was an old social studies textbook from his childhood, one he failed to return to his teacher many years ago.

He stared at the cover. When he started flipping through the pages he heard, "What you got there, sweetie?"

It was Candice. He didn't say anything. He couldn't. He swallowed hard as only one thing ran through his mind: *How was he going to tell her the truth?*

The Note

It was poised to be a busy and entertaining night at the Forgotten Coast Shrimp and Raw Bar. The place was getting an early start and buzzing with the usual mix of tourists and locals. The out-of-towners were there for the food and karaoke on the porch. The locals were there for their usual cocktail hour and socializing. Nigel was rolling down Gulf County Road 30A. He turned onto 30E, Cape San Blas Road, to pick up Red and Trixie. The three of them were also heading to the raw bar for the local scene.

They all started to pile into Nigel's truck. It would be a bit of a squeeze, but not too uncomfortable. And besides, the raw bar was just a few miles away. Yet, even though it would be a short trip, they still had to contend with Trixie's incessant complaining. Red chuckled as Trixie lamented, "I just can't believe it," she said before taking one last hard drag on her cigarette. She dropped it on the ground and drove the little butt deep into the oyster shell drive with her shoe. "The world has gone to shit. When's the next full moon?"

"What the hell's happened to get you all worked up, Trix?" Nigel asked jumping behind the wheel.

Trixie jumped in the middle as Red climbed in and closed the passenger side door with a snicker.

Trixie said, "What happened? It's more like what hasn't happened?"

"Huh?" asked Nigel.

Trixie said nothing.

Nigel looked at Red and asked, "What is she talking about?"

Red smiled and said, "She's a little upset with the moral compass of our Gulf County neighbors. They've been on their best behavior. It's bad for business."

Trixie chimed in, "Not one. Not one damn call in almost two weeks. Not a breaking and entering, not an assault and battery, no simple DUI, not even a simple jaywalking charge! Nothing! It's killing me and I'm overstocked with T-shirts. Our society has just gone to shit."

Trixie owns Trixie's Freedom Bail Bonds. And everyone that uses her gets a free international orange T-shirt that says *I got My Freedom at Trixie's*. Her phone number is on the back. It's not uncommon to see them worn about the county.

Trixie commented one last time as they rolled into the raw bar parking lot, "Bunch of damn goodie two shoes!" Neither Red nor Nigel said anything in hopes the subject would go away.

Nigel eased his way around the building. The likelihood of finding a good spot to park with the place so crowded was slim, but it's always worth a quick look. If he couldn't find anything, he'd let Red and Trixie jump out then find a spot on the side of the road.

As they came around the back corner of the building, Red said, "Look at that ass." He was pointing at a huge Hummer, an H3 with Illinois tags. Its driver had pulled in crooked to create space around his vehicle, taking up two spaces. "What a jerk!"

Nigel said, "I guess he thinks he's special." Nigel gave the Hummer a closer look and said, "Wait. Yeah .. I saw the same vehicle earlier today on Reid Ave. He did a similar thing by parking over a dividing line. He took up two spots."

Red asked, "You got some paper and a pen handy?"

"No. Why?"

"I'm leaving this idiot a note."

Trixie said, "Let it go, Red. We don't need the trouble." With her husky laugh she concluded, "And besides, I'm out of your size T-shirts."

Nigel said, "Yeah, Red. It isn't worth it. There is plenty of parking out on the street."

Red mumbled in personal protest as Nigel started to roll towards the street. The timing couldn't have been better. Nigel came to a stop to let another truck out. It opened up one of the most coveted spots at the end of the porch. Nigel smiled as he backed into the primo parking spot. Throwing on the emergency brake, Nigel said, "See, Red. Everything worked out. We got one of the best spots after all."

Climbing out of the truck Nigel said, "I do live a charmed life."

The place was packed. Folks were everywhere. Nigel dropped the tailgate while Red got each of them a fresh beer from the cooler in the truck bed. Nigel has an old, five-foot porch swing cushion he keeps in the truck. It fits great across the tailgate to make for comfy, front row seating.

Nigel evaluated the karaoke talent. It was worse than bad. The worst of the singers so far, he felt, was a toss up between two drunk girls trying to sing *Before He Cheats* by Carrie Underwood and an old guy wearing socks with his flip flops trying to sing both the Sonny and Cher parts of *I've Got You Babe*. Neither was pretty to watch or hear. Most of the singers were following an old karaoke philosophy, *if you can't sing good, sing loud*. It never works.

The best of the night were two adorable little girls. They both looked to be about four or five years old, friends on vacation together. Horrified and scared to death, they held their microphones and stared at the crowd. They stood there, never singing a single word or note as Taylor Swift music played in the background. It was perfect. When they were done, Nigel hollered, "Let them do another one." But that wasn't going to happen. The girls couldn't wait to get off the porch and seek refuge behind the legs of their smiling mothers.

Nigel reached behind him to get a fresh beer. As he looked over his shoulder, he noticed Red in the parking lot having words with some stranger. Nigel remained a casual observer until the guy shoved Red. It wasn't a big push, but it was enough to get Nigel off the tailgate.

"Hey, buddy!" Nigel directed towards the guy. "You need to check your ass right now and think about what you're doing."

The guy turned to see Nigel heading their way. The guy wasn't huge, but he was a pretty good size, bigger than Red, not quite as big as Nigel. The guy had a pretty little brunette with him, a wife or girlfriend perhaps. She stood to the side and didn't appear happy with her partner. "Just get in the car and let's go, Larry," she said.

The guy looked at her and said, "Hell no. I'm not going anywhere until this guy apologizes." The guy was pointing at Red.

Nigel said, "I don't know what this is all about. And to tell you the truth, I don't care. But the lady here is giving you some damn good advice. I'd take it, if I were you."

"Screw you!" the guy said.

Nigel threw his hands up in the air, shrugged his shoulders with a smile and said, "Okay, pal. If that's what you want. But I got to tell you right now, you ain't going to like it."

The guy didn't catch on, but his lady friend did as she turned and covered her mouth to giggle. Her reaction told Nigel she wasn't his wife. No wife would have let a stranger talk to her husband like that. Wives have too many *stand-by-their-man* qualities. This gal didn't have any.

Nigel looked at the guy and asked, "What's going on? What's this all about?"

The guy said nothing.

Nigel looked at the girlfriend and asked, "Miss?"

She shrugged her shoulders and said, "I don't know."

Nigel said to anyone that would listen, "Would somebody please tell me what's going on here?"

He looked at Red and Red pointed to a piece of paper in the guy's hand. At the same time someone on the porch was beginning the second most obnoxious karaoke song ever, Journey's *Don't Stop Believin'*, second only to *Love Shack* by the B-52s.

Nigel reached over and snatched the paper from the guy's hand and looked at it. It was a note. He read it and said, "Oh, hell. You're the Hummer guy."

The guy said nothing.

Nigel read the note again, smiled and asked, "Red, did you write this?"

Red said, "I didn't do it. Nobody saw me do it. Nobody can prove I did it."

"That guy saw you do it, asshole." The Hummer guy pointed over towards the porch; a guy was standing there watching. Trixie stood next to him.

"That guy? That guy standing with the woman?" Nigel asked.

"Damn right. He saw the whole thing. I was asking around and that fella pointed at this joker." The guy was thumbing towards Red.

Nigel looked over at the man standing next to Trixie. Trixie was smiling. Nigel looked back down at the note, then to the guy and asked, "So tell me. Is it true?"

"Is what true, asshole?"

"The note," asked Nigel. "Is there any truth to the note?"

The guy said nothing.

Then Nigel said, "Ah Shit. There's no sense asking you. I wouldn't get an honest answer anyway."

Nigel turned to the girlfriend, waving the note and said, "Miss, maybe you can tell me. Is there any truth to this?"

She said, "I don't know. I haven't seen it."

Nigel motioned for her to come his way and she did. He handed her the note. She read it. Her eyes widened as she looked back at the big Hummer, then back at her boyfriend. Again, she covered her mouth and giggled as she shook her head no and turned away laughing.

Nigel took the note back, turned back to the guy. He got close so most couldn't hear. Nigel kept his hands at his side, leaned in and said, "According to your girlfriend. You ain't worth a ..." Then Nigel got even closer and whispered the rest to him.

The Hummer guy shoved Nigel hard. Nigel almost slipped to the ground but maintained his balance. He straightened up and gave Trixie a smile and a look that spoke volumes. *You are going to owe me, big.*

He walked back towards the guy saying, "You really don't want to do this."

Hummer guy landed a right hook to Nigel's jaw and he went down to the ground. It was a good lick. Nigel stayed down rubbing his jaw. The man standing next to Trixie intervened. "That's enough. That's enough," he said as he walked towards the scene. He looked down at Nigel. "Are you okay?"

Nigel said nothing as he stood back up nodding his head.

"Nigel. Do you want to press charges?"

This got the attention of Hummer guy. "Charges?" he said. "What the hell you mean charges?"

Nigel looked at Hummer guy and said, "Yeah, that's right, dickhead ... charges. Meet Deputy Miller of the Gulf County Sheriff's office," Nigel paused for a breath and added, "asshole."

Nigel looked over at Trixie who was still standing on the sidelines. Trixie sent Nigel a wink. Nigel kept looking at Trixie as he spoke to the Deputy, "Yeah, seems like pressing charges is the thing to do."

Deputy Miller turned towards the guy and said, "Hands behind your back." The deputy produced a set of handcuffs from the back of his belt and clasped them on.

Hummer guy started to protest but shut up as soon as Deputy Miller went into the routine of reading him his Miranda rights.

As the deputy was leading the Hummer guy away, Red asked, "Hey, deputy. Can we get him for double parking too?"

The deputy stopped, looked at the Hummer, laughed and said, "No, Red. I'm afraid not."

"Dammit," mumbled Red.

Trixie stopped the deputy and stuffed several business cards in the shirt pocket of the Hummer guy. "Call me. I'm open 24 hours."

The guy didn't say anything.

Then Trixie said, "You look like you wear an extra-large shirt."

"Yeah," the guy said.

"No problem," said Trixie. "I got plenty of them."

The Hummer guy said, "Huh?" as the deputy took him away.

Trixie walked over to Red and Nigel. Hummer guy's girlfriend joined them. Nigel said to her, "I'm sorry, miss. It didn't have to happen that way."

The brunette stuck her hand out, "The name is Cindy, and don't worry about it. Larry can be a real shit."

Nigel took her hand and said, "Pleased to meet you. Is there anyplace we can take you? Maybe drop you off wherever you are staying?"

"Later maybe, unless you are going now."

Nigel looked at Red and Trixie. They both shook their heads. They weren't ready to leave yet either.

"That'll be fine. That's my truck over there. The cooler in the bed has beer. Grab one and hang out for awhile."

She nodded and walked that way. Nigel watched as she got a beer and made herself at home on the tailgate.

Trixie said, "So I got to ask. What did the note say?"

Nigel grinned as he handed her the piece of folded paper.

Trixie opened the note and read the words; *I hope you fuck better than you park.* Then she laughed and said, "Red! I love your crazy ass!"

The Awakening

Perhaps the only thing worse than being bullied is being the bully when the bullied have had enough. It doesn't work out that way in most instances, but isn't there something sweet about it when it does?

Nigel Logan was small for his age. That changed later in junior high school when his growth hormones woke up and took charge of his body. *The metamorphosis of puberty.* In grade school, however, he was smaller than the rest. He was quiet and withdrawn, even meek. He didn't fit in with the popular crowd, and he didn't make friends. He had a calm personality which made him susceptible to being picked on and bullied. He was an easy target.

He wasn't alone. Other kids fell into the same category, but those kids often migrated towards each other for protection. *Safety in numbers.* Nigel wasn't like that. He was a loner. He kept to himself and that didn't bother the other kids one bit. By Nigel not seeking refuge in the company of others, it made him an even bigger, easier target. He drew attention away from the others. And because of that Nigel took the brunt of the bullying.

Nigel was smart, much smarter than most of the other kids. He hated going to school, though, to that school anyway. Perhaps, if he didn't have to suffer the company of those that harassed him, it would be different. He didn't know; he had nothing to compare it to. School had always been that way.

The bullying was usually only simple, mean-spirited antics: name calling, pushing and shoving, knocking books out of hands, and slinging paperwork off desks. His mother always told him, "Ignore them, dear. Don't give them the satisfaction of knowing they are getting to you." She would go on to say, "Once they realize their bullying has no power over you, they will stop. It won't be fun anymore."

His Mom was wrong. It didn't stop. And on that second day of the new school year when Nigel started the fifth grade, the bullies stepped up their game.

There were several folks that picked on Nigel. Most were wannabe bullies. They were weak kids themselves, guys that had been bullied around much of their own lives and now sought strength and confidence by bullying others. Of all the bullies, Stan Hornbuckle was the worst. Hornbuckle had two buddies he ran with: Mark Teller and Chris Thompson. Teller and Thompson were not as tough as they let on. They were mean enough, but they found their strength and bravery from the company of Hornbuckle. They were followers, not leaders.

Stan Hornbuckle was bigger than his schoolmates. No surprise there; he flunked the third grade twice. He wasn't smart, but displayed promise as an exceptional athlete. The two school coaches liked him for that. He came from a broken family and lived with his mother who had little to no positive influence on him. His father, who drank too much, walked out on him and his mom for a Waffle House waitress when he was six. His summers and every other weekend were spent sneaking smokes, raiding his dad's liquor stash, and loading up on all the hash browns he could eat. Not a bad arrangement to his line of thinking.

It was the first gym class of the school year. For fifth graders it meant changing into actual gym clothes and sneakers, a transition from running around and playing in blue jeans, dress shirts and some variety of loafers. The gym clothes were typical: blue shorts and a white T-shirt with the words "Property of Eastside Elementary Athletic Department" printed on the front. All the kids were excited to wear them. It meant they had achieved a new and desired status. *The big kids at school.*

Gym is always a favorite for kids. The teachers are fans too, especially if they have students later in the day. *Wear their little asses out, Coach!* That was the mantra coming out of the teacher's lounge.

The coaches always did their best to beat the little bastards down. And they knew of no better way to burn off the excitement of a new school year than with a game of dodgeball. It was the perfect game to suppress the high energy that comes with preadolescence.

Young Nigel Logan was no athlete. It wasn't that he was weak and uncoordinated. He just never took to sports. He couldn't throw a baseball to save his life. He damn sure couldn't hit a softball, not even a slow lobbing one. And basketball was always a nightmare, he couldn't dribble, hit a layup, and he may have been the only kid in school--girls included--that couldn't hit the rim from the free throw line.

When it came time to pick teams, he was usually the last kid standing, but that didn't bother him. He understood. He wouldn't pick himself to be on a team either, unless it was dodgeball.

Dodgeball was different. Nigel liked dodgeball. He may have been small for his age, and lacking in certain athletic skills, but the one thing Nigel Logan could do was dodge. Nigel had lightning-fast reflexes and speed. He was quick, very quick.

The coaches had a habit of picking their favorite athletes as team captains. They called Bobbie Bain and Jamie Smith to duty. With great ceremony the two faced off for the traditional coin toss to determine who gets first pick. With dodgeball, the coin toss meant much more. It wasn't just to see who picks first. It was to see who gets Nigel Logan. He was almost always the first guy picked for a dodgeball team. Only a moron would pick someone else.

Nigel was sitting on the bleachers when Jamie Smith yelled out his name. Nigel got up and moved through the crowd to stand behind Jamie. He smiled when his captain offered a high five when he stepped up.

It was the typical back and forth, each captain snagging favorites until both teams were full. Then both teams faced off on the makeshift court set up by the coach. Nigel looked across the floor at Bain's team and saw Stan Hornbuckle and his two cronies, Teller and Thompson. Smith stepped up to Nigel and asked, "You ready?"

Nigel nodded his head.

The captain patted him on the back and said, "Same strategy as last year. Okay? Leave the offense to us."

Nigel said nothing again and nodded.

They were playing by standard dodgeball rules. There were four live balls at any given time. If you get hit by a ball, you're out. If you catch the ball, the guy doing the throwing is out. Plain and simple.

Nigel's athletic abilities being what they were, there would be no throwing or catching of the ball. Those two things were up to the rest of the team. It was too risky. Nigel was to do one thing: move, distract, and stay alive. DODGE!

With both teams set, the coach blew his whistle and the game began. The coach stood around and watched from the sideline. After a couple of minutes, he disappeared to his office for a fresh dip of Copenhagen and a peek at this month's *Hustler* magazine.

In dodgeball the number of players on each side drops fast, especially in the opening minutes of the game. This game was no different. It's like shooting fish in a barrel. Nigel was quick as ever, gliding out of the way of the big red balls that came towards him. He had to be careful; Stan Hornbuckle set out to collect Logan as a trophy, a confirmed kill. Every time Hornbuckle got his hands on a ball he focused on Nigel, but every throw was a frustrating miss. There were so many balls being thrown at Nigel he didn't have the luxury of time to see who was left on each team. As the players thinned out, he counted a total of seven folks still on the floor. Four were on the other side and three, including him, remained for his team. Jamie Smith was still alive and he yelled, "Keep moving Nigel, keep moving!"

Nigel said nothing, sliding to the floor as a ball thrown by Hornbuckle whizzed by his body. Nigel rolled on the floor and watched the ball glance off the hip of a teammate attempting to jump out of the way. *Dang!*

Nigel sprang to his feet and moved to the baseline to stand with his captain. It was now two against three, Nigel and Jamie against Hornbuckle, Teller, and another guy. Jamie had a ball in his hand. He gave a double pump towards Hornbuckle, but redirected his throw towards Teller who was preoccupied with his own throw at Nigel. At the precise moment Teller's throw skipped under Nigel's jumping feet, Jamie's throw creamed the side of Teller's head. He never saw it coming. A great kill.

The even matchup brought several exciting exchanges between the teams. Smith's team was at a severe disadvantage. While Nigel could dodge, his orders were clear. No throwing or catching the ball. This made it more like two against one and a half, and those odds brought about the demise of Jamie Smith.

Two balls were flung at the captain from different directions. Jamie caught one of the balls eliminating one opponent. But, while diving to get out of the way, the other ball thrown by Hornbuckle clipped his foot. Jamie Smith was out. It was Nigel's team now, leaving only him and Hornbuckle to face off.

Hornbuckle went around and collected all the loose balls and lined them up at midcourt. With a ball and a smile, Hornbuckle started his offensive. There were a few close calls, but Hornbuckle couldn't land a single shot. And with Nigel uninterested in collecting loose balls, each shot would bounce off the back wall and roll towards Hornbuckle. The barrage of shots continued, and with every missed shot, the cheers in support of Nigel and the laughing towards Hornbuckle grew.

Nigel welcomed the support. That had never happened before. For once, he had schoolmates on his side, cheering. He also sensed the fury and frustration building inside Hornbuckle. Every miss brought him extra laughter and embarrassment.

Nigel was feeling confident. It was a new sense the crowd gave him and it felt good. As he continued to duck, jump and dodge every oncoming shot, he decided to do something that, up until that moment, went against his quiet nature. He would go on the offensive and taunt his opponent.

It started with a little smile of sarcasm as a ball flew by his head. The crowd loved it and began to jeer and taunt Hornbuckle. *Come on Horny, what's your problem? Hey Hornbuckle ... You throw like a girl!*

Hornbuckle was furious and threw a ball that didn't even come close. Nigel stood on the baseline glaring at his enemy. For once, Nigel Logan was in control. He smiled big at his opponent, stuck out his chin and waved his fingers out in front. *Bring it on!*

A flurry of shots from Hornbuckle flew in Nigel's direction. They all missed. Hornbuckle gathered up all the balls again and again stood at midcourt. Nigel was opposite him on his baseline creating as much distance as possible. Then to everyone's amazement, Nigel spoke. "Stan. What's your problem? I'm getting tired. Really tired and bored."

"Shut your mouth, Logan."

"No. I won't. I'll make you a deal. I'll stand right here. I won't move out of the way when you throw. If you hit me, you win. If you miss, I win. I'm, betting you'll miss."

"You'll stand right there?"

"Yep."

"You won't move?"

"Nope ... I promise not to dodge the throw. Like I said ... I'm figuring you'll miss."

"That's a deal."

Hornbuckle picked up his last ball. The crowd got behind Logan. They started a chant: *Horny's gonna miss. Horny's gonna miss. Horny's gonna miss.*

Hornbuckle was boiling mad and Nigel took his final stance. He kept his feet together and placed his arms tight behind his back to decrease the target area. Nigel closed his eyes, lowered his head, and waited.

Hornbuckle smiled, and as he started his windup said, "You're going to wish you never made this deal, Logan."

The windup was huge. Hornbuckle twisted big with the ball way around his back. He unwound and grunted as he released the ball which was now rushing, straight as an arrow, towards Nigel's head.

When Hornbuckle grunted, Nigel opened his eyes and lifted his head. The ball was already half the distance. As the ball closed in, its speed seemed to increase. The Hornbuckle throw was true. He would not miss. Nigel had to think fast and all that came next came in a flash. *Use your speed Nigel. Use your speed!* Then words came that he had always heard. *Keep your eye on the ball, Nigel. Keep your eye on the ball.*

Nobody expected what happened next, not the crowd, not Stan Hornbuckle, not even Nigel Logan. It all happened so fast. The ball was getting closer and closer, a missile to the head. He never blinked and at the last second he used his speed to release his arms and hands from behind his back. Then he blinked, but not until the ball was in his hands. He caught it in front of his face. Point to Logan. The game was over and the schoolmates on the sidelines went crazy with cheers and laughter.

Not accustomed to losing in such an embarrassing fashion, Stan Hornbuckle became even more furious. He couldn't stand being at the center of jokes and ridicule. He had to save face, so he resorted to the only tactic he knew.

Hornbuckle looked to the crowd and found both Teller and Thompson. They both looked out of place, not laughing, embarrassed for themselves and their fearless leader. Hornbuckle yelled, "Get him!" And they did. Nigel tried to avoid their grasp but couldn't, not two against one. They tackled him to the floor as Hornbuckle walked over to join them.

Helpless, Nigel could do nothing. He flailed and kicked the best he could, but, in the end, Hornbuckle was able to collect Nigel's gym shorts and underwear as a prize. He stood smiling in triumph as he held the garments high in the air, a sign of victory. Nigel was naked, except for his t-shirt and sneakers.

The crowd made a huge circle leaving Hornbuckle and Nigel in the center. And once again, a Hornbuckle attack on a smaller, more vulnerable target worked in his favor. The students were now laughing at Nigel, not Hornbuckle.

Nigel stood there horrified, trying to cover himself. He had never felt such humiliation. He rotated in slow motion, looking at his schoolmates, looking for help, looking for the support that only an instant earlier was on his side. It didn't come. The group stood and laughed at him. They all laughed. All but one.

There was a new girl at school that year, and she was appalled. Her fingers were pressed tight against her open mouth. She couldn't believe what she was witnessing.

Nigel was now even more embarrassed. The new girl, he thought she was so pretty. He hated that she saw him like that. He removed one of his hands from his crotch and tried to grab his shorts, but Hornbuckle jerked them from his grasp. The crowd laughed even louder. Nigel tried again, this time with both hands, exposing himself. The result was the same except the crowd laughed even more.

Nigel heard the excited words, "Stop it! Just stop it! You're so mean." Nigel turned his head. It was the new girl. He didn't even know her name, and she was standing up for him. Tears began to fill his eyes. It was too much for him to bear, so he ran for the locker room, leaving the laughter in his wake. He passed the coach who was strolling into the gym to check on the commotion.

When the coached realized Nigel didn't have any gym shorts on, he spit his Copenhagen juice into a Royal Crown soda bottle and said, "Nigel. Son ... What do you think you are doing?"

Nigel never responded. He sprinted to the locker room to get dressed, absent his underwear.

Still horrified, Nigel was almost dressed. He was putting on his shoes as the other classmates started to filter back into the locker room. The laughter had been replaced with a quieter more serious tone. Everyone ignored him, but he didn't care. He wanted out of there and left the locker room running towards the gym exit. He couldn't get out of there soon enough. That's when the coach stopped him at the door.

"In my office, Logan."

"I can't," said Nigel. "I'll be late for my next class. I have to go."

"No you won't," said the coach. "In my office. Pronto!"

Nigel opened the office door and saw Stan Hornbuckle. The sight of Nigel made his eyes open wide. Nigel stood in the doorway until the coach pushed him into the office and shut the door. The coach walked around, sat at his desk, opened up his middle drawer and retrieved his custom-made paddle from underneath a short stack of *Hustler* and *Penthouse* magazines. He laid it on the desk.

While Nigel was alone and getting dressed, the coach interrogated the gym class to figure out what had happened. No one would say anything, except one person, the new girl. She spilled the beans. Nobody else was brave enough.

"So, Nigel," the coach asked. "Is it true? Is what I'm hearing what actually happened?"

Nigel looked at Hornbuckle who looked back, his eyes filled with hatred. Nigel looked back to the coach and said, "I don't know. What do you mean?"

Frustrated the coach reached in his back pocket, pulled out his can of Copenhagen and grabbed a pinch. Looking at Nigel, he worked the dip between his cheek and gum, getting it in place with his tongue. Then he said, "Nigel, I don't want to screw around here, so I'm going to ask you straight." He reached for his bottle and brought it to his lips and spit. "Did Teller and Thompson hold you down, while Hornbuckle pulled your shorts and underwear off?"

Nigel said nothing, but turned to look at Hornbuckle. Hornbuckle returned a look. *I'll kill you.* As his nemesis glared at him, Nigel thought about how humiliating it was to stand there naked on the gym floor, circled by his laughing classmates. The shame and embarrassment shifted to madness.

"Well, Logan," said the coach. "Let's have it. I don't have all day. What's your story?"

What's your story? That was a stupid question. Coach knew the truth. The new girl didn't have any reason to lie.

No. The coach knew damn well what had happened. He only wanted to force Logan to squeal on Hornbuckle. Not so much to punish Hornbuckle, but to make Logan out as a weak tattletale in front of the entire class. Then Logan remembered advice given to him by his father. Rule number one on growing up: *Never rat out your enemy.* Rule number two: *Save your anger for later, for when they don't expect it.*

It wasn't until then that Nigel understood what his father had taught him. Before then, they were only words. Then his mind took him back to the gym floor to relive the laughter, the pointing, and the jeers. His shame was now gone. For the first time in his life, he felt the adrenaline of anger.

The coach lost his temper. He picked up his paddle and slammed it down on his desk. "Nigel! Goddammit! Come on now. What happened? Did he or did he not..."

"No!" Nigel said, interrupting the coach. Logan looked at Hornbuckle to exchange looks of hatred and contempt. Logan's eyes burnt a hole through those of his adversary. It was a look Hornbuckle wasn't expecting. It even made him wince a little. Logan spoke to Hornbuckle's face. "No coach. He didn't touch me. Nobody did."

The coach shook his head in disbelief. "Then why were you running around naked in the gym. Explain that for me."

Logan turned to the coach and with almost the same look he had given Hornbuckle, Logan said, "I don't know. I can't remember."

The coach picked up his spit bottle and made a deposit and said, "Get out of here! Both of you!"

Logan was the first one out the door. The rest of the class bunched up around the office door trying to hear what was going on. Logan stopped and looked around at his schoolmates, and then he pushed his way through the crowd and stormed to the door.

Moments later Stan Hornbuckle emerged from the office with a smug look of victory. Thompson and Teller knew everything was alright. They met him at the door with celebratory cheers as they slapped high fives to each other.

The rest of the week was somewhat uneventful for Nigel. Some continued to giggle and laugh at him about the gym incident, but he ignored them. After a few days, it was as if it didn't happen. Memories and attention spans are short, even in elementary school.

There was a change, though, in the way Nigel carried himself. That fateful first day in the gym had made a difference in him. From the spectacular dodgeball victory, to the vulnerability and humiliation that followed, a profound shift had come over Nigel. The last thing he wanted was trouble. He just wanted to be left alone. Yet, where before he would avoid confrontations with the school bullies, now his encounters with them didn't give him cause to seek alternate routes or shrink in his desk. For some reason, he was no longer afraid.

It was Friday, the last day of the first week of school. The other kids couldn't wait for it to be over; neither could Nigel. The sooner it was over, the better. Monday would be the start of a new week, a chance to begin anew. Make it through that Friday without incident; that's all he wanted. But you don't always get what you want. And Nigel's case was no exception.

All the classrooms at Eastside Elementary had their own water fountains. It was an experiment to keep thirsty kids from leaving the classroom in search of a sip, which was nothing more than an excuse to roam the halls. However, what school administrators didn't figure on was how much water kids would drink between and during class. The copious amounts consumed created an urgency to piss, another great excuse to roam the halls.

It was third period, social studies, and the teacher was Mrs. McDaniels. She seemed old, but all adults do to grade school kids. She was a large woman, not so much fat, just big. She had huge hair of bouffant style, jet black except for a sizable gray streak that ran through the middle. Most of the kids called her *skunk*, which was disrespectful. But, truth be told, it was the first vivid image that popped into your head when you saw her.

Even Nigel's dad couldn't help himself. One day, while he was being picked up after school, Mrs. McDaniels was walking across the parking lot to her car. Nigel's dad said, "Holy shit! It's Pepe Le Pew." Nigel smiled. It was funny, but he liked Mrs. McDaniels and her social studies class. It was one of his favorites, and he enjoyed learning about places he hoped one day to visit. Little did he know, the Navy would later take him to many of the places he only read about in her class.

The line at the water fountain was long. Nigel waited his turn. Mrs. McDaniels was not yet in the room. He heard a slight commotion coming from behind. He turned to see Stan Hornbuckle cutting in line right behind him. It made him nervous, but for some reason it didn't last long.

When it was Nigel's turn to drink, he walked up and pushed the button. He liked this water fountain best over all the others. The water always seemed colder.

He watched as the spout made a sizable arch into the sink. Nigel never drank from the stream of water. He always cupped his free palm and placed it under the falling water and drank from his hand.

Nigel was drinking when he heard, "Hurry up, punk!" Nigel ignored the demand. Then he heard, "I said, hurry up!" The next thing Nigel knew his face was being pushed down into the water and sink. Hornbuckle held him there for a spell before letting him up.

As usual, the antics of Stan Hornbuckle aroused laughter amongst some in the room. With his face and hair now wet, Nigel turned to look at his classmates and frowned. Before, he didn't care if they laughed at him, but now he did. He'd had enough of being laughed at. He continued to ignore Hornbuckle and went back to the fountain for another drink.

The water filled his hand beyond the brim, cold water overflowed into the sink. Nigel waited until he heard the angry voice of Stan Hornbuckle another time. At that precise moment, Nigel turned and slung the cold water into the face of his enemy. Hornbuckle was caught off guard. The water hit and he let out a girlish hoot.

In that brief moment, Nigel was taken back to his dodgeball victory. As it was then, the classroom laughter was being directed at Hornbuckle. Logan smiled.

Embarrassed, the flustered Hornbuckle said, "You little punk!" and shoved Nigel hard, back into the water fountain and wall.

Logan said nothing. He sprang off the wall to attack. Hornbuckle met him with a hard punch to the stomach. Nigel went to the floor, but he didn't stay down long. He used his speed and agility to get back up and charge the larger Hornbuckle, driving his shoulder into his torso and wrapping his arms around his middle.

The arms and fists of Hornbuckle were free, and he used them on the side of Nigel's head. Nigel dropped to one knee, but sprang up again. Hornbuckle gave a huge shove that spun him around, landing his chin and face on the desk of another classmate.

Nigel stayed draped, face down on the desk. Blood began to pour from his mouth. He had bitten his tongue on impact. Nigel was slow to raise himself from the desk. He was staring down at the social studies text. It was one of the larger books students had to tote around. It was wide, thick and heavy, full of glossy photos from all around the world. A pool of blood was growing on the festive German dancers that made up the cover. As he looked at his own blood, his anger grew. Then he heard a gasp and a sniffle. Nigel looked up. It was the new girl. Her name was Melissa Hunter. She stood up for him in the gym earlier that week. He learned her name just yesterday but had not yet spoken to her. Not that he was much for talking to girls. He was still mighty shy about such things. But, there she was; it was her desk he had landed on. She was crying, a look of pity on her face.

Nigel turned his head and saw Hornbuckle standing right behind him, hands at his side, and palms out, fingers waving ... *Come on.* Nigel turned back to look at the book. Blood was still dripping from his mouth. The taste of his own blood made him shake and pushed his anger closer to the edge. He looked at Melissa. Her lips quivered as she read his mind. Her head slowly shook a gesture of no.

Nigel looked at her. Fear had kept him from speaking to her, but now there was none. Through his lips and teeth that were awash with blood, Nigel said, "Melissa, please don't cry ... Not for me."

She continued to shake her head no, now a begging gesture. Her eyes fell and watched his fingers and hands draw tight around the bottom of the big text book. He squeezed it with all his might and clenched his teeth even tighter. Melissa looked back up to Nigel and saw something in his eyes. Before she could say anything, Nigel launched himself off the desk, twisting around with the book lagging behind.

Stan Hornbuckle never saw it coming. He was clueless until he spotted the picture of the earth that made up the back cover, but by then it was too late. It whipped around too fast and with too much force. Logan planted Greenland or Iceland squarely to Hornbuckle's face, shattering his nose and backing him against the windows.

The classroom filled with gasps and screams. Nigel's bloody mouth paled in comparison to the blood that now poured from the nose of Stan Hornbuckle. It was everywhere. The corner of Logan's eye caught Mark Teller taking a step in. Logan didn't hesitate. He spun around and landed a solid blow to Teller's left ear which sent him to the floor. Logan turned around and found Chris Thompson, but Thompson backed off two or three steps. He wasn't going to play.

Logan turned back to find Hornbuckle. He was still up against the windows, stunned, bent over at the waist holding his nose and trying to wipe his eyes now awash with the automatic tears such a blow brings. Logan didn't hesitate. He reared the text book way back and swung for the fences connecting to the head which was presented like a baseball set atop a T-ball stand. It was another huge shot that sent Hornbuckle to the floor.

There were more screams from the girls and the boys were now shouting: *Fight! Fight! Fight!* Logan dropped the book and crawled on top of Hornbuckle and commenced to hitting his bloody face with his balled up fists. He never stopped swinging. Even when Mrs. McDaniels arrived and pulled him off his target, he continued to swing at the open air. She calmed him down enough that he stopped.

Mrs. McDaniels was kneeling on the floor, holding each of Logan's arms and looking into his eyes. He was shaking all over from the adrenaline rush he was feeling. She looked around the room at all the blood. She saw Hornbuckle being helped up by Chris Thompson. Mark Teller was sitting against the wall holding his head. Mrs. McDaniels said, "Get those two to the school nurse, immediately."

She continued to assess the room and couldn't believe what she was seeing. Above all, she couldn't believe who was involved. Nigel Logan was one of her favorite students. If she hadn't seen it with her own eyes, she wouldn't have believed in a million years he was capable of such. She knew different now.

The teacher looked into his eyes again and said, "My dear, Nigel. Oh ... Oh my God. What have you done?"

Logan said nothing, just looked through her with a cold, blank stare, still trembling.

Calvin Wheeler was the principal of Eastside Elementary. He was a good man, fair in his dealings with students and a good administrator. Logan sat outside his office door waiting for his dad to arrive. Stan Hornbuckle, sat across from him, waiting for his aunt.

He held a bag of ice on his face and nose. A bad case of raccoon bruising had already set in around the eyes. Logan said nothing, just looked at his enemy enjoying his new look. Stan tried to intimidate Logan. He said, "Logan, you jerk. You broke my nose. You broke it. I can't wait to get my hands on you."

Logan stared back, eyebrows raised and said nothing. *Really?*

It was in that moment Stan Hornbuckle knew he no longer had an emotional or psychological advantage over Nigel Logan. It was over. He couldn't be intimidated or scared any longer. His fear was gone. And after what happened in the classroom, it didn't take long for everyone in the school to know that Nigel Logan wasn't the same kid they used to know. He had changed.

Mr. Wheeler gave Nigel's father some general information about the fight over the phone, but he didn't go into great detail. When Nigel's dad came into the office, he took a look at his son half expecting to see him beaten up. But all he saw was a small swollen mouse on his cheek and a look of shame. He was embarrassed his dad had to leave work and come to school. Then Nigel's dad turned and saw Stan Hornbuckle. He did a double take then spoke to his son, "Crap, son! Did you do that?"

Nigel said nothing as he looked at his father with apologetic eyes.

Nigel's dad looked back at Hornbuckle and said, "Damn!" Then the principal's office door opened.

"Mr. Logan, I presume." They shook hands. "Calvin Wheeler. I'm the principal around here. Please, come into my office." Logan's dad looked at his boy as he walked into the office. They went in and closed the door. The principal's secretary was also in attendance, already sitting in a chair by the wall.

Wheeler said, "This is Ms. Culpepper. She's my assistant."

Barbara Culpepper was an icon at Eastside Elementary. She was in her seventies and had more continuous time working in education than anybody else in the district. She taught for more than twenty-seven years before ending up in the front office where she has broken in more than her fair share of new principals. Needless to say, she's seen a lot over the course of her career.

They all shook hands and Nigel's dad said, "Please, call me Howard. Nice to meet you both." Then he pointed over his shoulder with his thumb and said, "My son. Did my son do that to that boy?"

Both nodded their heads, Ms. Culpepper with a slight grin on her face.

Mr. Wheeler said, "He was provoked."

Nigel's dad said nothing.

"Howard," Wheeler started, "for good reason we've never had the pleasure of meeting. You've never had a need to come in. Nigel is a good boy and a better student. His grades are exceptional and the teaching staff loves him. We've never had an ounce of trouble." The room got quiet for moment. "Until today."

Howard Logan asked Wheeler, "Who is the other boy and how old is he? He looks a bit seasoned for grade school."

"His name is Stanley Hornbuckle. He's a bit older than your typical fifth grader having been held back on more than one occasion." Then he crossed his fingers and waved them in the air saying, "But we keep the faith and hope we'll be able to move him along to better things."

That was a kind way of saying we're tired of fucking with this shit-bird. Let him be somebody else's problem for once.

"Hornbuckle," said Nigel's dad. "I've heard the name. He's somewhat of a bully I gather."

From her chair, Ms. Culpepper injected without hesitation, "A worthless little bastard is more like it."

Principal Wheeler cut her a look and she responded, "Well ... it's true, Calvin, and you damn well know it. In all my years, he's one of the worst I've seen."

Wheeler looked back at Logan's dad and said, "What she means is ... he does have what you might call, a reputation."

Ms. Culpepper rolled her eyes into the top of their sockets and shook her head. She was the practical administrator while Wheeler played the part of political principal. No doubt, he needed her a lot more than she needed him. He could go tomorrow. She'd go when she was damn well good and ready.

Wheeler explained to Logan's dad everything he knew. He spoke about the week's earlier events in the gym and how Nigel had been humiliated in front of all his classmates. This was news to Howard Logan; Nigel had failed to mention the incident. The principal did his best to describe the events from earlier that afternoon, about how Nigel snapped and used a text book to punish the Hornbuckle boy in a brutal fashion. He went on to say again that Nigel had been provoked. But he also had concerns for the manner in which Nigel responded. It was so violent and he seemed to have little or no remorse.

Howard Logan said, "Well ... When enough is enough..." He let the rest fall off to an awkward silence.

"True, so true," said Wheeler. "We just wish he had handled it a little differently."

"What do you mean?" Logan's dad asked. "Squeal? Come tattle? Are you saying he should have come forward and said, 'Stanley is being mean to me. Make him stop.' Exactly what good would that have done?"

Ms. Culpepper jumped in before Wheeler had a chance to comment. She said, "Nothing. We could have given Hornbuckle detention. Maybe bang all the erasers after school. But that would have only fueled the fire, made him worse."

Principal Wheeler gave his assistant another cutting look but she dismissed it and went on to say, "No, Nigel did the right thing. Kids have a knack for policing themselves, putting each other into their place. That's what our sweet Nigel did today. Truth is ... I wish that he, or someone else, had done it a lot sooner. I don't think Nigel will have to worry about Mr. Hornbuckle anymore, and Stanley may think twice before sizing up another target. No ... Nigel did us all a favor today. He did what most of us around here would have liked to have done ourselves."

Wheeler was beside himself, "Ms. Culpepper! Please! Now that will be enough!"

She rolled her eyes again and said nothing. Not because he had told her to, but because she didn't have anything else to say.

Principal Wheeler said, "Mr. Logan. It has certainly been a long week and an even longer morning, especially for Nigel. Please, go ahead and take him home for the rest of the day. Let him rest. I'm sure next week will be much better."

Howard Logan walked out of the office, got his son's attention and motioned with his head. *Time to go.* Nigel got up, walked up next to his father and they left together down the hall towards the big double front doors. Principal Wheeler and Ms. Culpepper stood at the office door and watched as Howard Logan placed his hand on his son's back, a comforting gesture.

Principal Wheeler said, "Barbara, I still can't believe that Nigel was capable of what he did today. It just blows my mind. He's always been such a good student. A good kid."

Ms. Culpepper looked back at her boss and said, "Calvin, he is a good kid, always will be. I know that deep inside my core. It's just..." she paused for a beat or two. "Now, he's changed, awakened. He's not the same boy and, now ... I don't believe we have any idea what he's capable of. Greatness, I expect."

Nigel and his father were quiet all the way back to the car. Not a word was spoken, even during the drive to the house. In the driveway, Nigel turned to his dad and said, "I'm sorry, Dad."

"Sorry for what?" his dad replied.

Nigel didn't say anything.

"Let me ask you something, son?" They both turned to look at each other. "This Hornbuckle kid. Did he deserve it? Did he have it coming?"

"Yes, sir."

"Well ... If he had it coming, you didn't do anything wrong. You understand that don't you?"

"I guess."

"Always remember that, son. Those that get what they deserve get it by no fault of others. You did nothing wrong."

You did nothing wrong. Nigel would hang on to those words of wisdom from his father for the rest of his life.

The Juice

Nigel Logan was on I-10 heading west, five miles under the speed limit with Chum Bucket, his 17-foot Key West center console, in tow. He turned on the stereo, but the station his truck was always tuned to filled the cab with loud static. He was still out of range of Oyster Radio. Sometimes, when the weather is right, he can get lucky that far north. Unwilling to surf channels he threw in a Brian Bowen CD. As *Shoulda, Coulda, Woulda* started to play, he settled into the drive recounting the events of the weekend.

He was returning to Port St. Joe after spending a couple days behind the camera shooting the Mug Race over on the St. Johns River. It claims to be the world's longest river race regatta. It is hosted by The Rudder Club, an old and longstanding sailing club nestled on the banks of the St. Johns River just outside Jacksonville, FL.

The event is huge and taken serious by some, not so serious by most. This mix of determination attracts a large number of participants. Most do it just for fun and the party. It's an annual classic and local tradition. Close to 100 boats were in attendance.

Unlike a normal sailboat race where the boats are restricted to a small contained area or circle, the Mug Race starts at one end of the river and finishes at the other. Nigel would be running *Chum Bucket* all the way down the river. With this in mind, he knew he would be chasing boats as much as shooting them, so he decided to round up some help once he got into town. Jacksonville is a Navy town, so he wasn't worried about finding someone.

The cell phone of Navy Chief Marvin Snellings must have shown Logan's name on its screen. After only three rings, he answered, "Well I'll be damned. Look what crawled out of the woodwork. You son of a bitch. Where in the hell have you been hiding?"

Logan hadn't seen or spoken to Marvin since he retired and left Norfolk. Except for a brief phone encounter with his old girlfriend, Kim Tillman, he hadn't been in contact with any of his old shipmates since leaving service. That was a sad fact to swallow, so it felt good to hear Marvin's voice.

Marvin Snellings is a Chief Boatswain's Mate, a BMC, and a damn good one. He rules with an iron fist, and delivers results. They served together on Logan's last ship, and even before his retirement, Nigel knew Marvin had orders to the USS Samuel B. Roberts, an Oliver Perry Hazard class frigate out of Mayport, FL.

"Hey, brother. Not hiding, just going. It's good to hear your voice. I want you to meet me for dinner. I have a proposal for you."

They met at Singleton's, a local dive with exceptional seafood. It's a favorite on the historic waterfront of the Mayport Village. It lacks curb appeal, and unless you knew what was inside, you wouldn't be inclined to stop. That was how Logan felt years ago when he was first stationed on the base. It took a shipmate to drag him in there to discover what a jewel it was. What's not polished is more than made up for by good food.

Mayport isn't what you would call a tourist town, so there was a time when Singleton's only serviced the locals and sailors stationed there. That all changed when that Food Network fella showed up and featured the place on *Diners, Drive-Ins and Dives*. Now folks commute from all the surrounding beachfront towns to eat there. *Shit! There goes the neighborhood.*

Nigel found his old bar stool open, his favorite in the joint, so he grabbed it. Marvin mounted the one next to him. Nigel slapped the bar to get some service. The bartender, a tough-looking old bird turned and looked their way with a scowl. Skinny, but muscular, she had bad mascara and green eye shadow that clashed with her faded and stained Bobby Sherman T-shirt. A long gray ponytail ran down past her belt. "What's it take to get some damn beers around here?" Nigel barked.

The second she saw his face and heard his voice, the scowl and the fight in her gritted teeth fell away to a smile and she rushed over for a hug. Sally has been serving up drinks and beers at this bar for years. She doesn't forget a face and she damn sure didn't forget Nigel's. She dashed over, leaned her elbows on the bar and grabbed the cheeks of his face. She smiled and looked deep in his eyes and said, "You sure are a sight for sore eyes." Then she moved in closer and gave him a big kiss on the lips. Nigel kissed her back with equal enthusiasm, thinking the entire time; *Winstons ... probably three packs a day ... some things never change.*

Sally came up for air and Nigel said, "It's good to see you too, Sally. How you been?"

"Hell. Nothing changes. Same goddamn shit, different day."

"What about you, Sugar?" Sally straightened up, took on a more serious deportment. "I hear we had some trouble in Norfolk. Is all that taken care of now?"

"Everything is fine," replied Nigel. "Not even worth mentioning." Which was Nigel's way of saying, *Enough of that. Let's move on to something else.*

Sally examined and studied Nigel's eyes. Nigel looked at her face with a smile. Then she smiled back and said, "Fair enough! What are we having?" Then she shook her head and spoke to the ceiling, "Stupid question, Sally. Coors light, draft, squeeze of lime." she looked back at Nigel to find both thumps up.

Placing his hand on Marvin's back Nigel said, "And bring my friend whatever he'd like."

Sally's lips went from being pursed to a straight line and back to being pursed again before saying, "Nigel. Is this on your tab, baby?"

"Why sure. Of course."

"Good!" she said looking at Marvin. "Because this scallywag has a tendency to be a little late on settling his."

Marvin said, "What? How much could it be? You know I'm good for it."

Nigel laughed and said, "Don't you worry, Miss Sally. We'll be all settled and square before we leave."

Sally brought the beers.

They exchanged notes about all that had transpired over the last couple years. Marvin told him about reporting for duty on the Roberts. His new Deck Department was more screwed up than a soup sandwich. It took the whole first year for him to clean up the mess. He said, "Funny how expectations and a little heavy-handed discipline will bring out the best in people."

Marvin told him about his most recent divorce. "Number four is out the door and I'm done with it," he said. "Marriage that is. It's just a pain in the ass. Can't find anyone that's any good at it."

Number four's name was Judy, a bombshell beauty that was no stranger to the Navy. Marvin hooked up with her soon after arriving at Mayport; a month later they were hitched. It was a train-wreck marriage lasting a mere seven months. It ended one day when Marvin arrived home a little earlier than expected from a Mediterranean cruise, like six months earlier. Marvin explained in graphic detail the events of that dreadful morning.

He started. "You just ain't going to believe this shit, Nigel."

"Do I need a fresh beer?" Nigel asked. "Don't answer that." Logan turned, found Sally and ordered another round. When the frosty mugs appeared, he took a little sip and said, "You have my undivided attention."

Marvin explained that his ship was scheduled to deploy with the USS Ronald Reagan battle group, a typical six-month Mediterranean cruise. They were to shove off at 1000. Like most Navy wives, Judy drove him to the ship that morning. She gave him a long hug and a wet kiss goodbye, and she stood by the car and watched her sailor cross the brow of the ship and step aboard.

Not long after morning muster it was rumored that difficulties had developed in the engine spaces. The Chief Engineering Officer, or CHENG, and his Gas Turbine System Techs were having a hell of a time getting the propulsion systems to ignite. At 1100 they announced the sea and anchor detail would be pushed back to 1800. At 1400 it was announced they would try again in the morning. The Engineering Department would be burning the midnight oil.

Such a delay isn't good for a ship, especially its captain and CHENG. One of the most embarrassing things for a skipper is to be scheduled to deploy and not be ready. Sending the message to the battle group commander that *his* ship wasn't ready had to be a painful thing to do. Kiss the next promotion goodbye.

Marvin got a ride back to his house and that's when things got interesting. Marvin said, "Nigel, I literally walked in the front door, and, before I could hang up my ship's cap, I heard a familiar rhythmic chant coming from inside the house. 'Oh Baby! Oh Baby! Oh Baby! Yes! Oh Baby! Oh Baby! Oh Baby! Yes!'"

"None of this sounds good," said Nigel.

"Ya think? Just wait. It gets better." Marvin took a sip of his beer and continued, "I walked through the house and followed the sounds to the kitchen. I stood in the doorway and watched. They were so caught up in what they were doing; they didn't even notice I was there. Judy was naked on the breakfast table, her knees up around her ears. And this guy, some Hospital Corpsman from the clinic, is standing at the edge of the table banging my wife. The whole time Judy kept perfect time screaming, 'Oh Baby! Oh Baby! Oh Baby!'".

"Marvin. I'm so sorry. What happened?"

"No big deal. What can I say? I had my cell phone out videotaping the whole thing and when I caught a break between her moans and groans, I got their attention. I said, 'Hey Dude! Don't think you're some porn star. She's faking. You know that, right?'"

Nigel said, "Oh Shit!"

Marvin laughed and said, "That's exactly what he said."

"What about Judy? How did she take it?"

"The whole thing was no big deal to her either. When she saw me standing there, she was pretty calm about it all. She acted like, *Oh well. Caught again.* Then she looked up at her lover and said, 'Oops. Sorry 'bout this baby. I'm afraid this ain't your lucky day.'

The guy tried to jump back and run, but his dungarees were wadded up around his ankles. He fell straight to the deck. That's when I walked around the table, grabbed him, and introduced myself."

"Again, I'm sorry."

"Don't be. I got it out of my system that day. The poor guy. He was a pretty boy too, but a broken nose and three missing teeth later, not so much. And I got what I deserved, I guess. What is it we tell our sailors? 'Don't rush into anything.' I should practice what I preach."

Nigel said nothing.

"Enough about me, brother. Tell me. What's going on with you? Last I remember, you just up and disappeared after your retirement. Poof! You were gone. Not that I blame you, given the circumstances."

"There isn't much to tell," said Nigel.

Nigel told him about how he found Port St. Joe and the Forgotten Coast. Marvin was shocked beyond belief when Nigel told him about the little house he was renting. He said, "Damn, Nigel. A house? You're getting all domesticated and shit."

Nigel hadn't thought about it in those terms, but perhaps Marvin was right. He was settling down. On active duty, he always expected to be moving around. It comes with the territory. But now, at this stage of his life, the thought of leaving Port St. Joe has never entered his mind. All of a sudden his extended stay in Port St. Joe was more than just a long stopover. He looked at Marvin and said, "Funny you put it that way, but yeah. I guess you're right. Port St. Joe is home now."

There ... He said it. *Home*. And the sound of the word coming out of his own mouth made him realize how much he couldn't wait to get back. He was already missing the place and his peeps.

With all the catching up out of the way, Nigel got back to business. Marvin jumped at the opportunity to drink Nigel's beer and serve as his personal coxswain for the weekend. Marvin said, "Sounds great! When do we start?"

Again, some take the Mug Race much more serious than others and others not at all. Boats of all makes, models, and construction make it out for the event. There were even a couple homemade sailing thingies that had no business leaving the garage, much less getting underway. One Catalina 22 had, they counted them, seven big Igloo coolers on deck and the crew was tossing beers to the other boats. Of course, Marvin had to do a close flyby and get a couple from them.

Nigel couldn't have asked for a better driver. He explained what he needed with regard to angles and lighting from the sun, and Marvin was spot on keeping the camera in the heat of the action. Nigel's problem with Marvin, if you could even call it a problem, was his persistence in giving one boat, a catamaran, more attention than the others.

Nigel tapped on the windshield and got Marvin's attention. Pointing across the river, Nigel demanded, "Over there. Now!"

He spotted a gorgeous boat, an Alberg 37. She was aptly named *American Beauty*, a stunning classic designed by Carl Alberg. The breeze had built and she was all powered up. She heeled with grace, her port deck inches away from being awash. Her shiny gold lettering stood out against her slick black hull. You couldn't have asked for a better photo opportunity.

Marvin circled the boat and gave Nigel every possible angle. The lighting was perfect and frame after frame was fired off. Nigel was so excited to see such as gorgeous boat under sail he must have collected fifty or sixty images. He couldn't wait to get back home to study them in post production.

Nigel is a sucker for old sailboats. Their sleek sheer, low freeboard, and long overhangs are dead sexy. *MisChief*, his own boat, is a 1966 Vanguard 32, another fine example of classic design, a real head-turner. But, even Nigel would admit, she pales in comparison to the boat he now had framed through his lens. This boat deserves to be in a museum.

Marvin said, "Nigel. Are we done here?"

Nigel lowered his camera and watched as *American Beauty* powered away on a close reach. He was thinking, *Just beautiful.* Her proud skipper knew she was getting extra attention and waved back. Nigel couldn't help himself and fired off a few more frames. Then he took a sip of his beer and said, "Yeah. I'm done here." And before Nigel could point out the next boat to shoot, Marvin announced, "Okay, we're heading back towards that catamaran."

"Really?" Nigel asked. "We've already been over there twice."

Marvin ignored him and headed that way until the boat, a NACRA F-18, was headed straight towards them. Marvin throttled down, stopped the boat and waited. Again, Marvin gave Nigel a great camera angle with perfect lighting. It was a sight, even for the third time. The boat was flying a hull under the power of its patriotic American flag spinnaker. The crew was all grins and so was Marvin when he yelled, "Get that shot! Get that shot!"

It was a great shot. The boat was fast, it was on a starboard tack, its port hull slicing through the water. Both her crew, two gorgeous blonde females of college age were hiked out in perfect form under trapeze. Nigel found them in his viewfinder and zoomed in. Their backs were tight and straight. Their flat tanned bellies rippled with muscle. Their faces smiled again for the camera. Frame after frame was clicked off as they whizzed past *Chum Bucket*, buck naked, not a stitch. The only thing covering their well tanned bodies was a pair of ZHIK sailing sneakers, sunglasses, and their hiking harnesses. The girls blew them a kiss as they sailed by. Nigel lowered his camera and smiled back. Marvin said, "Thank you, sweet Jesus."

Nigel said nothing.

"And this is what you do for a living?"

"Yup," Nigel said. "It's like this every time I go out." He lied.

"Who do I have to kill to get a gig like this?"

The words hadn't been out of his mouth one second before he realized it wasn't the smartest thing to say. Nigel could tell by the look on his face; he regretted it. Marvin's eyes apologized, but Nigel played it off pretending not to make the connection. Then Marvin said, "Sorry 'bout that, brother. I didn't mean to..."

Nigel feigned a confused look, stopped him in mid-sentence and said, "Huh? Sorry about what?"

Marvin looked at Nigel, shook his head and smiled. Then he said, "Hey! You're going to share a few of those with me right? The guys in the goat locker are never going to believe this shit." He paused for a beat or two and said, "Hey! You don't suppose one of them cuties might be interested in becoming my number five, do you?"

Nigel smiled and said, "Marvin, either one of those girls could be your daughter."

"Ah, true brother, true. But that's just it. They're not, they're SEDs."

"SEDs?" I asked. "What the hell is a SED?"

"SED. S.E.D. Somebody Else's Daughter."

"You're not right," said Nigel. "You're a real sick bastard."

Pointing at himself with both index fingers he grinned and said, "Helloooo. Sailor."

Nigel turned down his street, smiling and laughing as he finished reminiscing over the last couple of days with Marvin. But as he pulled up in front of his little cottage, his smile dropped. He was expecting to see the lawn mowed. The grass where he backs his boat was already too high, and with his being gone all weekend, it was the perfect time for Luke McKenzie and Maxine to drop by and knock out the yard. That had been the arrangement anyway.

Old man Luke McKenzie is a crusty fella, another retired Chief Petty Officer, a brother in anchors. He has a small lawn care business to supplement his pension and social security. Maxine is his partner, a beer-drinking, television-watching goat that does all the trimming. She's a four-legged weedeater with a beard.

Nigel played a part in helping Luke recover Maxine awhile back after she went missing in what was labeled by local law enforcement as "The Great Kid-Napping". Funny to most, not so much to Luke.

Now they are tighter than ever, and Luke never lets Maxine out of his sight and vice versa.

Backing the boat into its spot he mumbled, "Dammit, Luke."

As he walked around to unhook the boat from the hitch he spotted Ms. Eleanor Johnson walking her little mutt, Fred. A goofy name for a dog, but there you have it. She's in her early seventies, well kept for her age and has never married. She lives by herself a couple blocks away and around the corner. He got her attention, "Ms. Eleanor, good afternoon. Have you seen Luke around? He was supposed to cut my grass while I was gone."

"Now that seems to be the million dollar question, doesn't it?"

"Huh?" Nigel grunted.

"Luke's whereabouts. I've been looking for him too. That rascal," she said. "Haven't seen him since last Friday. When you catch up to him, tell him to swing back by the house. I have a little something for him."

"A little something, huh?"

"Never mind that. You just tell him, ya hear."

"Yes, Ma'am."

He finished putting the boat away and grabbed his camera gear and headed to the back door. He stopped in his tracks and tilted his head to the side. *What the...* He took a couple steps closer; it was a huge rat, dead on the back stoop, flies swarming around its carcass. It looked and smelled like it had been there a couple of days, maybe since Friday when he left for Jacksonville. "How in hell did you get there?" he said aloud. Then it dawned on him. He knew what it was and why it was there. It was a trophy.

Nigel turned his head from side to side and looked around the yard. He smiled when he found him. He was sitting tall and proud by the fence. "There you are. Did you do this?"

The big grey tabby cat sprung to his feet and ran to Nigel. It drove its head into his ankles and rolled over on its back looking for praise and maybe a rub on the belly.

"Why in hell did you put it on my steps, you old cat." The big tabby comes around from time to time, quite often here lately. Nigel knelt down, rubbed its head and ears as he looked around wondering. *Who do you belong to? You're too friendly to be a feral stray.* Then he spoke to the cat like it might answer back, "So tell me ... Who's your owner? Just where in the world do you belong?"

41

The cat started to squirm a bit and Nigel stopped rubbing. The cat flipped to its feet and darted off around the corner of the house. Nigel made a casual effort to follow, but when he got to the corner, the cat was gone. Then he turned, looked back at the rat and went for the shovel. *Damn cat.*

His eyes opened an instant before the alarm went off. Even with only three and a half hours of sleep, his feet swung around and hit the floor. Nigel's personal reveille is 0400. Some old Navy habits won't budge, bend, or break. He rubbed his face and smelled the coffee that just finished brewing. A coffee maker with a clock and preset timer is one of life's simple pleasures.

He grabbed a cup and went into his office. Plenty of post-production and editing work awaited him from the images he took at the Mug Race. Twenty-five or thirty images into his work, a new image popped up on the screen. Nigel busted out in uncontrollable laughter, so loud he startled himself. After he pulled himself together, he was left shaking his head and smiling.

Nigel Logan doesn't take pictures of people, he finds portrait work boring. He agreed to shoot a wedding once. Never again. Dealing with humans as photography subjects just sucks. *Pose like this. Pose like that. Chin up. Let's do something with your hair. Dude, really? Your fly is open.* You don't have that in sailing photography. Any boat with an apt skipper just does it; they both know what to do. The guy behind the camera just has to be in the right position at the right time.

He smiled as he was looking at a perfect photo. It was of the girls on the catamaran, hiked out and smiling. He had several of them to edit, but he figured he would leave this one alone. Marvin photo bombed the shot jumping in the corner of the frame, big grin from ear to ear, tongue out, and thumbs up. Nigel decided to have it printed, framed and sent to Marvin for his pleasure, his own personal memento from the weekend.

At 0900 he took a break. He got up from his computer, poured the last of the coffee from a second pot and walked out on the front porch. It was already getting steamy. He looked at his lawn. *Dammit.* He grabbed his phone out of his pocket and dialed Luke McKenzie. No answer.

A few minutes later his phone rang. He looked at the screen. It wasn't Luke. It was Candice.

Nigel doesn't have a girlfriend, but if anyone resembled that description, it would be Candice Turner. She manages the Reid Avenue Bar and Bottle Shop and has been trying to land Nigel as her regular beau since the day he blew into town on *MisChief*.

He had just sailed in from Key West. After cleaning up, he went ashore. Her bar was the first he found and she became the first person he met. They spent the afternoon and evening together and he ended up getting a little over served. To end the night, she kept him out of jail when trouble later developed between him and one of her three ex-husbands.

Nigel looked at his phone and smiled at her name and picture on the screen. They see each other on occasion; things haven't yet developed to Candice's liking, but she is patient. He answered the phone.

"Good morning, Sunshine," he said.

"Oooo! Sunshine, huh? Well, back at you," she said. "When did you get back to town?"

Nigel doesn't like to chit chat on the phone, but he likes the sound of her voice, so he made an exception. He plopped down on his porch swing and they talked about his trip and her busy weekend at work. It was a nice conversation then she asked for a *sort of date*. "Let's have some dinner tonight?" she asked.

"Don't you have to work?"

"Yes, and that sucks, but you could pick us up something and we could eat at the bar. Call it a *working date*. That would be okay, wouldn't it?"

Nigel thought about it for a moment and realized that he did want to see her. He had missed her while he was gone. He said, "Sure. That sounds fine. Does sevenish sound alright?"

"Perfect," she said. "Who knows, maybe we'll both get lucky later."

"Candice," he said. "Knock it off."

"A girl can always wish, can't she?"

"Okay ... Enough of that. I got to go." Before saying goodbye he asked. "By the way, have you seen Luke?"

"Nope," she said. "He and Maxine usually come in every night, but he was a no-show this weekend."

"Okay, thanks. See you tonight."

"Can't wait."

He ended the call.

Later he strolled into Gloria's Salon and Spa. The visit was twofold. He was feeling a little bushy and needed a trim. Plus, if there was ever a place to get the inside scoop on what was going on, it was at Gloria's.

The top of the door raked across and rang the bell as he walked in. Gloria's head popped out from behind a curtain. "Come on in and have a seat, sweetie. I'm almost done here. As soon as I get her under a dryer, I'm all yours."

Nigel nodded with a smile and took a seat.

Minutes later Gloria walked up and took him by the hand and guided him to a warm chair. Across from him were three older ladies under dryers, each reading through magazines: *Cosmopolitan*, *Redbook*, and *Guns & Ammo*. "You look busy today," he said.

"Oh, dear. It's been crazy, but I never complain about too much business. What do we need today, the usual?"

"Yes. Clean me up. I'm feeling a bit shaggy."

Gloria pulled out her scissors and comb and went to work. A master of hair sculpting, she's also quite versed at collecting human intelligence. She began her normal line of questioning about how he's been, what he's been up to, stuff like that. They talked about everything, but Nigel knew it was just a matter of time before she would delve into the more important stuff: his love life. "So how are things going between you and Miss Candice?"

Nigel rolled his eyes and said, "Do I really have to answer that? I'm pretty sure you've already been briefed on the subject."

With her gorgeous southern accent and guilty smile she said, "Things can change from day to day, my dear. And a woman in my position can't rely just on the few sources that are available. I'm always looking to stay abreast, and there is nothing better than confirmation from the horse's mouth."

Nigel said nothing.

Gloria continued to trim his mop for a couple of minutes before stopping to say, "Nigel, sweetheart. Can I give you a little advice?"

He said nothing because he knew he was going to get it whether he wanted it or not. He smiled as she continued. "You really need to get off the fence. She really is the sweetest thing and absolutely adores you. Y'all are perfect for each other."

Nigel thought about those words for a beat. *Perfect for each other.* In many ways, Gloria was right. Over time he had come to know and appreciate Candice more and more. She was easy to be around, and aside from her tendency to be a bit forward and assertive, she wasn't demanding. But being perfect for each other is a two-way street. While Nigel has come to understand and grown closer to Candice, she and everyone else in Port St. Joe knew very little about Nigel, especially his past and previous troubles. Troubles he wasn't completely free of.

"Gloria," Nigel said. "What if I said, you may be right. That Candice is perfect for me."

She smiled back. Her expression said, *Really? You're doubting me. Of course I'm right.*

Nigel went on to say, "But what if I'm not right for Candice? I like her a lot, but I'm not all I appear to be. Let's just say, I have baggage. Baggage I would hate to bring into a relationship that could later destroy it."

Gloria let that sink in a bit and went back to cutting his hair, but she continued to talk. This time in more of a motherly tone, "I know not of what you speak." She paused from cutting and turned his chair so she could look him square in the eyes, "And contrary to what you might think, I don't care about your past. I'm a pretty good judge of character, and I've known you long enough to know a thing or two. I know your heart." She turned the chair back and went back to cutting.

Her words sank into Nigel's head. He said nothing, until Gloria ignited a little response. She said, "And besides, that other fella she's been seeing..."

Nigel jerked his head around and interrupted, "What other guy?"

Gloria stopped cutting and smiled, looked at him through the mirror and said, "Ah ha! It appears your interests run deeper than you let on."

Nigel played it off. "Nonsense. She can see anybody she wants. She's free to do what she pleases. She knows that. I was just ... just being curious."

She spun him around in the chair again. She started clipping his bangs. "There is no other guy, Nigel. That was a little white lie. I just wanted to see how you would react."

Dammit, Nigel thought, but said nothing. She stopped clipping again and looked into his eyes, "Nigel, baby. She is crazy about you, and you are crazy about her. Stop being a goofball and give the two of you a chance. Life is too short. And that's all I'll say about the matter. I'll never bring it up again."

Nigel thought, *Yeah. You'll never bring it up again. Sure. Whatever you say.* Then he changed the subject, "By the way. I've been meaning to ask you. Have you seen Luke McKenzie around?"

Gloria jumped back. She stood up straight, caught off guard by the question. She looked around and across the room to the ladies under the dryers, especially the one reading *Guns & Ammo*.

"What is it?" he asked. "I just want to know..."

Gloria hushed him, "Shhh... Hold your tongue, Nigel." She looked back around the room. The ladies were still reading their magazines. They didn't hear a thing. "Thank goodness for old, loud driers," she whispered.

"Gloria. What is going on?"

"Why do you...," she looked around the room to make sure the coast was clear and finished, "want to know where he is?"

"Because the son of a bitch was supposed to mow my grass while I was gone, and he didn't. What the hell is going on?"

That got the attention of the old gal reading *Guns & Ammo*. She looked up from the magazine and tilted the hair dryer canopy up a bit. Gloria looked at her and gave a small smile and a little shake of the head. *It's nothing dear, no, no, no.* She went back to looking at her magazine.

"Nigel, our old Luke has gotten carried away and painted himself into a big corner. He's in hiding, no doubt. It's been a sensitive subject around here for about a week and a half or more. I try my best not to let the subject surface. I would hate to cross-pollinate trouble amongst my customers."

"Gloria, what are you talking about? Cross-pollinate trouble? What is that supposed to mean."

Lowering her voice to a whisper, Gloria said. "What that means is, I'm done talking about ... Mr. McKenzie." She looked around the room and continued, "I suggest you find him and quick. He can fill you in on all the sordid details." She paused a beat, put on a big smile and asked, "Now, would you like a shampoo to go with this fancy new look you're sporting?"

Nigel declined and gave her a twenty and a kiss on the cheek before heading out the door.

Five minutes later, Nigel pulled his truck into Luke's driveway. Luke's truck was gone. He stared at the house. He thought about what Gloria said. *He's painted himself into a big old corner. He's in hiding.* For Ms. Gloria to have been so secretive was odd. She is always ready to pull the trigger on details. She loves to share, but not this time.

Nigel sat there for a few minutes and was about to leave when something caught his eye. It was an upstairs window curtain. It moved, along with a shadow. Nigel smiled. *Damn Luke. If you're hiding, you suck at it.* Nigel got out of his truck and walked up to the door and knocked. He waited. Luke never came to the door. He knocked again and called through the door. "Luke, dammit! Let me in. I know you're in there."

Nothing.

From the street Nigel heard the long, slow squeal of car brakes. He turned to look. It was an older lady, late sixties or early seventies. He didn't know her. She was driving a 1965 Ford Galaxie 500. It was dirty from being parked under a tree too long. There was a lot of sap built up on the top, and the blue paint was faded beyond repair, but it sounded good and looked to be in pretty good shape as far as the body goes. Nigel smiled as she came to a complete stop and rolled down her window.

She asked, "Is he in there, young man?"

From behind the front door, Nigel heard a low bark, "Hell no. That's the right answer. Hell no, he isn't home. Send her away."

Nigel smiled when he said, "No Ma'am. It doesn't appear so. I don't think anybody is at home," referring more to his mental state than anything else.

"Thank you, honey," she said. "If you see him, please tell him Vanessa came by."

"Yes, Ma'am. Miss Vanessa. Got it. Consider it done."

As Ms. Vanessa drove away, Luke asked, "Is she gone?"

"Yeah, Luke. She's gone."

"Come around to the back door. Let yourself in. Don't let anyone see you. Lock the door behind you."

Nigel closed the door and threw the deadbolt until it slammed home. He turned around. The kitchen was dark. The whole house was dark. With all the lights off and all the shades drawn, no sunshine was allowed in. Nigel looked around and from the shadows Luke emerged and sat at the kitchen table. As if ready to engage in high level espionage, he said, "Come. Sit."

Nigel didn't bite on all the cloak-and-dagger bullshit. He leaned up against the counter, crossed his arms and said, "Old man. What in the hell is going on? What have you gotten yourself into?"

Luke said nothing.

"And atop everything else, you didn't mow my grass like you were supposed to. My yard looks like ass."

"Couldn't risk it," he said.

"Don't be goofy, Luke. Risk what?"

"Being seen."

Nigel stood there in the dark shaking his head saying nothing.

"I've spread myself too thin. Let things get out of hand."

"Luke," Nigel said. "What in the blazes are you talking about?"

"It's the juice, man. The juice."

"You're starting to piss me off," Nigel said. "Juice. What juice?"

"It's powerful stuff, brother. More powerful than I ever imagined. He tried to warn me. He really did."

"Dammit, Luke! Will you just come out with it?"

He did.

Luke told Nigel about a recent trip to visit his brother, Val McKenzie. Val lives at the Broken Wood Center, a nice retirement community in Charleston, SC. The place has all the right amenities to keep their residents happy and occupied. It's a great place. Luke's brother is quite the commodity there, a big hit with the ladies. Luke said, "Val told me, he said, 'This place is great. I'm one of ten guys in the whole complex and there are over fifty little fillies running around. There's no broken wood here. I get plenty of action.'

"Nigel, it was incredible. I was there for three days and he had a different gal show up at the door every night. I couldn't sleep for the damn headboard slamming up against the wall. I tried banging on the wall, but it just made Val laugh."

"Holy shit, Luke. Really?"

"Yeah, really. And did I tell you he's three years older than me?"

Nigel said nothing as he tried to flush the image of promiscuous geriatric sex from his brain.

Luke continued, "On my last morning I asked him about it. About where he was getting all his stamina, his Mojo. That's when he told me about the juice."

The sound of Luke using the word *Mojo* brought a smile to Nigel's face. For a guy of his generation, it just didn't seem an age-appropriate reference. Nigel didn't interrupt the story. He continued to listen.

About a year ago, Luke's brother went on a trip to Venezuela with several of the other residents. Of the twelve that went, he was one of only two guys to make the trip. While in Caracas, he and the others visited the Parque del Este, one of the city's most important parks. The gals were wearing Val McKenzie out. The other guy had already had enough and didn't even get off the bus, but Val was willing to try and hang in there.

While walking the paths of the park's dense forested region, he fell behind. Taking a handkerchief out of his pocket and wiping his brow, he stopped and plopped down on a park bench next to a woman. She was a vibrant, older lady; not as seasoned as Val, but was well within her senior years. Val, a little out of breath, huffed and puffed as he looked at the stranger and said with a laugh of embarrassment, "Those old birds are trying to kill me. Leave me for dead I tell you."

The stranger looked deep into his eyes. Then she reached over and took his hand asking, "May I?" She rubbed both sides and studied the creases of his palm and fingers. Then she scooted close to him and rubbed his forearm. Much to Val's surprise she brought his hand up and placed his palm upon her right breast. She applied firm pressure, pulling him in tighter. Val flinched but didn't complain as he turned his head from side to side to see if anyone was watching.

She smiled at Val, kissed his palm and placed it back on his lap, patting it.

"No, my dear," she said in her broken English. "You far from death. Much strength left. Fuego deep inside, still. I help you." And that is when she introduced herself.

"Val told me her name. Christina Ortiz," said Luke. "She is a Santeria Priestess. A damn voodoo witchdoctor or something. She reached in her purse and gave him a small vial, a home-concocted potion. She has some spooky voodoo name for it, but Val just calls it *The Juice*. She told him, 'All you need is one little drop under the tongue and you will be new again.' Val threw all caution to the wind and allowed her to administer the first dose, right there on the bench." Luke went silent shaking his head with a sly grin.

"Yeah, and?" asked Nigel.

"And nothing. The rest is history. Within an hour he was jogging around the park and caught up with those old gals in no time. Later that evening they went to a salsa bar and he danced the night away. They made it back to the hotel and one of those old gals followed him back to his room. That's when the headboard banging started."

It didn't take Nigel long to connect the dots, piece together the connection between Val's good fortune and Luke's newfound troubles. Nigel was about to say something when they heard a faint noise on the front porch. *Shuffle Shuffle Scrape ... Shuffle Shuffle Scrape.* Then the doorbell rang. Luke almost jumped out of his skin. "Don't move, Nigel. They'll go away after a while."

"Luke, you're being silly." Nigel got up and snuck into the living room to take a peek. It was the old gal that drove by earlier. She rang the doorbell again. Nigel could see her shadow move to the windows. She was pushing a walker. *Shuffle Shuffle Scrape ... Shuffle Shuffle Scrape.* She was looking for a crack in the blinds to look through. She called through the glass, "Luke. Baby, open the door. It's Vanessa ... Luke, please let me in ... Luke ... are you in there?"

Nigel went back to the kitchen and asked straight away, "So how much of that potion did your brother give you?"

"A whole vial. He keeps a supply. He gets it in the mail. Buys it from that old voodoo gal in Venezuela." Luke went quiet.

"Go on. Tell me the rest."

"What can I say? The Juice is awesome. Powerful stuff. Just like Val said. Too powerful, actually. It all started the second day after giving it a try. I felt great, got more lawns mowed that day than ever before. My last stop was at Eleanor Johnson's house. She came out and sat on the front porch steps to watch me mow. When I finished she said, 'Something is different about you, Luke.' I smiled and walked over and noticed she was wearing shorts, lots of leg showing.

She didn't even have her compression stockings on. She was all legs. I hardly even noticed those varicose veins."

Nigel winced and said, "Oh hell. That's enough. I see where this is leading."

"Screw you, Nigel. I might be old, but I'm not dead."

Nigel said nothing shaking his head.

"There she was. There I was. I looked at her and she gave me a knowing smile. I smiled back and a fire started burning in my crotch. I swelled up like a hound dog tick. Old Eleanor noticed too. She stood up and said, 'Oh Luke, we need to do something with that.' That's when I followed her into the house."

"Okay," Nigel said. "That's all I need to hear. No more details are needed."

"I gave her a good going over, Nigel. It was incredible. I ..."

"Enough, Luke! That's enough. I don't need a play-by-play."

Luke went quiet.

"So, who is the lady at the door? This Ms. Vanessa? What's her story?"

"What? Vanessa Helms? She's from Wewa. I cut her grass on Wednesdays."

Nigel looked down the hall towards the front door. She was still out there. *Shuffle Shuffle Scrape ... Shuffle Shuffle Scrape.*

Luke said, "Hey, Nigel. Don't let that walker fool you. She's an animal in the sack. She doesn't need that thing in the bed." He went silent for a beat or two then continued. "Unless she wants some position she can't quite manage on her own. Then we'll pull it in, but that's it brother. Promise."

Nigel thought about it for a minute and out of the blue he asked, "Luke. Exactly how old are you?"

"I'll be eighty-four next month. Why?"

"Just curious." Nigel continued to think. He's eighty-four. Getting more action in one week than I've had in the past three years possibly. He chuckled to himself and looked over at Luke.

"Luke," Nigel asked, "exactly how many gals are you using The Juice on?"

Luke held up both hands. Nigel counted the fingers through the darkness.

"Seven!" Nigel said.

"Yeah and they're trying to kill me. They can't get enough. They want it over and over again. Then they want some more. It's awful."

Nigel said nothing.

"There's this little gal that works at the general store. I cut her grass every other Friday. Well, I was in the store the other day picking up some beer for me and Maxine. She grabbed my arm and led me back into the storeroom. She had my pants off like nobody's business. The next thing I knew we were doing it on a pallet of Trail Blazer dog food." Luke thought it over and said, "The stuff has made me into a porn star, brother. And the cameras, they just keep on rolling."

Nigel said, "But there's more to this than just seven horny gals with almost 600 years of experience, isn't there?"

Luke looked up and nodded his head.

Nigel thought some more and then it dawned on him, "Shit! They don't know about each other, do they?"

Luke shook his head and said, "It seems somehow each of them got the idea they have exclusive access to the Luke machine. That I'm their private boy toy. "

"And why would they think that?"

Luke looked up at Nigel. Nigel was looking back, his eyebrows raised and a thin smile on his face.

"Don't look at me like that, dammit," argued Luke. "You have no idea. The Juice is powerful stuff. You get caught up in the moment. Has you saying things … things you otherwise wouldn't."

Nigel started to laugh under his breath, "Things like what, Luke?"

"Damn you, Nigel. Stop laughing at me. I got a situation here…"

Nigel's phone rang. He held his hand up. "Hush, let me get this." It was Gloria from the beauty parlor.

"Hey, sugar. You found Luke yet?" asked Gloria.

"Yeah, he's here at the house holed up like a scared rabbit."

"Has he told you everything?"

"About his little secret harem? Yeah, he told me," said Nigel.

"Well, it was only a matter of time, but you can tell Luke it's not such a secret anymore. Remember those three gals under the dyers?"

"Oh, no. You're kidding me? All three of them?"

"Oh, yes. And they started comparing notes. Each one of them thinks they have a special date with him tonight. He's in trouble, doll."

Nigel said, "Hold on a sec, Gloria." He covered the mouthpiece and looked at Luke with a grin and said, "I guess you overbooked the flight tonight, huh?"

"Go to hell, brother. You're not being much help here."

"Okay, Gloria. I'm back."

"Nigel, it gets worse."

"How can it get worse?" Nigel listened to everything Gloria had to say. Luke watched with great concern. Nigel was shaking his head and finally spoke. He said, "Gloria. Come on. He didn't. All three of them?" Nigel listened some more and thanked her for calling. Luke could hear her laughing on the other end of the line as Nigel ended the call.

"You are in deep shit, brother. You've proposed marriage to these gals?"

"Not all of them dammit! Just ... four." Luke said nothing then looked at Nigel and pleaded, "What am I going to do?"

"Beats the shit out of me, brother. But you better think of something fast. There's a herd of them heading over here right now."

"What? Not here? Oh, no."

No sooner did Luke start shaking his head from side to side when a loud banging began at the front door.

"Oh my God, Nigel," pleaded Luke. "What on earth am I going to do?"

Nigel said nothing, but he walked over and started flipping on the kitchen lights. Then he headed down the hall towards the door flipping on more lights.

Luke called out, "What are you doing? Shit! Don't let them in!"

Nigel stopped and turned around and said, "Love you, brother. But you are going to have to set this mess straight. Right now. I have faith in you, you're a Navy Chief. You'll think of something."

The banging at the door stopped when Nigel grabbed the doorknob and flung it open.

The ladies said nothing at first; startled that anyone even answered the door. One of them, the gal Nigel saw under a dryer reading *Guns & Ammo*, finally asked, "Where is he?"

"He's in the kitchen, ladies. In the kitchen. But go easy on him. He's made some big mistakes and he is very sorry."

Miss Guns & Ammo brushed by Nigel and said, "Sorry and no good. That's what I say."

Nigel was patient and stepped aside as the old gals filed in one by one. He smiled at the last one as she passed by. *Shuffle Shuffle Scrape ... Shuffle Shuffle Scrape.*

Later that evening Nigel strolled into the Reid Avenue Bar and Bottle Shop with a couple of Piggly Wiggly sacks, dinner for two. Candice could have asked for anything, from any restaurant, but she insisted on fried catfish, green beans, black-eyed peas, and cornbread from the Pig Deli. She smiled as he approached the bar. He placed the food on the counter and she said, "That looks ridiculous on you."

"What?" Nigel replied. He ran his hand over his new T-shirt from the Piggly Wiggly and turned around modeling it. "You mean this? ... I like it." There is never a shortage of T-shirts for sale at the Pig. They have developed somewhat of a *cult* following. Collecting Piggly Wiggly T-shirts has become quite popular. This one had the famous pig's face on the front with, *What happens at the Pig ... Stays at the Pig,* written on the back.

Candice worked the bar. Between patrons she would slip over to stool 17 and enjoy a bite or two and a quick word with Nigel. He shared the highlights of his photo shoot with Marvin at the Mug Race. He told her about the girls on the catamaran and how Marvin was just beside himself. Candice leaned over the bar, got in his face and said, "And I guess having two smok'n hot, naked girls sail by you didn't excite you at all, huh?"

"I was working, Candice. Hazards of the job," replied Nigel with a smile. "Um ... Um ... I'm a pro. Yeah ... I'm a pro. I see that kind of stuff all the time, and it never affects my ability to focus on the work. I'm a pro."

"My ass," said Candice. "Yeah ... You're a pro. A professional man." She reached closer and kissed him on the cheek. "That's why I love you." Then she took off down the bar to pour more drinks.

Nigel watched her go. A great walk.

Nigel didn't realize until she was already pouring a draft that she had dropped the "L" word. *Love.* He wasn't sure what to do with that. How exactly had she meant it? *Friendly love. Couple's love.* He didn't know. It couldn't have been *lover's love.* They haven't slept together. Not yet anyway. The one thing he realized was he didn't mind hearing it. That he could admit to himself; he liked the sound of those words coming from her.

He's been in town now for a little over two years, and things between him and Candice have not been allowed to progress beyond a very tight friendship. He's made sure of that. They've dated on a regular basis, but it has been Nigel holding back, failing to commit or take things to the next level.

If Candice could have things her way, they would already be connected at the hip, an item. For the most part, she has already staked her claim over him. *Stay away ladies. He's mine.* She is ready for more, but she's patient. She's confident he wants to move things along too. She sees it in his eyes, but there's something holding him back. *What?*

Nigel likes watching her work. She's the ideal bartender. She's a hot, sexy mess and knows how to use it to maximize tips without being too flirtatious. Sexy or not, none of it is worth a damn if you can't pour a good drink. She does. Even the most mundane task, like pulling a draft draws a lot of attention. She was at the draft station now, and Nigel, along with almost every red-blooded guy in the joint, was keeping a close eye. Eric Church's *Springsteen* was blasting on the jukebox, and she was swinging her hips and dancing to the music as she filled two pints to the brim, no foam.

She then turned to the whiskey and charmed a long pour of Jim Beam Black on the rocks into a glass. She caught Nigel watching her and she grinned as she bit her bottom lip. Nigel smiled and called her over with his finger. She served the drink then swaggered over toward him and leaned over the bar. "What, baby?" she said.

"You're gonna have to stop all that," he said with a smile, pointing and twirling his fingers towards the draft station. "That's what."

"What's wrong, baby? You don't like the way I dance? I do it for you, sweetie," she said with a wink.

"You do it for every wandering eye in the house. That's who you do it for," he said.

"Well, my goodness," she said reaching over to run her fingers across his cheek. "If I didn't know better, I'd say that my Nigel is starting to show little signs of jealousy." She stood up tall, crossed her arms for a beat then placed them on her hips. "Perhaps I'm starting to get through to you, you big lug."

Nigel said nothing, just smiled at her.

Candice said, "Well, if you're uncomfortable with how I operate, I can change. I can, but it's up to you. All I need is a good reason." Then she pursed her lips and walked away giving it a little extra swing. She looked back over her shoulder and shot Nigel a private wink and a nod, then went back to working the bar.

Nigel smiled thinking about what she said. *Give her a reason.* He watched her mix some concoction. He lost count of what all she was putting in it; because, he couldn't concentrate. Her hips and shoulders were moving in perfect time to Kenny Chesney's *Pirate Flag.* He got her attention and raised his voice so she could hear and said, "I wouldn't have you change a thing."

She winked back. And as she went back to work, he said to himself, "But maybe I will one day. Give you a good reason that is."

Nigel settled back on his stool and shook his head. *Mercy.* Then the opening of the front door caught his eye. *What did he just see?* He strained to look over the heads at the bar and through the crowd out on the floor. Was he seeing what he thought he was seeing? He moved his head from side to side, trying to catch a glimpse. Then ... Yes ... Leading the way and heading towards the bar, spreading the crowd like a boat makes a wake, was Maxine. Behind her was Luke McKenzie. And behind Luke was ... Nigel stopped to count: one, two, three, four, five, six, seven. Yes. There were seven gals in Luke's presence, four of which he had already had the pleasure of meeting, even if only for a brief moment.

Luke found Nigel and worked his way over to stool 17 with a big grin on his face. His harem closed in tight. Candice came over to join them. Luke Bryan's *Country Girl, Shake It For Me* was pumping through the speakers. Luke looked at Candice and said, "Honey, turn that candy cane country shit off and put on some Waylon. For Christ's sake, my girls here need something good to dance to."

Candice smiled and walked over to the stereo.

Nigel looked at Luke with a big smile and said, "Well, it looks like you've gotten over your troubles."

"Yeah, brother. It couldn't be more perfect." Luke turned to the ladies and said, "Girls, come close. I want to introduce y'all to someone. Another damn, fine Navy Chief."

The girls came closer. Luke said, "Girls, this is Nigel Logan. A dear friend of mine. A brother in anchors." Nigel smiled and nodded. Luke continued with his introduction, "This right here is ..." He had to think about it for a moment. Then he smiled and said, "Ms. Tuesday. Yeah, this one is Ms. Tuesday. And this one over here is Ms. Thursday. And right behind her is Ms. Wednesday."

Nigel started to laugh as Luke continued to introduce his lady friends, one named for each day of the week. Then Luke said, "And last but not least is Ms. Friday. But I think y'all have already met haven't you?"

Luke nodded as she moved closer to take his hand: *Shuffle, Shuffle, Scrape ... Shuffle, Shuffle, Scrape.*

KIRK S. JOCKELL

The Home Opener

All national holidays are great, but for some, especially those living in an American tourist town, Labor Day is one of the best. It serves as a fresh start, a new season for the locals. For the communities of the Forgotten Coast, it's no exception. While the calendar might not reflect it, summer is over. Summer, that is, as defined by a coastal town that thrives on the almighty vacation dollar. The heavy invasion of tourists is all but gone and the coast is clearing. Thank God!

It is the main break in economic activity, and they will miss the tourist dollars, but only for a while. This is when the locals get to take back their town, their beach, and their sanity. That is until January, when they welcome back the annual migration of snowbirds. The micro tourist season that provides stability dollars during the winter months.

The days and weeks following Labor Day are a time of transition. Parents everywhere are getting their kids, whether they like it or not, ready to return to school. The same goes for the locals too. Those in Port St. Joe do their best to get their kids excited about going back to class. It's tough, moving kids away from the lazy, carefree times of summer life. It's even tougher in a coastal town where the main attraction is the beach or the bay. Yet, one thing always helps ... the smell and excitement of high school football.

The Port St. Joe Sharks are defending another Class "A" state championship, and that is enough to get everybody excited, regardless of age.

The town loves its football and there is plenty of spirited energy floating around leading up to this year's home opener. On Friday the Sharks will be hosting the Wewa Gators, a huge local rivalry slated as *The Clash of the County*. The little town of Wewahitchka, Wewa for short, is only about 25 miles up Highway 71, so bragging rights are important between the two towns.

But for Candice, the game is more than just a home opener. Her favorite niece is Kay, a sixteen-year-old starting her junior year at Wewa High. And on top of everything else, she is a cheerleader on the varsity squad. Much like her aunt, Kay is a looker and a most sweet young lady. During her sophomore year she was voted *Friendliest* by her classmates.

Candice is a graduate of Port St. Joe High. She was never a cheerleader, but she was the Homecoming Queen three times straight. An old classmate of hers told Nigel once, "Dude, if she had flunked and had to repeat her senior year, she would have taken it again. No doubt." Several years later, Candice still has it and her local popularity hasn't waned one bit.

Nigel met Kay on two occasions. Once when Candice brought Nigel to a family reunion, and again when she was staying with Candice for a long weekend. Nigel liked her. She was pretty, smart, respectful, and refreshingly naive.

To Nigel, the best thing about Kay was the insight it gave him to Candice's past, how she looked way back when. At the family reunion, Candice's mother paraded him through an old family photo album. There were pages and pages of Candice. Nigel enjoyed the pride her mother took in showing off her little girl. "Wasn't she just beautiful?" she said, making it more a statement than a question.

Nigel said, "Was? ... Still is. She still is."

"And look at that little darling," she said referring to Kay as she walked through the room with two cousins. She snapped the album shut. "Every time I see her, I see my little Candice. She is the spitting image."

It was true. There was no denying the resemblance. It was astonishing. Even now, years later, the amount they favor each other is nothing short of amazing. That told Nigel something. Kay was on her way to being a gorgeous woman, and Candice hadn't changed a bit. She was aging quite well, better than him, and he liked that.

Leading up to the game, Nigel witnessed many phone calls and messages exchanged between Candice and her niece. They prodded each other about the big game all week, a rivalry thicker than the blood that bound them. Nigel enjoyed the friendly banter between the two. The game was going to be a showdown, no doubt. And Candice had already told Nigel, "You're going." Nigel didn't protest.

Candice was sporting a Salt Life ball cap. Her hair was in a ponytail that ran out the gap in the back. She had on an old jersey from her high school days, a memento from a senior year powder-puff game. The jersey has been well loved over the years and the school colors had seen better days. Below that she had on a pair of her best blue jeans. Not best as in new, best as in old, faded, tight, and torn in all the right places. On her feet, she sported a simple pair of black flip-flops that showed off her new pedicure, toe nails painted the school colors: purple and gold.

It was a juvenile look, but fitting for a women attending, not just a football game, but a snapshot of her old life in high school. She wasn't alone either. Plenty of others dressed in a similar fashion, a glimpse of how they might have looked back in the day. To Nigel, it was obvious; everyone was exhuming their past, revisiting the glory days. It was fun to watch. Hugs and kisses were being passed around to old friends as if they hadn't seen each other in ages. When, in reality, most had seen each other in the Piggly Wiggly in recent days. It was Friday night in Port St. Joe. Come Saturday morning, it would be business as usual.

The stands were full. The crowds were bouncing to the music, both sides waiting for their team to take the field. Candice and Nigel strolled through the visitor's side of the field. Candice saw and chatted with several of her old Wewa High friends and finally stopped behind the fence where the visiting cheerleaders would lead their student body.

Down towards one end zone, the Wewa team gathered behind a huge banner made by Kay and the other cheerleaders. It had a cartoon image of a shark suspended by its tail; a rope dangled the big fish. The words *Catch the Sharks for Dinner* and other motivational slogans such as *Win! Fight!* and *Go! Go! Go!* surrounded the image.

Moments later Candice, Nigel, and the Gator fans watched as the Wewa team busted through the banner. The visiting Gators filled the air with cheers and excitement as their team dashed to their side of the field.

On the field there was a lot of jumping up and down, grunting and cheering. Fists pumped in the air while others slapped the helmets of their teammates. They were doing everything and anything to get each other fired up to face the Port St. Joe Sharks. But despite all their best efforts, it was tough to erase from their minds the fact that the Sharks were defending state champions. The Sharks were good and the Gators were bringing a butter knife to a gun fight. *But hell, don't give up. Anything could happen.*

The Gator cheerleaders cleaned up the field and ran over to join their fans. Kay saw Candice standing by the fence and ran over, finger waving and pointing as she proclaimed, "You're going down, Auntie. You're going down."

"Yeah, we'll see. We'll see," returned Candice.

They were all smiling when Nigel said, "Good luck tonight, Kay. Tonight, I'm pulling for you guys."

Candice slapped Nigel's arm. Then Kay reached over the fence and gave Nigel a big, tight hug and a kiss on the cheek.

She bounced back to her side of the fence and with her bubbly cheerleader smile said, "Thanks, Nigel."

"You're welcome."

She hugged him over the fence again. She held tight as she cut a look to Candice, winked and said, "Isn't he just the sweetest thing."

She let go and was doing the cheerleader bounce thing when she looked at Candice and said, "He's a keeper!" Three bounces later she was in formation with her squad. As Candice and Nigel started to walk away they heard the girls start a classic cheer, worn out over decades of use. *Two! four! six! eight! Who do we appreciate...* Nigel reached down and took Candice's hand. She squeezed her fingers in approval.

Nigel said, "I feel like a goofy kid again."

Candice stopped and spun him around so she could look at him. She said, "That's the whole idea you big lug."

"Okay then." Nigel thought for a couple beats and said, "Here. Jump up on my back. I'll carry you around."

She didn't hesitate and jumped before he was ready. They almost fell to the ground, but Nigel recovered. Nigel had the back of her knees cradled in his arms and she held tight around his neck. He couldn't see her face, but he knew she was happy. He was too.

They found a place to sit in the home team bleacher section just in time for the kickoff. She wanted to sit in the student section with the rest of the *Old Kids*. The alumni crowd outnumbered the entire student body which made the home team cheering section a huge force to reckon with.

The Gators won the coin toss and elected to receive. With both teams on the field, the Shark cheerleaders raised their hands, wiggled their fingers, and led the crowd in a prolonged, "Goooooooooooooo....Sharks!" And the ball was in the air.

It was a fine kick, high and long. It was dropping towards a patient Gator wearing the number 21 on his jersey. He was standing on the two-yard line. The kick had great height giving the Shark's special teams unit plenty of time to bear down on their opponent. There were three Sharks running fast, no one left to block or slow them down. Number 21 was in their sights, they planned to collide with the Gator as he caught the ball. It was something they practiced time and time again, something they called *The Perfect Train Wreck*.

In a low voice to himself, Nigel said, "If this kid catches the ball, he's going to get creamed." Nigel saw 21 take his eyes off the ball for a quick look down field. Now he saw the Sharks coming. Nigel thought, *Good. Now just let the ball go into the end zone. Take your touchback and your twenty yards. No shame in that.*

The Gator ignored Nigel's mental suggestion. He picked up the balls trajectory, shifted a bit to the right, backed up a step and caught the ball on the Shark one-yard line. He spun around to his left and skirted one Shark who fell and rolled into the end zone. The other two Shark players hit 21 as he was again spinning to his left. The hit drove all three players into the middle of the end zone. All three were going down when the Wewa Gator put his left hand down on the field looking for balance. He found it and neither Shark had a good hold. They were grabbing and clawing at their man, but the Gator kicked away, tripping, and stumbling to his freedom. Number 21 was off and running. He gathered both balance and speed as he exited the end zone.

He headed straight up field and sidestepped the next two Sharks. He moved to his left, diagonally towards the middle where he found a small hole and exploded ahead. Now he was on the twenty-five yard line. He was hit from the left by a Shark and it slowed him down, but he spun around again to avoid the tackle. Now he was running towards the sidelines. Another Shark was bearing down on his position. At the last instant, the quick Gator stopped and let the Shark slip by. Then it was straight up field again: the thirty, the thirty-five, the forty, the forty-five. He was finally run down and tackled around midfield.

The excitement coming from the visitor's stands was electric. Number 21 came up from the tackle holding the ball high in the air for his teammates and supporters to see. He began to strut, waving both hands up in the air trying to get his side of the field fired up. It worked. It was an explosion of noise.

Nigel looked over at Candice and said, "Now, that's how you start a football game."

"Oh, shut up you. You traitor."

The momentum from the kickoff return stayed with the Gators. The first play was a screen pass to the right where a receiver caught it and turned it into a seven-yard gain. Then they went to the running game, a fullback up the middle for four yards. "First down, Wewa," said the Shark announcer, in a flat, lifeless voice.

It was good fundamental football. The Gators were moving the ball downfield, converting every third-down opportunity into a first down. The fans loved it.

Wewa was in the Red Zone, inside the fifteen-yard line. Nigel looked at Candice and saw the genuine worry in her eyes. He smiled but said nothing. He knew better.

The Gators set up with two wide receivers to the left, one to the right, and the backfield set behind the quarterback.

Things were quiet on the home front. The Shark fans watched with quiet concern and feigned enthusiasm as they focused on the situation on the field. The visitor's side projected a cacophony of belief, optimism, and excitement. Nigel thought he could see the entire bleachers sway, rocking from side to side and bouncing up and down.

The quarterback took the snap and dropped back to hand off to one of the halfbacks. The halfback charged through the line, but it had been a fake. The quarterback was bootlegging the ball towards his right. He looked down field and that's when he saw one of his wide receivers down field and cutting across the end zone. He was wide open.

Still moving to his right, the quarterback launched the ball. It was a great throw. The spiral was perfect, the target was still running, waiting for the ball, and the Wewa crowd was expecting the best, while the Port St. Joe fans awaited the worst.

It all seemed perfect for Wewa, until this Shark nobody had been paying attention to appeared out of nowhere and jumped in the path of the ball. He had great height in his leap as he intercepted the pass, catching it on his left side. He was fast and never missed a stride. By the time he exited the end zone, the fan participation took a drastic turn. He bounced off a couple of Gators, now playing defense, but kept going. By the time the Shark flew past the quarterback, he had an open field in front of him, nothing but grass between him and six points. Now the home team announcer had something exciting to report on. The loud speaker, which now seemed to be turned up a notch or two reported, "Twenty-five, Thirty, Thirty-five, Forty ... Nobody can catch him! He's got an open field!"

The announcer was running out of breath when he yelled in a squeaky voice, "Touchdown! Tiger Sharks!"

Nigel thought she was going to kill him. Candice had converted her worry into furious excitement. They were both standing now, everybody was, and she was beating on him with her fists as she watched and cheered the young man all the way down the field. Then she grabbed Nigel and kissed him.

After that, it was all over for the Gators. The tide of momentum they enjoyed during the opening minutes of the game had turned against them. The deflation of excitement and hope was too great. They would never recover.

With seven and a half minutes left in the game, Candice and Nigel walked back over to see Kay, not to gloat or rub it in, but to finalize some post-game details. Kay was staying the night with Candice, and she had a date with a young man from Port St. Joe after the game. Kay would get ready at Candice's house, and the boy would pick her up there.

Candice and Kay exchanged hugs. Then Kay put her arms out towards Nigel. He snuck in for a quick squeeze. Candice said, "See you in a bit, kiddo."

When Candice and Nigel were in the car they heard the final buzzer. Nigel looked back to see the score board. It was an impressive win. Final score: 53 to 12.

Later at the house, Kay was in the bathroom changing when the doorbell rang. Nigel answered the door. "Yes. Can I help you?"

A young man stood at the door. He was a little on the thick side, about six feet tall, maybe 200 pounds. He still had boyish features, but Nigel could see he was coming into his own. He was giving his facial hair a chance to fill in, and he wore his best serious look on his face. And he was respectful. Nigel liked that.

"Yes, sir," the young man said. "I'm Teddy. I'm here to pick up Kay."

Teddy, Nigel thought. He's hasn't graduated to Ted or Theodore yet. Still going by a name used most likely by his mother. *Not a bad sign.* Nigel let him stand in the doorway for a beat or two before saying, "Sure, come on in and have a seat. She'll be right out."

They sat down in the living room. Nigel took a chair. Teddy took the couch. He looked nervous. *Good.* His mood lightened up a bit when they both heard Candice yell from the kitchen, "Hey, Teddy. How are you?"

"Fine, Ms. Candice. Thank you, ma'am."

He was still being respectful. *Good.* Sometimes faking respect can be tough for a young man.

Teddy's nerves returned the second Nigel started asking questions. He wasn't expecting the preliminary date questions. Nigel reached out his hand and said, "My name's Nigel, Teddy. What's your last name?"

"Mason, sir. Teddy Mason."

"Nice to meet you, Teddy Mason." Nigel made sure to include his last name, to let the young man know he wasn't going to forget.

Teddy said nothing.

"So, you're from St. Joe?"

"Yes, sir. Born and raised. Graduated last year."

"Nice. Lucky guy. Getting to grow up in such a cool place and all. I'm from Virginia."

Teddy started to relax a little. This wasn't so bad. Then his sphincter tightened when Nigel asked, "So what exactly do you have planned for my Kay tonight? What are you going to do?"

The young man squirmed on the couch a bit and finally said, "Oh, I don't know. Get a bite to eat, maybe. Then maybe head out for a drive on the beach."

With eyebrows raised Nigel asked, "You plan to take her out on the beach, huh? What you plan to do there?"

Now Teddy was shifting in his seat. Nigel was enjoying himself. Plus, he wanted to make sure that Teddy remained just a little uneasy for the rest of the night. Little did Nigel know, he was about to be more successful than planned.

KIRK S. JOCKELL

"Well, sir. Umm... You see. Some friends are going out..."

Teddy was interrupted when Kay came in the room. "Oh, he's just disgusting. Ugh!" she said. Then she saw Teddy and said, "Oh ... Hello, Teddy. I didn't know you were here. I'm almost ready."

"You look scrumptious," said Teddy.

Nigel held a stare until Teddy turned his head to catch it and the silent message behind his eyes. *Scrumptious? Really?*

Nigel let that sink in before turning to Kay to ask, "Disgusting? Who is disgusting? What's the fuss?"

She held her phone up in the air and said, "Michael Stephens. That's who. He's a creep and he keeps texting me all these little nasty messages."

"Really?" asked Nigel. "Show me."

Kay came over and sat next to Nigel and started going through her texts. Nigel looked them over as she scrolled through them: *I want to see you in a wet T-Shirt ... I bet you're hot in a string bikini.* And the latest one sent just minutes ago: *You've got the best ass of all the cheerleaders.*

Nigel looked at Kay and asked, "Who is this chuckle-knuckle, again?"

"Michael Stephens. A guy from school. He's in my class. Been after me since the year started."

"You want him to quit, right?"

"Like, Yeah! He's a total Creepoid."

"Okay," said Nigel. "Why don't you leave your phone with me and go finish getting ready."

"What are you going to do?"

"Everything will be just fine. Just give me a minute."

Kay leaned over and kissed him on the cheek before she stood up. It almost made him blush, but he had other things on his mind. Teddy got up to leave too, but Nigel told him to sit back down. He did, but with great hesitation.

Both Nigel and Teddy watched as Kay exited the room. Then Nigel found the number the texts were coming from and dialed it. It rang twice before he heard a voice say, "Well, hello sugar britches."

Nigel was silent for a beat then said, "Don't even think of hanging up, Michael Stephens. See, I even know your name. And I have your number, Michael Stephens. Again, don't even think of hanging up."

The line was quiet. Nigel said, "Did you hear me?"

The line was still quiet but Nigel could hear nervous breathing on the other end of the line. Then he heard a single, "Yeah." Nigel smiled.

Teddy watched as Nigel let the young man on the phone anticipate what was to come next. After a bit of silence, Nigel asked, "How old are you, Michael Stephens?"

"Seventeen," Michael answered.

"Seventeen, huh? That's too bad," Nigel said. "That means you're still a minor and I can't find you to whip your little ass."

Michael asked in a broken voice, "Who is this?"

"This is Kay's uncle, and she's my favorite niece."

The young man on the phone said nothing.

"I've been reading the text messages. The ones you've been sending Kay. I'm not happy."

The young man on the phone still said nothing.

"Are you still there?"

There was dead silence on the phone. Then the young man said, "I'm still here."

"Good, then listen up. As soon as we get done here, you are going to text Kay an apology. Are we clear? And if I ever hear of you sending her any more inappropriate text messages, I promise you son this is no threat, I will hunt your father down, rip his eyeballs out and skull fuck him. Do you hear me? He should have raised you better."

Nigel heard the line go dead. Michael ended the call. Nigel put the phone down on the coffee table and sat back. Teddy was looking at the phone resting on the table. He was sweating with a slight case of the shakes.

Nigel looked at Teddy and said, "Sorry for the interruption. Where were we? Oh yeah, the beach... you were telling me your plans."

Teddy looked at Nigel and was relieved to hear Kay come back in the room. He stood up and asked her, "Are we ready?"

Kay looked at Teddy with concern and asked, "Are you alright, Teddy?"

Nigel answered for him with a smile, "Oh, he's going to be just fine. You kids go off and have a good time. It's getting late."

Seconds later Kay's cell phone buzzed and vibrated on the table. She grabbed it, another incoming text message. She was reading it as

Teddy had her by the other hand and marched her towards the door. Candice came in from the kitchen and said, "Y'all have fun. Not too late. Okay?"

Teddy had the doorknob in his hand when Nigel said, "Hey, Teddy."

Teddy turned and answered, "Yes, sir."

Nigel said, "I like you."

"Thank you, sir."

"Let me ask you one last question."

"Yes, sir."

"How old did you say you were?"

"I didn't, sir. But, I'm ... eighteen, sir."

With a big smile Nigel said, "Good ... Good ... Now, you kids get out of here. Be safe."

They would be. It was a guarantee.

The Stranger

It was late on a hot and steamy Thursday afternoon when the stranger walked into the Reid Avenue Bar and Bottle Shop. Candice, the bar manager, looked up and took notice of the attractive female as she stopped just inside the closing door. A blond with an exceptional tan, she stood there enjoying the refreshing air conditioning, a blast of cold air coming down from the ceiling. The sudden change in temperature gave the stranger a chill, and her nipples tightened as she walked towards the bar.

Candice noticed how the stranger's white blouse, moistened from sweat, defined her reaction to the cold. Candice offered a smile and said, "A bit nipply in here, huh?"

The stranger looked down and touched her breasts. A little embarrassed she looked back at Candice and said, "Yeah ... I guess you could say that. But it beats that damn sauna out there." She grabbed a stool.

Phil Stewart, a local deckhand shrimper, was a little overserved and sitting at the end of the bar. He too took notice of the new beauty and decided to move in for a closer look. Candice saw him get up and tried to stop him saying, "Sit your ass back down, Phil. Leave the nice lady alone. She doesn't want to talk to you."

He kept coming, a starboard list to his swagger. "Free country, Candice. And we'll let her decide who she wants to talk to." He took a stool right next to her and began to gaze up and down her blouse.

Candice looked back at the stranger and said, "Ignore him. What Phil, my ex-husband, lacks in discretion, he makes up for in stupidity."

The stranger reached out to shake Phil's hand, "Nice to meet you, Phil." Phil took her hand as he turned to look at Candice, smart-ass grin on his face.

Things got a little awkward when Phil wasn't quite ready to let go of her hand. He held tight even as she was loosening up her grip. She continued to smile but had to jerk her hand away. Phil gave her an offended look, but instead of adding tension to the situation, the stranger offered up a compliment. "My, that's some grip you have there, Phil. I bet you don't even know your own strength."

Phil smiled, lifting and lowering his eyebrows in quick succession. "Don't bet on it, sweetheart."

"I'm sorry," said Candice. "He's a pest. Pay him no mind. What can I get you? ... Beer? Wine? You look like the wine type."

"Actually," the stranger said, "I'll take a whiskey."

Phil looked at her and said, "A whiskey girl ... I think I love you..."

Candice said, "Shut your hole, Phil."

The stranger ignored both of them and strained to look around Candice to see what was available. She looked back at Candice and said, "The Maker's Mark will be fine. On the rocks, please."

"Makers on the rocks. Coming right up." Candice turned to grab the bottle and make the drink. While she had her back turned, Candice continued the normal bartender small talk, "So, where are you from?

"Virginia," said the stranger.

"That's a pretty state," said Candice. "Never been, but I've seen pictures. What brings you to our neck of the woods?"

As Candice turned around with the drink, the stranger pulled a picture out of her purse. She lifted it up for Candice to see.

"Do you know this man?" asked the stranger.

Candice looked at the picture and let out a small gasp. It was of a handsome man. He was in uniform. Warm eyes, firm jaw bones, and chiseled chin. He didn't smile, but he wasn't frowning either. It was a serious look, all business. Candice placed the drink in front of the stranger.

"Who wants to know?" It was the only thing Candice could think to say.

"Well," said the woman, "based on your reaction, it would appear you do know him. Where can I find him?"

"I have no idea who he is. Never seen him before." Candice lied.

The stranger gave Candice a look of sarcasm. *Really?*

"Really," Candice said. "I've never seen him before, ever."

Phil Stewart grabbed the picture and took a look. Then he slammed it down on the bar, face up. "I know the son of a bitch. It's that bastard, Logan."

"Nigel Logan?" asked the woman.

"Yeah ... Nigel Logan." Phil thumbed towards Candice. "The asshole is her boyfriend."

"Shut your damn hole, Phil. Shut it now. He's not my boyfriend." Candice went quiet for a beat or two then said, "Not yet anyway."

The woman took a sip of her cocktail, offered a simple smile and said, "You could do a lot worse, honey. Now, do you know where I can find him?"

Candice said nothing, but Phil Stewart did. "He hangs out at the Forgotten Coast Raw Bar. I'd start there. If you find him, tell him I said, 'hello' and that I haven't forgotten him."

The stranger took another sip of her whiskey and set it down. She gathered her stuff and slipped three fives under the glass. "I gather this will cover it?"

Candice nodded her head. Her mind was racing as the stranger headed towards the door. *Who was this woman? What did she want with her Nigel? And why did she have to be so damn beautiful and classy looking?* Then Candice stopped her, "Miss ... What's your name? You know ... In case I see him."

The woman looked back with a mischievous smile, "Doesn't really matter, honey. I'm just an old friend from way back." She lied.

Right before she got to the door, Phil picked up her drink and hollered, "Hey! You gonna finish this?"

Candice said nothing but her mind was running a thousand miles per hour. *What should I do? Call him. That's what I'm gonna do. Call and warn him. No ... Maybe that isn't best. Maybe he'll think I'm checking up on him. I'll come across as pushy and overprotective. He might not like that.*

The whole time she was thinking, she was dialing his number into the phone. She was about to press the call button when she decided against it. She cancelled the call and put the phone down. Her frustration built and she grabbed the whiskey from Phil's hand and threw the glass, smashing it up against the wall, "Son of a bitch!"

Nigel sat atop stool 17. Red was next to him. Trixie, Red's wife, sat next to Red. Trixie held her head in her hands as Nigel and Red argued the existence of Bigfoot.

"I'm telling you, Nigel. Folks round here have heard it, seen it even."

71

"That's bullshit, Red. Just bullshit."

"I'm telling you brother. Just telling you what other folks are saying. They've seen it."

"Okay ... I won't deny that folks hear some mighty strange things out there. Hell, I've heard some of the creatures, cats usually. They'll make your skin crawl. But actually seeing it. That's just bullshit."

"I'm jus' say'n, man. Jus' say'n."

"Okay, Red. What does the damn thing sound like?"

Red went into a wailing, high pitched moan, mouth open, his head swaying in a circle. The whole bar turned to look at them. It was pathetic. Trixie slapped his arm, "Stop that, Red! Knock it off." She looked around the room and offered a look of apology. *Sorry folks. Sorry 'bout that.* She slapped him on the arm again, "You're embarrassing the hell out of me."

"Crap, Trixie. Quit your hitting. He's the one that asked."

Nigel looked at Red and said, "So ... You've actually heard it yourself, huh?

"Well, no. But folks tell me..."

Nigel interrupted him, "Well, if you've never heard the damn thing, how in hell can you sit here and ...." Nigel let it drop off and shook his head.

"What?" asked Red. "What is it?"

"Red this is just stupid. There is no fucking Bigfoot, alright. It's all bullshit. Bigfoot doesn't exist."

"Stop calling him Bigfoot. I hate it when people do that. The term Bigfoot trivializes its existence. Makes it sound like a cartoon character or something. It's a Yeti, alright. A damn, Yeti!"

"There is no fucking Yeti, Red. Give it up!"

Trixie sat there, shrinking into her stool. She'd had enough. She pulled back her arm to swat at Red, but he caught her in the corner of his eye and said, "Don't you hit me again."

She stopped her windup and said, "Shut up then. The both of you, you hear me. I've had enough of this silly-ass conversation."

Red became appalled, "Silly-ass conversation, huh. So I guess you're picking sides. Is that it?"

"I'm not picking any side, Red. I just want the both of you to shut the hell up. Get it?"

Red turned to face the bar and drink his beer. He brought the cup to his face and whispered under the lip of the cup. "It's a Yeti, dammit."

Nigel was just about to say something in reply when his phone bonged. A text message. The name on the screen almost made his heart stop. He reached into his back pocket for his wallet. Then he pulled out a stack full of business cards and shuffled through them until he found the one he was looking for. He compared the name on the card to the name on the phone. They were identical. But, of course they were identical. He had used the card, long ago, to program the information into his phone.

He put the cards away and stuck his wallet back in his pocket. Then he looked at the ceiling as if there were answers up there to the questions that raced through his head. He didn't like being caught off guard. He grabbed the phone and opened the message.

Hello, Nigel. This is Sherry Stone of Channel 7 News, Norfolk, Virginia.

Nigel looked at the screen and put his phone down and got up to recharge his beer. He sat back down.

"Everything okay, buddy?" asked Red.

"Yeah ... Yeah ... Everything is fine. Just thinking is all."

The phone bonged again. It was Sherry Stone again. He took a sip of beer and opened the message.

We call them Bigfoot where I come from.

His heart skipped a beat. He looked around and surveyed the room. It didn't take long. There she was on a stool at the end of the bar, sitting, listening, watching and waiting.

Their eyes found each other and locked. Hers hadn't changed; they were the same beautiful shade of aquamarine he remembered. She was stunning, as beautiful as he remembered, maybe even more. Her denim shorts and white blouse revealed all her best qualities: great tan, toned legs, a tight figure that didn't look manufactured. No, these were all her own attributes, gifts from God. Then there is the smile. It will turn you to putty.

She got up and walked over to Nigel. On top of everything else, she smelled great, of faint gardenia. She smiled and said, "It's been a long time, Chief Logan. I thought you would have called me by now."

"When I was ready," said Nigel. "I thought that was what we agreed to."

There was awkward silence as Ms. Stone made eye contact with Red and then Trixie. She looked back to Nigel and said, "Well, what does it take to get a sailor to buy a girl a beer around here?"

Nigel turned to Red and Trixie, "Red, Trixie ... Let me introduce you to Sherry Stone. She's from my old stomp'n grounds around Norfolk." He left out the part about her being a television news reporter on purpose.

Both Red and Trixie exchanged pleasantries and shook hands with Ms. Stone as Nigel looked on. Trixie asked, "So what brings you to our little part of the world?"

"I'm here on a little business...," said Ms. Stone. Shooting a glance at Nigel she continued, "or at least I'm trying to be."

Nigel could see that Red was about to continue the conversation with a follow-up question, so he intervened, "I'm sorry, y'all. You'll have to excuse us. I'll need to speak with Ms. Stone in private." Nigel gave Ms. Stone a slight glare. "We have a few matters to discuss."

Nigel's glare turned to a smile which was returned by Ms. Stone. He got up and took her by the elbow and escorted her back to where she had been sitting. As she sat down, she asked for a Corona. He got it for her and occupied the stool next to her and said, "I don't like being surprised like this. Tell me three things right now. How did you know I was in Port St. Joe? Who gave you my cell phone number? And ..."

He stopped, didn't ask the third question. It would have been a stupid one. He knew exactly why she was there.

She said, "And the third thing?"

"Forget it. Just answer the first two."

"I'm a reporter. You know I have to respect and protect my sources."

"I know you're a reporter that risked coming a hell of a long way for nothing. Now, spit it out. How did you find me?"

Sherry Stone gave it some thought and realized that it didn't matter if she revealed her source. As a matter of fact, the source had said, "If you find the son of a bitch, tell the asshole I said to go to hell."

They looked at each other in silence. She thought. He waited. "Well ... My source," she said, "had choice words for me to pass along if I found you. Would you like to hear them?"

"Ah! Kim Tillman. That won't be necessary. I can imagine just fine. I can't believe she is still holding a grudge."

"It would appear your old girlfriend took the breakup badly. A woman doesn't easily forget. The pain runs deep."

"The bitch doesn't feel pain. She's a spoiled, selfish, one-sided brat. It appears she hasn't changed much."

Sherry Stone said nothing.

"Enough about that. That was a period of my life I will never get back, and it isn't worth discussing any further. I had forgotten about her a long time ago, and I just forgot about her again, seconds ago. Let's move on. Now answer my third question."

"You never asked it."

"I don't have too."

She said nothing.

Nigel realized the conversation was moving into areas he wasn't prepared to go, so he shifted gears, "Excuse my manners, Ms. Stone ..."

"Please ... Call me Sherry."

"Fair enough, Sherry," he said. "Have you eaten?"

She hadn't. Nigel ordered baked oysters and steamed shrimp. He got fresh beers and they made small talk. It was the thing to do. Aside from knowing she was a local television news reporter, Nigel knew nothing else about her. He figured, as a reporter, she will have done plenty of research on his life, more than he'd be comfortable with.

The conversation was more one-sided than she wanted. He made her talk all about herself. Where she was from? Where she went to school? How she got into broadcasting? Everything. It became frustrating for her. She would try to turn the tide, change the conversation back towards him, but he would smile and say, "When I'm ready."

Nigel liked listening to her talk. At first she spoke in her broadcast voice. He liked that. But as she became more comfortable around him, her voice softened to a more natural conversational tone. It felt like two old friends, just chatting. She began to smile and laugh more too. He liked that too.

She was a homegrown Tidewater girl. Born at the historic Naval Hospital, Building #1, in Portsmouth, Virginia; she was raised in Virginia Beach. Her father had been a Naval Officer, a brown shoe aviator flying A-6 Intruders out of Oceana Naval Base. He had been able to work the system and homestead the Norfolk area for fourteen years. When his detailer gave him no option to stay in the area, he bailed on the active duty Navy. He took a lucrative position as a contractor at the base and joined the Navy Reserves to finish his career. He refused to disrupt his family by dragging them all over the world. Nigel didn't know her father, but he liked him. He had heard enough to determine that.

She went to Princess Anne High School and later to Old Dominion University, studied broadcasting and interned at the television station. Her smarts, good looks, ability to deliver a message and local knowledge of the area made her a perfect match for the station. She was offered full-time employment before she even graduated.

He never asked her age, but by his calculations, he was about 10-12 years her senior. She was in her late twenties, early thirties. He was in his mid forties. He let the math sink in to see if he cared. He didn't.

"What about a boyfriend?" asked Nigel.

"That's getting a bit personal, wouldn't you say?"

"Well, your entire trip down here is about getting a bit personal, wouldn't you say?"

She smiled. He liked it when she did that. A great smile. She reached over and grabbed his forearm, squeezed it. Leaning in she said, "Touché ... Fair enough..."

She continued to speak to him. There was nobody special in her life. Not yet anyway. There had been some potential candidates, but they were unable to handle her ambition for career and independence.

Sherry Stone went on talking. Trixie did her best to hear every word, but couldn't make out anything that was being said. Then she elbowed Red and said, "Oh, shit. Red ... Look."

Red turned his head and saw Ms. Stone had moved much closer to Nigel, talking to him with smiles, holding his arm with both hands. He smiled and turned back to Trixie, "Stop being so damn nosy, Trixie." They're just talking for all you know. Plus ... it's none of our business."

"That's not what I wanted you to see. Look out the window, you idiot."

He did, and it only took him a second to see what Trixie was talking about. He repeated Trixie's own words, "Oh shit."

Just outside the window, off to the side, looking in, was Candice. She stood there and watched from where Nigel and the stranger couldn't see her. How long she had been there was anyone's guess, but she had been there long enough to see enough.

When the stranger got too cozy for comfort, and he didn't protest, that was it. Candice turned and ran back to her Jeep, half mad, half crying. She tore out of the parking lot under full throttle, slinging gravel and squealing tires once they hit pavement. The commotion outside got Nigel's attention and he looked up. All he saw was a cloud of scattered gravel and dust.

Nigel felt a hand being placed upon his shoulder. He turned his head and saw Red leaning in. Nigel tilted his head and offered his ear. Red got close and whispered, "Candice."

Nigel snapped around and looked back out the window, then back at Red and said, "Oh shit!"

Red chuckled and said, "That seems to be the common response."

Nigel was speeding back into town. He excused himself from the impromptu meeting with Sherry Stone and told her their interview would have to wait. Ms. Stone asked, "When then?"

Nigel never answered.

His mind was on Candice now as he was driving down the road. Neither of them had an exclusive on the other. Yet he didn't want to hurt her. They were as close to a steady thing as any two people could be, but Nigel wanted options, for Candice mainly.

He had given great consideration to opening up to Candice, letting her into his past. It was all about the timing, waiting for when it felt right. It still didn't, but, now that his past had followed him to town in the form of Sherry Stone, he might have no choice. He might have to tell her anyway, good timing or not.

There was also the matter of trust. The things he would need to share with her would need to be held close; she wouldn't be able to share them with anyone. He knew she was trustworthy, but knowing your favorite guy is the prime suspect in an active murder investigation isn't your typical pillow talk. These were details he didn't want anyone to know. He just wanted to move on with his life, pretend like it never happened. It was looking like that was going to be harder and harder to do.

The thought crossed his mind again ... *He didn't want anyone to know.* The focus jumped from Candice and back to Sherry Stone. Depending on how things transpired during her visit, everybody on the Forgotten Coast could know everything by the end of the day. Such news would move like wildfire. For all he knew, she was still at the Raw Bar discussing everything with Red and Trixie right then. He had a gut feeling she wouldn't go into those details, but her sudden appearance at the Raw Bar would draw questions from both Red and Trixie. Questions that could lead to a natural progression of information swapping. He had to handle her, give her something to go back with. The sooner he could get her out of town, the sooner his life could return to a sense of normalcy or some semblance of it anyway. The longer she hung around, the more dangerous she became. He pulled off to the side of the road.

The phone rang a fourth time. He thought it was about to go to voicemail, but she answered instead. "Sherry Stone."

Nigel apologized for leaving in the manner which he did. He didn't mean to be so rude. He inquired about what she was doing and she confirmed the worst. She was spending time talking and getting to know Red and Trixie.

"They were telling me about when you first arrived in town," she said, "about how you landed with both feet, taking no time to jump into trouble. Beat up a guy pretty good it sounds."

"The guy was an ass," said Nigel. "He had it coming."

"Had it coming, did he? Seems there might be a history of folks getting what they deserve when you're around."

Nigel didn't say anything.

"So when do I get to see you again?" she asked.

"What else have you been discussing with Red and Trixie?"

Sherry looked up and smiled at Red. He was sipping his beer. Trixie was listening to the one-sided telephone conversation, trying to piece together the context without seeming too interested. Stone said, "Nothing of great interest. That I can assure you, so what about that date?"

"Tonight," Nigel said. "Where are you staying?"

"I'm at The Harbor Hotel, room 213."

"Perfect. Meet me in the hotel lobby ... Say around eight o'clock. We'll figure it out from there."

He ended the call and dialed Candice's number. She answered on the second ring but never said hello. He could only hear her sniffling and labored breathing. He knew she was crying. "Candice," he said, "it's me."

She said nothing.

"Please talk to me."

She ended the call. He tried to call her back but it went straight to voicemail. She had turned off her phone. He sat quiet for a few moments then left a simple message, "Candice. Honey. It's me. Please call, okay?" Then he threw his phone down on the seat. "Dammit!"

Nigel parked out on the street, right in front of the hotel. He walked through the front door, right on time. He looked around for her. Nothing.

The guy behind the counter said, "Mr. Logan?"

Nigel answered with a nod.

"The lady wanted me to tell you she is waiting in the bar."

He walked in and stopped. She wasn't alone. Three guys surrounded her at the bar. Each working hard for her attention, buying her drinks and anything else she wanted, trying with extra effort to impress. She wasn't. She toyed with them all the same. Nigel stood at the door and watched. He noticed a variety of libations in front of her. He stood there thinking. *What all was she having these stooges buy? Do these guys really think they have a chance?* It was almost comical.

After awhile she turned and found Nigel standing there, a smile on his face from watching her work the room. She smiled and winked at him. She stood up, backed away from the bar and grabbed what looked like a Cosmo and a glass of whiskey off the bar. One of the three guys commented in protest, "Where you going, baby? Come on, we want to party." She ignored them and approached Nigel with a seductive walk. She pulled up close, got up on the tips of her toes and kissed him on the lips. She backed off and smiled at him.

She reached up to kiss him again, but this time he met her halfway slipping a hand behind her back to pull her in close. It was a long wet kiss; they allowed their tongues to explore each other. She pressed hard towards him and he let her in. He used his free hand to find her waist, gave it a squeeze. She responded. It was part of the game.

They backed off each other and she smiled and said, "Thanks for saving me from those guys."

"You looked like you were doing just fine all by yourself."

She smiled back and said, "Can a girl buy you a drink?" She handed him the whiskey. He smelled it, bourbon. He took a sip.

From over at the bar, one of the guys said, "Hey, asshole! That drink isn't for you. I bought it for her."

Nigel gave her a look. *Really. You used these guys to buy us both drinks.* Then he said, "You are so bad."

She smiled back as he handed her back the drink and stepped around. He approached the guys at the bar and said, "Sorry 'bout that fellas. She can be a cold one."

One of the other guys said, "Screw you, dude. You're the one that stepped into our party."

Nigel looked back at Sherry. Another look. *See what you started.*

He looked back at the three guys and said, "Listen. Contrary to what you're thinking, there is no party. The lady is with me. End of story."

"That's bullshit, man. She was with us first."

Nigel read the name tag on the bartender. Her name was Tracy. He gave her a comforting look. She didn't return one. The bartender was burning holes through Nigel's face with her eyes. Tracy the bartender said, "I know who you are."

The comment caught Nigel off guard and he returned a confused look. Then he looked back at the guys and said, "So, here's the deal. I am willing to forget about your calling me an asshole and I'll take care of the drinks." He pulled a fifty dollar bill out of his wallet and handed it to Tracy. "Will this cover it?" he asked her. She snatched it out of his hand and said nothing. Nigel returned another confused look and under his breath said, "Keep the change."

He continued talking to the three guys, "I'll pay for the drinks. In exchange, all of you will chalk this up as a valuable learning experience and forget the whole thing. Because I already have."

Testosterone is the one thing that gets more guys into trouble than anything else. When it starts pumping through the blood stream, a guy will lose all rational thought and responsibility, allowing one's self to be driven by emotion. Never a good thing, usually.

Nigel had turned to walk away, but noticed from the mirror behind the bar that one of the three followed after him. It was the guy who claimed to buy the bourbon drink. Nigel watched as the guy reached to grab his right shoulder. Nigel used his left hand to reach across and back over his right shoulder to take quick possession of the guy's fingers. Nigel squeezed hard and spun around to his right bringing the guy's hand down, then turning it palm up and into the air, fingers bent back. Way back. The guy let out a whimper.

Nigel made eye contact with the guy and said, "Your stupidity brings out the worst in me. So ..." He squeezed harder. "You need to wise up. Until now, all you have is a little broken ego. Unless you want to add a couple broken fingers to the list, you best do the smart thing and back off."

The guy's head was nodding in exaggerated agreement before he said, "Yeah! Yeah! I get it! I get it! Just turn me loose, dammit."

Nigel squeezed a little harder and brought the guy to his knees before letting go. He looked up at the other two and took a step towards them. One of them held up a halting hand and said, "Good night, y'all. Have a nice evening."

Nigel and Sherry Stone left the inn and started walking down the sidewalk towards town, which is only one block away. Once they crossed over Highway 71 Nigel stopped and took Ms. Stone's elbow and turned her around to face him. "What the hell was that back there? I don't like surprises and I damn sure don't like games. So far today, you are two for two."

She was caught off guard by his reaction and said, "Ah ... Ah. I don't know. I was just having a little fun. I didn't mean to..."

Nigel cut her off, "Well, if that's your idea of fun, take that shit back to Virginia. You hear me? We don't need it around here."

She tried to speak again, "I'm ... I'm, so..."

"This is where I live now," he said. "These are my people and I care about them. They are the finest in the world, willing to give a perfect stranger the last shirt off their backs. I don't fancy outsiders, none of us do, coming in here and fucking with their generosity whatever their motivations might have been. Are we clear?"

She looked at him very close, deep into his eyes. She saw it: the caring. It was there, and it was genuine. He was upset, more for the three guys back at the inn than anything else. She nodded her head as she reached out and took his hand, squeezed it tight. "I'm so sorry. Please..."

Nigel let her talk.

"I was wrong, very wrong. Nothing like that will ever happen again. I promise. Do you forgive me?"

Turning away to start walking again, Nigel said, "We'll see how dinner goes."

Dinner was good. He took her to a new restaurant in town, Boneyard Cove. It's on highway 98, in the middle of the Port St. Joe strip. If you could call it a strip, all five blocks and two traffic lights of it.

The place is small, warm, and cozy. The staff was friendly and attentive. And the food was good. They shared the seared tuna and two dozen raw oysters, washing it all down with ice cold beer. It was great, and she was on her best behavior, looking more gorgeous with each passing minute. To avoid the temptation of being pulled in by her sex appeal, he made small talk.

He tried to get her to talk more about herself, but she wouldn't stand for it. She told him that she had already shared enough. Now it was his turn.

"Where do you want me to start?" he asked.

"I like stories that start at the beginning," she said. "That's always best."

Nigel thought about it for a moment. He took a long pull off his beer and set it back down on the table. He leaned in closer and captured her eyes and attention when he said, "In the beginning ... It wasn't perfect. I was born Nigel Mulholland, a bastard. I never knew my real father. My mother never told me anything about him. As far as..."

Sherry Stone interrupted, held up a hand with a smile. She went through her purse and grabbed a small Dictaphone and held it up for him to see. "May I?"

The sight of the recorder brought a whole new meaning to their dinner date and made him realize, even more, the true purpose of her visit. She wasn't there to get to know him better, or to have a personal interest in him. She was there because it's her job. It was the story she was after, a story he would give her to send her packing back to Virginia. He was reluctant, but nodded his head in agreement. She turned the thing on and asked him to start from the top.

He did.

She asked him, "So, to this day, you know nothing about your real father? Not even his name?"

"Nope. He wasn't listed on my original birth certificate. And I never asked."

"Did that bother you growing up?" she asked.

He shook his head and said, "Not really." Then he paused and said, "Well … maybe a little in the beginning." Then he looked her in the eyes and finished, "But I learned quick not to give a shit. Why would I? He wouldn't have been worth a piss anyway, right? A guy like that. No, I don't care, nor do I think about it. The way I see it, he did us all a favor."

"How did you get the name Logan?"

"My mother met a wonderful man when I was five years old. We all fell in love with each other. Mom found the husband she always deserved, and I found out what it's like to have a father. It's like he's been there my entire life. He adopted me."

"Are they still alive? Your parents?"

"Yes."

Nigel left it at that. Said nothing more. She was quiet, pausing to give him time to elaborate. It's an old interviewing trick. People like to talk. When a question is asked, if the interviewer pauses long enough after an answer, awkward silence fills the room and the subject will usually volunteer more. People like to talk. Not Nigel. She got nothing, so she let it go.

"Nigel," she said, "I want to talk about Norfolk. Can we do that?"

Norfolk. That was a gentle way of saying Terrance Lundsford, aka T-Daddy Lundsford.

Lundsford was a local rapper, a real piece of work back in Norfolk. He was no stranger to trouble. He was arrested for kidnapping, beating and raping a young girl during a carjacking. Lundsford was released without a trial. The prosecution's key evidence, ironclad DNA, was compromised. Its chain of custody was mishandled and the judge handling the case had no choice but to throw the evidence out the door. Lundsford was a free man.

Lundsford was a lot of things. Now he's dead.

The rape victim is the daughter of a Navy Captain, and the commanding officer of the last ship Nigel Logan had been assigned to before retiring. The captain, Charlie Matthews, was more than Chief Logan's skipper. And Grace Matthews is more than just a captain's daughter. They were family, but not of the blood variety. Nigel Logan and Charlie Matthews served together under many commands during their careers. Their careers developed together and through the admiration and friendship that developed, they became close, very close.

Nigel nodded his head and said, "Ask what you'd like. It's the reason you came here. We both know that. No sense playing games."

Sherry Stone picked up the Dictaphone to make sure it was running. She placed it back on the table so the little microphone pointed right at him. She was careful not to be too loud when she said, "Mr. Logan ... regarding Terrance Lundsford. Did you kill him?"

Mr. Logan. Earlier she was kissing and rubbing up against him, but now it was Mr. Logan, a professional touch to remove any signs of favoritism. Nigel looked down at the Dictaphone. A little red light flashed indicating it was recording. He looked back up at Sherry Stone and said, "You jump straight in with both feet don't you?"

"I'd be remiss in my duties if I didn't ask the tough questions."

"So, exactly how do you suppose I answer that?"

"Honestly, I would hope."

He repeated the question, "Did I kill Terrance Lundsford?" He paused ... "Well, the Grand Jury didn't think so. Isn't that enough?"

"That doesn't answer my question, Mr. Logan."

"No, I guess it doesn't. So let me put it to you this way. And you can put it all in print if you'd like. You're here for a story. I'll give you exactly what you want, an exclusive. That's what you came for, isn't it?"

She gave him a caring smiled and said, "You could say that. Go on."

Nigel looked around the restaurant. It was too full and too cozy to talk about such things. No privacy. Nigel said, "Not here."

They decided on her hotel room, private and quiet. She settled the bill. Nigel let her. He knew she would expense it at her office later.

He opened the door for her and watched her walk to the sidewalk. He liked what he saw. She turned around to wait for him to catch up. She liked what she saw too. They walked back to the hotel at a snails pace, letting good food and drink settle. She tried to make small talk, but Nigel was preoccupied with thoughts of Terrance Lundsford, and what he would tell her. She broke his train of thought as she grabbed one of his arms with both hands, pulled him close saying, "Hello. Anybody home in there?"

"Yeah, I'm here." He said nothing more.

As they approached the front door of the hotel, Nigel noticed something on the windshield of his truck. He walked over for a better look. It was a note. He pulled it out from underneath the driver-side wiper blade and opened it. It wasn't signed, but it didn't need to be. *When you get done doing whatever it is that you are doing, we need to talk.* It was from Candice. He looked in the air and thought, *crap.*

"What is it, Chief?" Sherry asked.

Nigel looked around, and shoved the note into his pocket. "Nothing," he lied and walked around the front of the truck to the sidewalk.

She touched his arm and asked, "Are you sure everything's alright?"

"Yes," he said. "Everything's just fine. Come on let's get this over with before I change my mind."

"You make it sound like being with me is such a chore."

Nigel held the door for her and said, "This isn't exactly a date, you know."

She smiled walking past and said, "You never know. It could turn into one before the morning."

Nigel took a deep breath and held it, lips tight, cheeks expanded. He watched her as she crossed the small lobby floor. She looked great, an abundance of sex appeal. His lungs couldn't take it any longer, he exhaled. He thought to himself, *Easy brother, Easy now.*

From across the street in a bank parking lot, Candice watched everything from her Jeep. She saw them as they were walking towards the hotel from the restaurant. She watched as the stranger pulled herself close, and she noticed Nigel didn't protest. She saw Nigel read her note, dismiss it, wad it up, and stick it in his pocket. She watched as the stranger grabbed Nigel's arm as he walked back

85

to the sidewalk. And she couldn't help notice the smiles the stranger had for him. Her heart sank as he opened and held the door for her. And she gasped when they disappeared through the hotel lobby door.

Candice waited fifteen minutes, then fifteen more before getting out of her Jeep to cross the street and enter the hotel. Perhaps they were just in the bar. They weren't.

Tracy, the hotel bartender, knows Candice very well. Tracy moonlights on occasion at the bar and bottle shop Candice manages. She saw the look on Candice's face when she walked in the room. It was obvious she was upset, perhaps even crying.

"Tracy, have you seen Nigel in here tonight?" asked Candice

Tracy didn't say anything at first, so Candice continued, "In the past 30 minutes or so? Did he come into the bar? Have you seen him?"

Tracy said, "Not that recent. He was in here earlier tonight."

"Was he with a woman, a blond?"

Tracy said nothing, just nodded her head.

"I saw them walk into the hotel." Candice looked back to the door and up towards the ceiling, as if she could see through the floor. "They must have gone to her room." She turned back around and looked at Tracy who was starting to cry herself.

"Oh, Candice," Tracy said with an alligator tear rolling down her cheek. "I am so sorry."

Tracy has known Candice long enough to know how she feels about Nigel Logan, how crazy she is about him. She has been since the day he blew into her life. Over time and from afar, Tracy has watched them grow closer and closer together, but never sealing the deal as a full-on couple. Nigel has made it clear that she is free to see other people, but she doesn't. She tried seeing other guys a few times, but never enjoyed it the way she enjoyed spending time with Nigel.

Candice never had reason to think of the consequences of being free to see other people. That being, he was free to see other people too. There had never been any evidence of his seeing anybody else, so it didn't bother her to place all her hopes and wishes in one basket. To work on him and be patient was a bet she was willing to make. That was, until now.

Tracy and Candice were both crying. Wiping her own face Candice started talking to herself, "Stop it, dammit! Stop this silly crying!" she grabbed a hand full of bar napkins and dried her eyes. She looked at Tracy, put on a feigned smile and said, "Goodnight, I'm going home."

But she didn't. Not right away. She sat in her Jeep looking at the hotel and the room windows. It was getting late and all but four windows were dark. She sat and wondered which window he was behind and what they were doing. She hated all the possibilities as her imagination ran wide open. It was tearing her up inside. She waited another thirty minutes, but couldn't stand it anymore. She started her Jeep and eased out of the parking lot.

Upstairs, outside room 213, Nigel leaned against the wall as Sherry Stone fumbled in her purse to find her door key. He looked at his watch, 2230. It's been a long day. *Click ... click.* He looked up to see her opening the door.

The room was a suite. There was a small living area complete with a refrigerator, and a huge widescreen Plasma TV. Furnishings included a sofa, love seat and two plush chairs, all matching leather. Everything was well coordinated with the rest of the décor, a small hallway led back to a bedroom.

Heading back to the bedroom she said, "I'm going to wash up and loosen up a bit. Please, make yourself at home and pour yourself a cocktail. Plenty to choose from on the counter."

He looked around and found the booze. A nice selection. He was going to decline until he saw the bottle of Four Roses Single Barrel. "Don't mind if I do," he said.

She popped her head around the door and said, "Will you be a dear and fix me a vodka tonic, extra lime."

He did.

She came out and joined him in the living quarters and sat next to him on the sofa. She had washed her face and her hair looked different, falling in places it didn't before, a few barrettes missing perhaps. She had changed blouses too, a loose fitting, silky blue, sleeveless oxford, top two buttons undone, no bra. *Damn*, he thought. *She looked great.* She reached over towards the table where her libation sat, allowing her blouse to open and reveal the lack of tan lines about her breasts. A swelling warmth filled his gut as she picked up her glass and sat back turning towards him, holding it up, "Salute."

Nigel lifted his own glass and tipped it her way. Said nothing.

They took the obligatory sip and Stone set her glass back down on the table revealing herself again and adjusted her position on the couch, moving ever closer to Logan.

In that moment Logan realized how long it had been since he had been with a woman. It had been a long time. Long enough that he didn't want to think about it anymore. It wasn't that he hadn't had his opportunities. It was, like everything else, all about the timing. The timing, the person, and the circumstances. And all three of those things were starting to look pretty good.

Stone smiled placing her left arm across the back of the couch and touched his shoulder. Then she edged forward reaching with her right hand and took hold of his right knee, squeezed it with care and released it.

"So," she said. "Tell me. Tell me everything."

Logan wasn't expecting the next moments to go in that direction, but deep down he was glad they had. It was time to get under control and his emotions back in check. He stood up, grabbed his bourbon and asked where the head was, any excuse to stand up and move. Stone was an old Navy brat, so Logan didn't have to explain that he wanted the bathroom.

Logan spent a couple minutes in there. He didn't have to go, so he just washed his hands and rubbed cold water on his face pressing hard around his eyes. He looked at himself in the mirror and smiled. *Sometimes buddy; you are your own worst knucklehead.*

When he returned, Stone was watching him approach her. She looked fabulous and sexy. She had her legs and knees tucked up underneath her on the couch. Her back was straight which accentuated her breasts, now aroused and engorged to maximum tightness. Nigel stopped and watched her for a moment, watched her body rise and fall with each deep breath. *Damn.*

Nigel smiled, took a sip of bourbon, walked around and sat in one of the chairs. Stone's own smile faded some when he said, "You realize. I have never talked about this with anyone. Formulating my thoughts about all this into actual words ... That is something I've never done before."

Stone changed her posture. She unfolded herself and placed her feet on the floor. She reached into her back pocket and produced the

Dictaphone and powered it up. She set it on the table, real business-like and said, "Go ahead. Everything, from the top."

"Everything?" Nigel said. "If I told you everything I knew about the Lundsford murder, it would be a short conversation." He lied.

"So, what are you prepared to tell me?"

"I don't get you," said Logan. "One minute you are trying to seduce me, and in the next instant you're playing hardcore news journalist."

"I don't let my personal and professional lives mix, Mr. Logan."

Oh, we're back to the Mr. Logan stuff.

Stone continued, "What's business is business, and what's pleasure is pleasure. You were right to get us back on track. I'm sorry for having derailed the purpose of our meeting. I am interested in hearing what you have to say." She gave a long smile and said, "We can always return to those things we both might find pleasing later, after we get through with this."

Logan admitted to himself that he liked that possibility. Only an idiot would think otherwise. Then he got his wits about him and said, "If you think I am going to sit here and give some confessional, or incriminate myself, you're crazy."

She said nothing.

"What I have to say, to share with you is my perspective. My honest thoughts about the entire ordeal."

"Alright," she said. "Let's have it."

"I've never spoken to anyone about this until now, to anyone. I've had this bottled up inside of me for a long time. I'm glad to get it out. I hope doing so will make me feel better, but that depends on one thing."

With a raised eyebrow, Stone said, "And that one thing is?"

Logan paused a bit and finished, "What you write as a result of your being here."

"I don't think I follow you, Mr. Logan."

"Would you please stop calling me that? For Christ's sake ... Mr. Logan? I don't like it. I'm not a mister, or a sir for that matter. That mister shit is for officers. If you want to formalize this interview slash conversation, call me Chief. Clear?"

Stone nodded as she heard the voice of her own father in her head. *Chiefs aren't sirs. They work for a living.* "Okay," Stone said with a big smile. "Chief it is."

"What's the smile for? Did I say something funny?"

"Nothing. Go ahead. You just reminded me of my daddy for a second, that's all. So, go ahead."

They paused for a while and smiled at each other. Then Logan said, "Let me start all this by asking you a question. Why are you so interested in me? Why should anyone care?"

"I'm not following, Chief."

"Me goddammit. Why should anyone be interested in anything I have to say?"

In a slight smartass tone Stone replied, "I don't know. Terrance Lundsford, maybe. You're the leading suspect in his murder. You're still free and at large despite enough evidence to warrant at least an indictment. How does that happen? How exactly does one get away with murder? To me, that sounds like a pretty good story."

Eyes set, not blinking, Logan smiled. He didn't reply.

Now frustrated, Stone said, "What, dammit?"

"Lundsford," Logan said. "You mentioned his name again."

Stone was now angered but in silence. She looked away.

"You see? That's the problem. You, and everyone else, are focused on me and Lundsford. There's no story there. Nobody gives a damn about either one of us, especially Lundsford. Terrance Lundsford was a worthless piece of shit, a cancer roaming the streets. Can I put it in any easier terms?"

Stone said nothing. She let him continue, but looked down at the Dictaphone to make sure the red light was still on. It was.

"As for me, I'm just a guy. A guy that dodged an indictment for a murder that nobody really cares about. Why doesn't anyone care? Because it was Lundsford. Not exactly a jewel citizen of Tidewater Virginia was he? I doubt seriously many mourn his untimely demise."

"What about his family? His mother?" Stone asked. "Don't you think she might care?"

Logan said, "I don't know anything about Lundsford's mother. She might be a fine woman for all I know. She may have done everything she could do, exhausted every option, to keep her boy off the streets. To this day, she may carry overwhelming guilt for not being more successful. I don't know. It could be the opposite as well."

Stone said. "Well ... if you were to stop for a minute and focus on the feelings of Lundsford's mother, what would you say?"

Logan didn't say anything at first. He wanted to think before he spoke. Always a wise approach. He reached for his bourbon and took a deep sip and allowed the aromatic burn to help formulate his answer.

"It's like war, really," he said. "In every war, and in almost every battle where the final outcome benefits a greater good, there is always collateral damage."

"Collateral damage?" Stone asked surprised. "Really? Is that what you would call it?"

"Sure. It is what it is. There's always collateral damage in battle. As much as it is planned to prevent, it is unavoidable and certainly always comes with regret."

Stone asked, "Are you saying you now have regrets?"

Logan gave her a stare, a slight grin on his face. He said nothing at first, but his glare sent a silent message. *Nice try, Stone. I'm not biting.* Then he said, "Regrets? Why would I have regrets? All I'm saying is, if Lundsford's mother is a fine, respectable woman, whatever pain she feels is a shame. A mother should never have to bury their own child. It's regrettable."

Stone grabbed a pad and pen off the table as Logan spoke. Despite the Dictaphone, she jotted down a few notes. She looked up from her pad when Logan said, "Grace Matthews."

"What was that?" asked Stone.

Logan looked away frustrated. He said the name again while looking at the wall. His eyes filled with hurt when he turned back to Stone. "Grace. Grace Matthews," he said to her. "Has everyone forgotten who she is?"

"No, not at all. Grace Matthews," said Stone, "the girl Lundsford allegedly raped. You caught me off guard. I wasn't expecting to hear her name."

Logan has never married and has never had children of his own. Grace Matthews, along with her two younger brothers are as close as he has ever been to having children. He's been there their entire lives, the colloquial Uncle Nigel. He watched them grow up. He helped Grace learn to drive when her own father wasn't patient enough for the task. And he spent countless hours helping each of them with homework. Nigel loves the Matthews children as if they were his own; the only difference is blood.

Grace Matthews had just turned eighteen when Lundsford took away her purity, her innocence, and her dignity. She was beaten and raped by Lundsford, but due to the ineptness of local law enforcement, Grace never got to witness the judicial justice she was entitled to.

"You weren't expecting to hear her name because you don't care, or you stopped caring. Either way, she is the most important part of this entire crazy triangle. She's the real victim, but her story is discounted and overlooked for some dead scumbag and a retired sailor that nobody in the world gives a shit about."

Stone said nothing, just kept taking notes on occasion.

"Getting away with murder. Do you really think that is a story, especially when it can only be told through conjecture and speculation? How about all the injustices to Grace? Huh? She is the only real victim in all this. Let me ask you. When the case against Lundsford went south and fell apart, did anyone do a piece on how law enforcement and the prosecution screwed up the case? Did any of y'all in the media do your homework and try and hold the system accountable?"

Stone didn't answer.

"Hell no. None of you did. Not you or any of your cronies. But the second Lundsford's body was discovered, and I became a person of interest and later suspect number one, you guys were all over that."

Stone said, "You also remember, of course, that of all the local reporters ... who gave you the most room? Who didn't hound you with a microphone at every opportunity? Who stood off in the wings?"

It was Logan's turn to say nothing. He knew the answer.

"Exactly. It was me. I gave you all the space in the world, didn't I?"

"Yes," said Logan. "I never quite understood why. It was something I not only remember, but I appreciated as well."

"Do you want to know why?" she asked.

Logan said nothing.

Stone reached down and turned off the Dictaphone. She reached for her cocktail. Logan noticed her hand begin to shake as she took a sip. The bottom of the glass rattled against the table top as she placed it back down. She swallowed and said, "Because Grace

Matthews and I have more in common than you know. That son of a bitch raped me too."

That was the last thing Logan was expecting to hear and made him a little suspicious. *Was it a trap?* But he dismissed those notions after observing her. She was shaking all over as she looked at her feet. She looked at him and said, "You see. You're not the only one with bottled-up feelings. I have never spoken those words until just a few seconds ago."

Logan leaned forward. Said nothing. Gave her all the time she needed.

She looked at the ceiling and took a big breath and continued, "I was nineteen. Stupid. Lundsford was a young local rapper. He was just starting his career. My girlfriends and I used to love that rap music, primarily because it allowed us to be a little rebellious with our parents. Daddy hated that stuff." She stopped to reflect a moment and said, speaking to the floor, "We were all so stupid way back then."

Logan smiled and said, "Youth and stupidity. They are a package deal."

Stone looked at Logan and smiled back.

"Anyway," she said. "A bunch of us went to a small theater in Portsmouth to attend a T-Daddy concert. Like I said, he was just starting out, so the venue was small, very up close and personal. I remember, we had third-row seats and Lundsford kept making eye contact with me. Always with a big smile and occasional wink. We were having a great time, so I'd wink back."

Stone took her drink and finished it off, the remaining ice cubes clanked against the walls of the glass. She handed Logan the glass and said, "Could you make me another, please. This time a bit more vodka and a lot less tonic."

He got up to fix her a new drink and recharge his own glass. He was making his way back when she continued.

"When the show was over, he came off stage to mingle with the crowd. When he found me, he invited my whole group to a backstage party. All the other girls politely declined, but since I had driven myself I figured a backstage party sounded cool. I accepted. My girl friends looked at me like I was crazy. I was."

Logan handed her the drink and sat down next to her on the couch. She took a stiff pull from the glass and held it tight in both hands.

"At first it was really cool. Lots of people. Lots of booze. Booze that T-Daddy was pouring down me freely. Time flew by and the next thing I knew the crowd had cleared out. It was only the two of us. We were sitting on a sofa and he kissed me. I kissed back. He slid his hand up my shirt. I was so drunk. I didn't realize what was going on until he started to unbutton my jeans. I protested, tried to stop him, but..."

Stone was shaking as she relived the horrors of that night. Her drink shook and started to wash over the side of the glass and into her lap. Logan took it from her and placed it on the table, then took Stone in his arms. He pulled her close and hugged her. She accepted him and hugged back. Logan held tight for a long time as she began to cry.

From over his shoulder, Logan heard her whisper, "I never told anybody after it happened. I felt so ashamed. That son of a bitch." She tightened her grip on Logan, then backed away to face him, kissing him on the neck as she passed.

"That is why I'm so interested in you. Don't you see? I needed to see you, spend a little time with you. I wanted to get to know you better, so I could better understand the man that freed me from that nightmare. You were the one to give Grace, me, and God knows who else their justice."

Logan was about say something, but Stone cut him off. "Don't say a word. Don't deny it. I don't want to hear you lie. You're better than that. It's best if you just don't say a word."

Logan took her advice and remained silent.

"I researched you thoroughly. I already know what kind of man you are. I spoke with Charlie Matthews, your old captain and friend, strictly off the record. He told me what kind of guy you were. How you are. It was tough for him to talk about it all: Grace, the rape, his relationship with you, and your arrest. It has been especially difficult for him because he hasn't spoken to you since you disappeared. He misses you so. You should know that."

It was true. Logan hasn't spoken to his dear friend since he retired and left the ship. Logan missed him too, but thought it best to stay away. He didn't want to tarnish his captain's career and reputation any further than he already had.

Logan stopped to remember his last meeting with Charlie. It was in the captain's stateroom, the morning after the Grand Jury failed to indict him. Logan came by at the captain's request. It was then that he told Charlie about his retirement. It was then that Charlie wanted to ask him if he had done it. It was then that Logan told him some questions are better left unasked. It was then that Logan last saw or spoke to his friend.

"You see," she said. "We know you killed Lundsford. We know it in our hearts, and we like it that way. You will never fully know the appreciation we feel for you and the sacrifices you have made to set us free."

Logan looked at Stone. She was smiling. She leaned in towards him and whispered, "Thank you."

Their lips met, a gentle kiss at first. She smelled great. They pulled away and looked at each other. She smiled. He touched her face along her cheek; a final tear was streaking down the side of her nose. He wiped it away with his thumb and cradled her head in his hand and pulled her into a long passionate kiss. She moved closer as he was doing the same.

Her hands began to explore underneath his shirt tracing the contours of his muscular chest. He slid his hand up the back of her shirt, rubbed and squeezed her bare back working his hand to the back of her neck. She came up for air, tilting her head back and exposing the underside of her chin. Logan moved his lips to her neck and nibbled his way to her left ear. Stone moaned and began pulling up on Logan's shirt. He didn't protest as he moved and shifted making it easier for her to untuck it all around his waist.

Their lips and tongues found each other again. No place inside their mouths went unexplored. She backed away to look at him. She was smiling, biting her bottom lip, a sexy look of guilt. Then she took his hand, licked his palm and placed it over her left breast. He felt her hard nipple in the center of his hand. He pressed, spreading his fingers out to explore. She was as firm as he expected when he tightened his fingers. She groaned and began to open his shirt, making quick work of the buttons until his tight chest was exposed. She ran her fingers through the hairs on his chest.

Then it was his turn. He began to unbutton her blouse but took his sweet time of it. He could tell she wanted him to move faster, but he was slow and methodical about it. When he cleared the last button he slid the silky material back off her shoulders and allowed her blouse to fall away past her fingers. Her body was perfect, one hundred percent tanned. He reached with both hands and with a soft touch allowed his fingers to trace every contour.

Stone reached over with her hands, grabbed both sides of his head and pulled him into her breasts. He took in a nipple with his lips and sucked until it found its way between his teeth. He gave it a nibble and she arched her back and whimpered, "Harder." And he did.

He spent ample time working on her perfect body, giving each breast equal time until she pushed him away towards the back of the sofa. She moved off the couch and knelt on the floor between his legs. She spread his knees wide so she could get as close to him as possible, then she buried her face and lips into his chest. Logan tilted his head back, enjoying every moment; then he felt her move to his belt. It was unbuckled in no time revealing the top button of his jeans. It gave a little pop. It was undone.

When she moved to his zipper, there was none. She looked up at him and said, "Oh ... button fly. Perfect."

He brought his head down to watch. She was about halfway down his fly, working the buttons off when he noticed something sticking out of his pocket. He took a free hand and pulled it out. It was a piece of paper, a note. Not just any note, the note. *Whenever you get through doing whatever it is you are doing, we need to talk.*

Whatever excitement and arousal he was feeling disappeared at that precise moment. He looked at the note and read it again, and again. His body relaxed, enough so that Sherry Stone could tell a change in his mood and state of mind. She felt him deflate. After getting the last button cleared, she looked up and asked, "What's wrong?"

Disappointed with himself, he gestured with a slight nod of the head. "Sherry," he said. "I'm so sorry. I just can't do this."

They both looked at each other for several beats before she said, "You're kidding me, right?"

"No. I'm sorry. I'm afraid not."

Stone sat back on her heels and took a deep breath. "Damn, Logan. You sure know how to break a girl's heart."

"I'm sorry. Actually, that's what I'm trying to prevent."

Stone looked up and saw the note in his hand. "It's from her, isn't it? That bartender girl?"

"Her name is Candice."

Stone said nothing.

"Again, I'm sorry. You are so attractive and drop-dead gorgeous. I lost my head. You see, I..."

Stone put her hand out and motioned for him to stop. She reached over and found her blouse, started to put it back on and said, "You don't have to explain anything. Really you don't. As bad as I wanted this to happen, I understand. Rejection is hard to accept, but I understand."

"So you're not mad?"

"Mad? No, not mad. Maybe a little hurt and embarrassed, but not mad."

She stood up and walked across the room to put herself back together. Logan did the same, tucking in his shirt and fixing his jeans and belt. He sat back down on the sofa.

She had her back to him as she spoke, "One thing is for sure."

Logan said nothing.

"As bad as I would have liked to have woken up with you in the morning, you didn't disappoint."

"How do you mean?"

She turned around and walked back towards him looking like nothing ever happened, she looked great. She sat next to him and said, "You are every bit the man, if not more, that Captain Matthews described. He said you were a guy of incredible honor and dignity ... How did he put it? Oh yeah, he said, 'Logan doesn't just do what's right. He does the right thing. There's a difference.' I would say he hit that nail square on the head."

Logan smiled. He knew she wasn't lying. Those were Charlie's words, no doubt. The difference between *what's right* and *the right thing* was a conversation they often had. Doing what's right follows a convention that there are rules and regulations to be followed. It's a path of action and expected behavior that is supposed to contain everything in some neat, safe package. Doing the right thing often means stepping outside, often way outside what one might often expect. The rules don't always fit the circumstances, so they need bending, maybe even breaking to achieve the results which best serves the greater good.

Logan said, "Charlie speaks a little too highly of me I'm afraid. I'm just a results-driven guy, and achieving those results isn't often very pretty."

Stone took his hand and said, "You will never be able to convince me of that, ever." She leaned in to kiss him one last time. He kissed her back, but not to the degree that Stone had hoped.

"What about your story?"

She held up her hand again and said, "Don't worry. I have all the material I need, more than enough actually. I'll send you a copy when it runs."

Logan nodded his head and stood up to leave. Stone remained seated as he headed towards the door. When he grabbed the doorknob, she said, "Hey, Logan."

He turned around and looked at her as she said, "That Candice is one lucky girl. Don't be an idiot and fuck it up. You'll piss me off."

Logan smiled at her words, and then walked out the door.

Promises

It had been two days since Logan left a very hot and bothered Sherry Stone to a cold shower in her hotel room, and he still hadn't seen or spoken with Candice. It wasn't for lack of trying though. He drove past her house that night, but her Jeep wasn't in the drive. He tried calling, but was unable to leave a message. He would dial her number, but the call would end after a few rings. No Candice and no voicemail. She wasn't taking his calls. She was answering, but ending them right after picking up. *Dammit.*

Logan isn't one to play head games. He hates them. But, he also knew, this one was on him. He had to take ownership of that.

He dropped by the Reid Avenue Bar and Bottle Shop on a couple of occasions, but she was never there. His last trip found Tracy, the Harbor Hotel bartender, working the bar and draft beer station. He approached her and asked, "Tracy, what are you doing here?"

Tracy didn't acknowledge him. She ignored him while pulling a pint of brew for another patron. Logan stood there as she stepped around the draft station and hollered down the bar, "Hey, Mikey! Heads up." Tracy took the mug of beer and launched it down the bar. Logan turned his head and watched as it slid down the runway on a collision course with another glass which was lifted just in time. Two or three stools later, Logan saw a hand pop out and bring the mug to a gentle stop. Nigel smiled as he turned his attention back to Tracy.

Tracy gave him a cold stare before asking, "What do you want?"

"Where is Candice?"

"I'm filling in for her. She's taking a few days off. Against my recommendation I might add, but she wouldn't listen."

"What do you mean? Against your recommendation."

Tracy didn't say anything. She looked at Logan with contempt, eyes wide; her lips formed a tight line. *None of your business.*

"Do me a favor, please?" Logan asked. "Tell her I came by to see her."

Logan turned to leave. After a few steps, Tracy yelled after him with a lie, "You know she won't care, right?"

Logan stepped out onto the sidewalk and jumped into his truck. He stopped to think about what Tracy had said: Candice was taking a few days off. He could understand that, but the part about doing so despite Tracy's recommendation bothered him. What did she mean by that?

He shook his head and thought to himself. *Don't be a worry wart. Candice is a smart and savvy gal. She can take care of herself.* She couldn't ignore him for long. It was a small town. He'd catch up to her sooner or later. He didn't give it much more thought as he started his truck and drove away.

At the end of Reid Avenue he made a snap decision to drive around the block. As he turned down Main Street, he saw an extraordinary number of cars parked in front of a small, old retail space. Painted in big letters across the top of the wide picture window were the letters R. I. D. D. Underneath in much smaller letters were the words, Red's Institution for Drunk Drivers.

Curious, Logan decided to stop. He parked across the street and had to walk about a block and a half. As he approached the big window to get a better look, the place was full of all sorts of folks including children. He saw one of the reporters from the local newspaper, *The Star*. Most everyone was dressed up in their Sunday best; smiles were everywhere. Logan became startled when his buddy Red popped his knuckles on the window and motioned for him to come in. He did.

When he got to the door, his questions were answered. A cardboard sign was taped to the front door glass: No class today. Graduation, 1:00 PM. Logan looked at his watch. It said 1255. Things were preparing to kick off. He stepped inside and took a spot in the back of the room and watched as the chaotic, social mingling began to organize itself into some semblance of order.

Six individuals, four men and two women stood tall in front of chairs facing the crowd. The room was set up like a small auditorium with folded chairs in neat rows, an aisle down the middle. Family and friends began taking their seats, but Logan decided to remain standing in the back, a fly on the wall.

With the small assembly seated, Red was preparing to address the crowd and graduates. Red took his position off to the side and faced the attendees. He looked good. He was clean-shaven, in shorts and flip flops, but he dressed it up by wearing a clean and pressed shirt, a white short-sleeved oxford.

At precisely 1300 Red nodded to the graduates and they took their seats. Then he spoke, addressing the attendees with grand ceremonious flair, "Ladies and gentlemen..." He paused a bit to squat down so he could address the children in attendance, "... boys and girls." He stood back up straight to refocus on the entire assembly, "Thank you for coming. Today is a big day for some folks in the room." He chuckled looking down the line of soon-to-be graduates and said, "I don't think there's any secret who those folks are." There was courteous laughter coming from the rest of the room and the occasional flash from the reporter's camera. "But the truth is," Red continued, "it's a big day for all of you. To the families and friends of the class here before you, they couldn't have made it this far without your unconditional love and support. For it is only through..."

Nigel could not keep a straight face. This was a DUI school, a path of education where attendance and participation is part of some legal requirement, usually court-ordered. It isn't vocational training designed to help discover some awaiting career path. However, there was Red, carrying on with much grandiose fanfare. Earning one's long sought after doctorate never warranted as much.

For most of the graduates, it appeared painful and embarrassing to sit there and be part of such a drawn-out proceeding. Nigel figured it must be one of Red's requirements of the school: *Successful completion of the course is only satisfied after suffering through a humiliating graduation ceremony complete with media coverage.* The look on their faces spoke volumes: *Give me my goddamn certificate or fucking shoot me now. Put me out of my misery.*

Nigel stopped his internal laughing and returned, best he could, to paying attention to Red and the event.

"...so their hard work has finally paid off. The long hours of studying after work, of burning the midnight oil late into the night has finally come to an end. Their efforts have yielded much fruit." Red paused for theatrical effect before continuing. "I can't even imagine the sacrifices they have made to get to this moment. Think about it for a moment. How many piano and dance recitals have been missed? Think of the baseball games that had to be played without mom or dad in the stands. It really is amazing. But *that* is what dedication is all about." Red stopped to look at the class as they sat before the audience. Then he said, "Ladies and gentlemen ... boys and girls, I give you the latest RIDD graduates. Let's give them a heartfelt round of applause."

The clapping went on longer than expected; everyone took their applause cue from Red. As long as he was clapping, everyone else would too. He stopped once the local reporter indicated he had gotten enough pictures. The room went quiet with abrupt quickness. It seemed the graduation was coming to an end. Everyone, including Nigel, was ready for it to be over. They wouldn't get that lucky.

"Family and friends," Red started, "I have a special treat for you. Something I've never done before. I'm surprised I haven't thought of it sooner, and I'm actually contemplating making it a part of the regular program in the future." Red paused for a beat and continued, "As I've described, graduation day is a big deal. Getting here isn't easy, so wouldn't it be fitting to allow the class valedictorian an opportunity to address his or her classmates and the assembly?"

Nigel watched as the graduates seemed to deflate before his very eyes. Most of them anyway, one graduate seemed to do the opposite. The mention of the word *valedictorian* caused one graduate to inflate with excitement and pride. Another graduate turned his head and said to Red, "Valedictorian! Red ... You got to be shitting me. Really?"

In a lower voice, but loud enough that everyone else could hear, Red said, "I wouldn't shit you, Steve. You're my favorite turd. Now hush up. If you had studied harder, it could have been you."

The student named Steve turned his head back towards the crowd, but not without letting the words, "Fuck me," slip though his lips. *Poor fella.*

Red said, "Ladies and gentlemen, the student you are about to hear from is graduating with an "A+" average. I've checked my records, and it stands as one of the highest grades ever achieved here at the institute. So, without any further delay, I'd like to introduce Dan Masters."

The student sitting closest to Red stood. There was a mixture of applause, some more enthusiastic than others. It wasn't hard to figure out who was and wasn't family. Red stepped back and sat at his desk.

He took his coffee cup in one hand and reached down to open a lower desk drawer with the other. There was no doubt in Nigel's mind what Red was doing. He knew all too well about the handle of seven year old Jim Beam he kept there.

In short order, the cup reappeared and Red took a sip as young Dan addressed the crowd.

At first, young Dan said nothing. He gazed out at the crowd, and then with beaming enthusiasm he picked someone out in the audience and said, "I made it, Momma. I really made it."

From the audience Nigel heard, "Love you, Junior. We're so proud."

It was an emotional moment for the young man. He couldn't have been more than 20 years old, but he held it together and said, "My name is Dan Masters. I'm from Wewa. For those of you that don't know, that's short for Wewahitchka." Everybody already knew that. "When Judge Rawlings ordered me to attend a DUI school, I got scared. I thought to myself, 'A school? Really? I hate schools.' Truth is, it wasn't so much that I hate schools, but I am afraid of them. I've never graduated from anything." He paused as gentle cooing sounds of sympathy oozed out of the audience. *Bless his heart.*

"But I knew," he continued, "that failure just wasn't an option this time. I knew that if I ever wanted to drive again, I'd have to pass. I was nervous, so I began asking around. Most all my buddies have had a DUI at one point or another, so I knew they would have an inside scoop on what school was best. They told me that Red's Institute for Drunk Divers was by far the best."

Nigel noticed Red sit up a little taller and smile proud. He wasn't expecting such a glowing endorsement. Nor was he expecting what followed.

Dan said, "Yeah, that's right. They said, 'You got to go to RIDD. Red is so cool, and it is easy as shit.'"

Red's smile started to straighten out to a thin line and his eyes started to flutter in concern. It got worse when young Dan went on to explain, "My buddy Ned said, 'He doesn't ever take roll and all the tests are open book.' And my good friend Bobby said, 'And he sleeps at his desk all the time.' But that wasn't really true. I only saw him sleep like twice, maybe three times."

The rest of the graduates were no longer frowning. They were all smiles. They were enjoying the address by Mr. Masters, chuckling as he continued, "My other friend Bubba said, 'There was this time...'"

Red jumped up and said, "Well ... That was interesting. Thank you, Mr. Masters. I appreciate you sharing your positive experience here."

Red's star student said, "But Red ... I'm not finished. I still..."

"Oh, hell yeah you're done. That was a fabulous speech. I can't tell you how much I appreciate those heartfelt remarks." Through the corner of his mouth Red said, "Now sit your little ass down."

Turning to the rest of the audience Red gave a big smile and said, "What y'all think? Let's get to some certificates."

Later, after everyone was gone, it was just Red and Nigel sitting around the desk. Red pulled out another coffee cup and poured Nigel a bump of Jim Beam. They clanked their cups and Red said, "Cheers, my friend. Hell of a day."

They took a sip and Nigel said, "So the valedictorian thing didn't turn out to be such a smart thing after all, huh?"

"That little bastard," Red said. "I never went to sleep during class. I may have dozed a time or two, but that ain't sleeping. The little fucker."

"Don't let it bother you. Forget about it. It was some funny shit though."

"Shut your hole, Nigel. How can I forget about it if you keep on?"

"Fair enough." Nigel changed the subject, "Hey ... Let me take you and Trixie out to dinner tonight."

"That sounds great but Trixie's in Tallahassee for the next few days visiting a girlfriend."

"Okay ... Then just you and me, my treat. But I got to go. I need to run down to the marina and check on the boat. I've neglected her and she needs some cleaning. Meet me at The Seaside Cafe around eight. I hear the special tonight is going to be great. They got in some monster flounder, so it should be good."

As Nigel was walking down the dock he tried to call Candice. It went straight to voicemail. Putting the phone back in his pocket he said, "Shit!"

MisChief was still and comfortable in her slip. She wasn't as dirty as he let on, but Nigel likes to stay ahead of the dirt and salt. Above all else, there are fewer things he likes more than spending time on the boat. It is a good place to be quiet and think, and he had plenty to think about. Candice mostly.

He spent the next two hours giving her a rub with the boat brush and a freshwater wash down. The entire time he thought of Candice and about what he was going to do. He liked her more than just a little. It's a lot, a whole bunch. That was something he had already come to terms with. To move things along, though, would mean he would need to talk to her about his past. But how much of his past should he reveal? That was the question.

The deck and topsides were clean; *MisChief* looked great. Nigel put away his cleaning gear and went below to grab a cold beer out of the fridge. He returned to the cockpit and got comfortable. Thoughts of Candice returned.

He sat in the very spot where Candice once settled into a cozy embrace with him and fell asleep. It was after a late evening sail. They had dropped the hook so they could ride on the anchor and enjoy the night sky. The chill of the air brought blankets, more red wine, and the need to exchange body heat. They got warm and comfortable in a tight wrap. Candice dozed off first and Nigel watched her face as she fell deeper into slumber. He held her until he too fell away in sleep.

That was the night Nigel was thinking about now. He took a sip of beer and remembered how he felt when he awoke several hours later. It was still dark, but the morning sun was just starting to illuminate the edges of the eastern sky. When his eyes adjusted to the dark, he saw her face through the shadows of the early morning. He remembered how beautiful she looked and how comfortable it seemed to wake up together like that.

Nigel caught himself smiling as he sipped his beer. Then he contemplated a serious question. If it was all over, if she was removed from his life, never to return, how would that make him feel?

The smile faded. He let the thought of her being only a memory sink in. He wasn't enjoying the hypothetical. Then he realized it might not be a hypothetical. She hadn't answered any of his calls, and she wasn't allowing herself to be found. *What if it was too late?*

He felt miserable. That was it. That was the honest answer to the question. *Misery.* The thought of her not being there, or something happening to her made him sick to his stomach.

His mind returned to *MisChief.* Again, it was the perfect place to think things through. He looked about the deck and noticed the hot sun had done a fine job of drying the boat, including the teak.

He needed something to do while his mind worked through the details about Candice. He grabbed a bottle of teak oil and some rags and started on the handrails. He worked and rubbed the oil into the wood being careful not to get any on the deck. As the handrails absorbed the oil, the teak took on a rich appearance, a color that popped in contrast to *MisChief's* white deck. That made him happy.

Nigel loves the look of oiled teak. Most sailors do, but most hate doing the actual brightwork. Nigel loves it. It serves as good therapy during those times when he needs to let his mind wander. This was such a time. It served as the perfect distraction and allowed other truths to settle into his brain. By the time he was halfway through the second set of handrails, the misery was gone. Like the oil and the teak, the truth about him and Candice soaked in. He was smiling again, but to keep smiling he'd have to set things right.

Red was late. Nigel expected it. He is rarely on time for anything. It's not that Red always runs behind. He's just not in a big hurry to get anywhere. If he spots a bald eagle, or a pod of dolphin working a school of jumping mullet, he will take a moment to stop and watch. Taking in nature ranks high on his list of priorities, much higher than meeting the likes of Nigel Logan or anyone else for that matter. He once told Nigel, "Nature is far more interesting than humans." His twenty-minute delay wasn't taken with offense.

There was no hurry; the wait was quite pleasant. Brian Bowen and another waterfront guitar player, Sailor Larry, were both on the outside deck entertaining the tourists. Brian plays a 60-minute set followed by Sailor Larry with his own 60-minute set. Then, after a short break, they play the last 90 minutes together. It's a perfect arrangement. The type of music each plays is different enough that there is no overlap of tunes and near non-stop music for the patrons.

When Red slipped into the bar, Brian was still playing out his set. He was between songs when Red walked over to the window and hollered down to the deck, "*Nets,* dammit. Play *Nets.*"

Brian pointed at Red and gave him a nod and said, "Right on! You got it brother."

Nets is one of Brian's newer original tunes, written about the downfall of a mullet fishing industry ravaged by tree huggers and silly state regulations imposed by the Florida Wildlife Commission. The song is a favorite of Nigel's too, and it gets quite a bit of airplay on Oyster Radio. Nigel sings along in the truck and gets especially loud when it comes time to sing ...*the huggers and the state can kiss my ass.*

Nigel turned the ringer off on his phone and checked his watch when Red slipped into the booth. He was wearing the same shorts from earlier in the day, but had dressed down a bit sporting a Florida State Seminole visor and a gold colored T-shirt that said, **Still Drunker Than You.** Nigel said, "Twenty-two minutes late. I've seen better. I've seen worse. What marvel of nature detained you this time?"

"Tourists," said Red. "I was stocking up on beer and the CVS checkout line was full of them. It was murder."

They were interrupted by their waitress, a pretty little blonde. She brought waters and menus. She looked to be in her mid-twenties, and she was gorgeous except for her nonstop gum smacking, the over-done eye shadow, and the pack of Marlboro Lights that showed at the top of her skimpy apron. Her name tag told them her name was Cindy. A sassy attitude peeked through when she asked, "You don't ... like ... want anything to drink or anything, do you?" Then she blew and popped a quick bubble.

Nigel said, "Well ... Hello, Cindy. This here," pointing with an open palm, "is my buddy Red."

Red and Cindy acknowledged each other with a nod as Nigel continued, "Now Cindy, Red and I definitely want to start things off with a couple beers. Bring us a couple of drafts; two of those Oyster City blonde ales would be nice."

"You want anything else, an appetizer or something?" Another bubble. *Pop!*

Nigel ignored the question. He found it fascinating how she could talk and never miss a beat with the vicious bubblegum chewing. It would be impossible for a deaf person to read her lips. The motion of her mouth never once matched a single word that was uttered. It was like watching an old Japanese movie dubbed in

English. Then on top of everything else, to throw in a quick bubble for effect; that was classy.

Nigel was feeling pretty good. He had made a decision about him and Candice, one he felt good about. In addition, he was about to have dinner with his crazy, best buddy. It was a night poised to be entertaining, so why not have a little fun with their waitress Cindy. If she plays nice and tolerates the two of them, she'd be well compensated later.

Nigel said, "Now, Cindy. Before you go off and bring us those frosty mugs topped off with tasty beer, there's something I need to make perfectly clear." Pointing back and forth between himself and Red, Nigel said, "We. The two of us. Me and Red. We are here together, just the two of us. Do you get where I'm going with this?"

Cindy looked at both of them. *Smack ... Smack ... Pop. Smack ... Smack ... Pop.* "Are you two like on a date or something?"

Nigel said, "Exactly my point. Lord, no. You shouldn't make such rash assumptions. Just because we are here, two men..."

"Two, damn good-looking men I might add," Red interjected.

"Exactly, Red," Nigel responded. "Let's not forget some of the finer details," Nigel returned his attention to the waitress. "Just because we are here together, two ... damn good-looking men, you shouldn't automatically think we are gay."

Cindy starting to look at the ceiling as Nigel went on. "I can promise you. Unequivocally, and beyond a shadow of any doubt, we are not a couple."

Smack ... Smack ... Pop. "Whatever you say. Can I go now?"

"Not that there would be anything wrong with it, if we were ... a couple, you know. Isn't that right, Red?"

"Exactly," Red said, "We might be straight, but we're a couple of pretty hip dudes."

Nigel didn't let up, "Cindy, even if you witness me cutting up his food for him, or you see him, God forbid, eating off my plate, which is highly possible ... under no circumstances whatsoever should you..."

Nigel felt Red reach across the table with both hands and take hold of his left hand. Nigel continued while Red rubbed and patted the top of Nigel's hand. "...ever think ... that for one second we're a couple. Nope, We're just a couple of regular dudes, promise."

Nigel saw Cindy look over at Red, so he glanced across the booth. Red was still holding Nigel's hand. His lips held a pursed smile as his eye lashes fluttered.

Nigel turned back to Cindy and said, "Pay no attention to him. Hey! What about those beers?"

Cindy rolled her eyes into the top of her head. *Smack ... Smack ... Pop.* "You two are sick."

After a few minutes she brought the beers. They were served in decorative glasses; two palm trees were painted on the front with a huge rainbow that arched over them.

Nigel looked at his beer, then to Red, and then to Cindy and said, "Nice touch."

Smack ... Smack ... Pop. Smack ... Smack ... Pop. "I thought you'd like that."

"Touché."

They ordered the baked flounder. They were as described: monsters. The beasts engulfed the plates, hanging over the side. They were scored with a decorative diamond design and cooked to perfection; the meat was light and flaky. The hush puppies and slaw had to be delivered on separate plates. Yummy!

Over dinner they talked about the graduation, about how naming young Dan Masters as valedictorian was probably a mistake. Red said, "Sleeping? Really? Doesn't the little bastard know the difference between sleeping and dozing? Even Einstein was known for his catnaps." Several times during the conversation Red referred to young Dan as Mr. Bastards.

The subject of Mr. Bastards fell away and the both of them started chuckling like a couple of school boys when, sure enough, Nigel reached over and stabbed a piece of fish from Red's plate. Red retaliated by nabbing a couple of Nigel's hush puppies.

Their chuckles and smiles retreated into thin, straight-lipped expressions as Brian Bowen approached the booth. Red scooted over to make room. Brian looked sick. Nigel said, "What is it?"

"Is your phone dead, dude?" Brian asked.

"No. The ringer's off. I'm at dinner."

Nigel reached over to look at his phone. He had missed five calls, all from Ms. Gloria the hairdresser. Confused, he looked back at Brian and said, "Gloria's been calling."

The booth went quiet for an uncomfortable period. Becoming frustrated, Nigel demanded, "What, goddammit? What's going on?"

"You've got to get over there," said Brian. "To the shop. It's Candice." Brian paused for a beat and finished, "Gloria says it's pretty bad."

Nigel froze for a moment. He was letting the news sink in. Then he called out, "Cindy! Over here. Now … Please."

As Nigel was gathering his things off the table, he pulled a hundred dollar bill out of his wallet. Standing up he handed it to her. "This should cover everything. Keep the change." Then he bolted out the door.

Brian moved over to Nigel's side of the booth as Red asked, "What's going on?"

"Gloria said she's been beaten up. Pretty bad by the sounds of it."

Red said, "Oh … That's terrible." He got quiet. He was thinking. Brian watched Red's eyes open wide. Red said, "Oh shit!"

"What is it?"

"It's Nigel. We've got to get over there and help. Make sure he doesn't do something stupid. Something he'll regret later."

"Whatcha mean?"

"I'm not at liberty to say right now. We just got to get our asses over there. Do you have time to come with me?"

Brian looked at his watch and nodded. Sailor Larry had just started his set. That would provide plenty of time.

When Sherry Stone, the news reporter from Norfolk was snooping around, it was obvious to Red she had a specific interest in Nigel. *But why?* He did a little snooping around himself and a Google search of Nigel's name revealed details about Norfolk and the Terrance "T-Daddy" Lundsford murder.

Red studied the news reports, read all about it. Nigel was the primary suspect. It was believed by law enforcement and the prosecution that his motive was to avenge the rape of a young girl in her late teens, the daughter of his commanding officer. The rape was particularly brutal and in connection to a carjacking. The prosecution team screwed up the handling of the critical DNA evidence, and with the victim unable to identify her assailant, the case was dropped by the district attorney. T-Daddy was released back into society. It was theorized that Chief Petty Officer Nigel Logan decided to take the law into his own hands. His own 9MM Beretta was found at the scene, his partial fingerprints all over it. His whereabouts couldn't be accounted for during the time of the homicide, and there was surveillance camera evidence that placed him in the vicinity of the crime earlier that evening.

Despite the evidence, the Grand Jury did not hand down an indictment. It was an embarrassing moment for the district attorney. Many speculated that some reviewing the evidence became sympathetic to the young girl Lundsford allegedly raped and to the Chief whose record was above reproach. Lundsford was notorious for being bad news, a nasty sort, and few in the community mourned his ultimate demise.

Nigel stormed through the door of the beauty parlor. Gloria's head popped out from behind a curtain that shielded one of the station chairs. She had a pained look on her face and was shaking her head no. She had been crying.

Nigel eased over towards the station. Gloria said, "She told me not to call you. But..."

He stepped around the curtain. Candice was sitting there with her face leaned over in a bag of ice. Known for her frequent changes, Nigel noticed she had dyed her hair. It was jet black. A look she knew wasn't his favorite.

Gloria said, "Candice, baby. It's Nigel. He's here, sweetheart."

Nigel kneeled down to look at her. He reached out and touched the side of her head and coaxed, "Candice. Look at me."

"Go away."

Nigel gave Gloria a quick glance looking for assistance. Gloria coaxed him on. He turned back to Candice. "No. I'm not going anywhere. I'm right here. Where I belong. With you."

Nigel looked back at Gloria and watched as she was nodding her head in approval. *You're doing fine. Keep it up.*

"Candice," Nigel said, "please look at me."

"Go away ... I don't want you to see me like this."

"Candice. Please." Nigel reached over and took hold of the ice. She was reluctant, but surrendered it and looked up.

Through the swelling of her left eye she was able to see Nigel smiling at her. Her right eye was swollen shut, black and blue with bruising. Her right jaw was puffy too, highlighted by a fat and busted lip. She looked at him and busted out in tears. The bleeding inside her mouth was still active. Blood was around her teeth when she said, "I'm so sorry. Please forgive me."

Nigel shook his head. His heart was aching. He looked up at the ceiling for answers. Then he reached to touch her face, to ease a tear away from her cheek and said, "Don't be silly. You have nothing to apologize for."

"But this is my entire fault."

Nigel said nothing. It hurt him even more to hear those words. *My fault.* How she could even begin to blame herself was beyond him. Never before, in his life, had he ever been shouldered with a greater feeling of guilt. This was his fault, not hers, and he took ownership of it.

She said, "I'm such an idiot."

"You can stop that kind of talk right now. You're not the idiot here."

It was a quiet moment between the two as they looked at each other. Nigel inched closer and closer. She saw his pain. His insides were being ripped apart. She reached over to touch his face. Now she was comforting him. Tears were pooling up in his lower lids. She tried her best to smile when she said, "I know. You're the idiot."

Nigel smiled back. He sniffled back the emotion and wiped away the tears. "I see you changed your hair color. Did you do that for me?"

It hurt her to do so, but they laughed and Nigel came in for a gentle hug. Then they cried together.

It's funny what emotions tears can muster. At first, they were tears of sympathy. They felt the other's pain, guilt, regret, sadness, and embarrassment. Then there was a slow shift. Candice's tears became those of happiness. She was being held by the man she cared for most, and she felt his sincerity. Nigel's tears became those of happiness too. He knew she was going to be alright. *They* were going to be alright. Then his tears boiled away as the fire of anger grew on his cheeks.

Nigel took her by the shoulders and stood back so he could look in her eyes. "Candice, baby. Who did this?"

She said nothing.

"I'm serious, Candice. Who did this to you? Tell me. I want to know, now."

She started to cry again.

Nigel looked up at Gloria and she motioned with her finger. *Come here.* When he stood, Gloria leaned in and whispered in his ear, "She's incredibly embarrassed."

Nigel wasn't whispering, but kept his voice down. "I don't care about that. Who was it?"

Gloria whispered a name and Nigel jumped back to look at her in disbelief. She was nodding her head in affirmation. Nigel repeated the name to make sure he heard her correctly, "Phil Stewart. You're sure about that." Gloria never stopped nodding her head. Nigel looked down at Candice. She returned a look of shame and humiliation. He knelt back down and took her into his arms and said, "Oh, I'm so sorry. Please forgive me."

Phil Stewart was Candice's first husband, a controlling, nasty bastard. He worked the shrimp boats. Nigel met him once and wasn't impressed, but lazy shits never do. Phil Stewart could not stand Nigel. He knew Nigel was seeing Candice and he couldn't stand the thought. Candice warned Nigel once about Phil that he was looking to make trouble. Little did Phil know, but at the moment ... the tables of trouble had turned.

"Where is he?"

Candice said nothing. Nigel looked to Gloria, but she shrugged her shoulders. He looked back at Candice and asked again.

Candice reached out and took his hands. "Forget about that piece of shit. Let's just move on. I did something very stupid, to hurt you, and it backfired. I ended up getting what I deserved."

Nigel started to shake. He slung her hands back into her lap and stood up saying, "Stop talking like that. Nobody deserves..." He bit his lip in a feeble attempt to control his anger. Then he asked again, "Now. Where is he?"

From behind him he heard a familiar voice, "He's at the city bar." The city bar was a euphemism for the Reid Avenue Bar and Bottle Shop, the bar Candice manages.

Nigel turned to see Brian Bowen and Red standing there. They had snuck in while Nigel was holding Candice.

Red shot Brian a look. Brian said, "What? I saw his truck there on our way over here."

113

Red said nothing.

Nigel said, "Thanks, Brian."

Nigel looked down at Candice. She was giving him a look of her own. *Let it go, baby. Just let it go.*

He wouldn't.

He knelt down again and took her hands. She looked down at her lap. He said, "This. All of this … it's my fault. I'm so sorry." He reached up and placed a finger under her chin and lifted so he could see her face. "Listen to me." She did her best to open her right eye. "He will never do this to you, ever again. I promise. Do you understand me? I promise. You will never again have to worry about Phil Stewart."

He reached in and kissed her on the lips. She twitched in pain, but tolerated it kissing him back.

He stood and asked Gloria if she would take Candice home and stay with her until he could get over there. She smiled and nodded.

Nigel walked up and hugged Gloria kissing her on the cheek. Gloria hugged back and whispered in his ear, "Bust his ass."

Nigel said nothing. He headed towards the door passing Red and Brian without even an acknowledgement. Once the bells of the door stopped ringing, Red looked at Brian and said, "Come on. We got to go after him."

The Reid Avenue Bar and Bottle Shop isn't far from Gloria's beauty shop. Just a few blocks away and around a couple corners. Nigel headed there with singular purpose. He was studying in his mind the layout of the joint. It's a long and deep room, not skinny, but much deeper in proportion to its width. The bar runs along the right wall, a little less than half the depth of the room. High top tables and chairs line the wall opposite the bar. Mirrors run the entire length of the bar on each side, giving the appearance of a much larger establishment. Further back in the room sat a few tables, mostly pool tables.

Nigel published in his mind the blueprint of the bar like a nautical chart. He knew he couldn't plan anything until he got inside, but several scenarios ran through his head as he walked.

Red called after him, "Nigel. Hold up. Wait for us."

He didn't.

Red said, "What exactly, dammit, do you think you are going to do?"

Nigel turned his head to the side and said, "Won't know until I get there. Making this up as I go along." Then he tore off in a run and disappeared around the corner.

Red said, "Oh, shit. Not good."

Nigel barged through the door but only a few took notice. It was loud with music and conversation. He stood in the doorway scanning the entire place with his eyes. His lower lip was close to bleeding as he was biting and thinking, *Show yourself. Where are you?*

Tracy was down at the far end of the bar listening on the phone. A few stools down from her, on the very end, and facing towards the door was Billy Townsend. Billy saw Nigel at the door and could tell he was looking for somebody. Billy dropped down to hide behind his beer.

Billy was Candice's third and latest ex-husband. When Nigel first made landfall in Port St. Joe, he was the town's newest stranger. It was his first visit into town when Billy made the mistake of getting a little too physical with Candice, Nigel's newest, favorite bartender. Nigel stepped in to introduce himself. Things didn't work out so well for Billy. It was Billy's memory of that night that caused him to duck and cower behind his beer. He relaxed though when he saw Nigel's eyes lock on Phil Stewart. Billy took a sip of beer and said, "Uh ... Oh."

Tracy heard Billy and she asked, "Uh Oh, what?"

Billy pointed towards the door with his head.

Tracy smiled.

Phil Stewart was about halfway down the bar. He was drinking beer and talking smack with a couple of other shrimpers. Nigel recognized one of them as Luther Collins, otherwise known as Little Bit, a true contradiction in terms.

Nigel wasted no time making his way towards the bar. He found Tracy watching him, so he raised his voice and said to her, "You need to call an ambulance." Shifting his focus to the target he yelled, "Phil Stewart. I got something to tell you."

Phil looked up and turned to his right to see Nigel heading his way and said, "Fuck you, ass..."

Before Phil could finish Nigel held nothing back and hit him with a bitch slap to the left side of his face. It ripped his head around

115

and knocked him off his bar stool. Nigel kept walking towards the pool tables, never looked back. He didn't have to. The mirrors told him everything he needed to know. By now, all eyes were on Nigel. He pulled a ten dollar bill out of his pocket and tossed it on one of the pool tables and said, "Sorry, guys. I'm going to need this table."

He could see Phil charging after him in the mirror. Nigel reached down and grabbed the cue ball and wrapped his fist around it tight. In a single motion he turned around and brought the loaded fist from behind, a fast hook, and connected with Phil's jaw. A cracking noise came from his mouth. Phil dropped to his knees.

The next thing Nigel knew, he was on his own knees. One of Phil's buddies sucker punched Nigel from behind. His hand still loaded with the cue ball, Nigel drove his fist into the guy's groin. The guy folded over and Nigel sprang to his feet and drove four hard blows to his left kidney which was now a prominent target. The guy dropped and rolled away.

A voice came out from the crowd, "Nigel! Watch out!" It was Brian Bowen.

Nigel turned his head in time to see Phil Stewart swinging a billiard stick, the fat end arching around towards his head. Phil didn't choke up on the stick, so the swing was long and slow. Nigel ducked for the miss. Phil got ready for another swing and worked closer towards Nigel who was now backed against the pool table. Phil did his best to speak through his cracked jaw, but it came out more like a growl than actual speech, "You son bitch. I'm gonna kill..."

Phil swung again. The stick moved faster this time, but Nigel was faster yet. He moved his head back leaving just enough space so the end of the stick passed by the tip of his nose. Then Nigel launched off the pool table. With the cue ball still wrapped in his fist and Phil Stewart now a little off balance, Nigel connected another blow to Phil's face. A clear shot to the nose.

Phil dropped the stick and began to sway and fall backwards, but Nigel grabbed him by the shirt and slung him around and onto the pool table. Phil landed on his back and Nigel crawled on top. Phil Stewart was out of it for the most part; he had stopped fighting back. But Nigel didn't care; he wailed another shot to his jaw and then another. That's when Little Bit stepped in.

Nigel was about to hit Phil again, but Little Bit caught and stopped his arm saying, "Enough, Nigel. He's done".

Nigel stood up, shaking from his adrenaline high. Little Bit spoke up, "Now, what's this all about?"

Nigel was so worked up and mad he couldn't speak. He was panting trying to catch his breath. He looked at Phil who was rolling around on the pool table.

From behind the bar Tracy called out, "The son of a bitch beat up Candice. That's what this is all about."

Little Bit looked at Nigel and asked, "Is that true? He beat up Candice?"

Nigel gritted his teeth and nodded his head.

Again, Tracy followed up, "Beat her up bad. Real bad."

This was news to everybody in the bar, disturbing news. Candice is everybody's favorite barkeep and Phil just made plenty of enemies in the house. Little Bit had to hold a few of the others back. They too wanted a piece of him.

Nigel could hear the shrill of sirens in the distance, faint at first but grew closer and closer. He handed the cue ball to Little Bit then turned and walked back to the pool table where Phil Stewart rested looking at the ceiling. Nigel crawled back up on the table and loomed over Phil and said, "Look at me."

Phil turned his head to the side and looked away. Then he shifted it to the other side, ignoring Nigel. Blood continued to drip from his nose and mouth. Impatient, Nigel said, "I said, look at me!" Nigel reached down and grabbed his jaw. He could feel the bones shift as he squeezed. Phil squirmed and hollered in agony. Their eyes locked. Nigel smiled and said, "Like I said earlier, I have something to tell you." Nigel maintained a firm grip on his jaw and drew close to his right ear and whispered, "If you ever, ever touch her again. If you even so much as look at Candice ... I promise. I won't make the same mistake twice. There won't be a body. There'll be nothing left to find. Are we clear on that?"

The sirens were right outside the door now. Nigel watched Phil's eyes for an answer. It didn't come quick enough, so he squeezed his jaw. Phil's eyes squinted hard trying to fight off the pain, his head nodding in agreement. Nigel crawled off the table as the doors swung open. Two police and an EMT entered. Little Bit yelled, "Over here."

The cops approached and assessed the scene. The EMT went straight to Phil Stewart, to evaluate his condition. One of the cops said, "So ... what in hell happened here?"

There was quiet in the room. Then Little Bit said, "He's drunk. He fell down."

"Fell down, really?" the cop asked. "You expect us to believe that?"

From behind the cops came a voice, "Yeah. That's what happened. His clumsy ass fell down." It was Phil's buddy, the one that came to his defense, the one with balls the size of grapefruit and a kidney the size of a watermelon.

Then it was Tracy. From behind the bar, she said, "Yup. Fell down."

Everyone in the bar started to confirm the demise of Phil Stewart, writing it off as another typical mishap of drunken misfortune. The one cop looked at Nigel. Nigel said nothing. Then he looked over at the bar and saw Billy Townsend and asked, "Well? Billy ... what do you have to say?"

Billy took a sip of his beer and said, "What can I say, the guy has a tendency to drink too much. He falls down a lot, always hard too."

The cops were shaking their heads as they walked over to the pool table where Phil Stewart was now sitting up. "So ... What's your story?" said the one cop. "You fall down?"

Phil Stewart looked over at Nigel, then to Little Bit. He glanced around the room at all the faces that were now glaring at him. He looked at the cops and nodded his head.

Nigel headed for the door and the second cop stopped him, "Where do you think you're going? We'll need to collect statements from everybody."

"I'm not going far. I'll be outside, sitting on the curb. I need some air."

Tracy came out a few minutes later. She watched as Nigel rubbed his swollen knuckles. She walked over and sat down next to him. She brought him a long pour of Jim Beam Black and reached over kissing him on the cheek. Making a joke she said, "I think I love you."

He smiled, took a sip and said, "You're too late. I'm already taken. And besides, I thought you hated my guts."

"That was before Gloria called me. That's who I was on the phone with when you walked in. She told me everything. Told me not to interfere. That you'd take care of everything. I guess you did."

Nigel said, "Thanks. You're sweet and a good friend to Candice. I appreciate that. Loyalty is hard to find these days."

She smiled back at him.

Moments later the door opened. Red and Brian came out and joined them at the curb. Brian asked, "You okay, brother? I need to run. I'm going to be late for my next set if I don't get my ass in gear."

"I'm fine. Get out of here."

Brian took off in a run. Nigel called after him, "And open with an original, dammit. *Hey Lover* would be good."

Brian provided a thumbs-up as he hurried away.

Red sat down next to Nigel and took his bourbon, helped himself to a deep sip and said, "You need to get your ass in there and give your statement. Somebody is at home waiting for you."

The front door to Candice's house was unlocked. He rapped on the door as he opened it. Two quick knocks … a pause … and a third. He stepped inside and looked around. It was quiet. He found Gloria on the phone sitting on the living room couch. He heard her say, "He just got here. Thanks for calling. I need to go."

She got up and walked across the room and gave him a hug. Then she got on her toes and he leaned over so she could kiss him on the forehead. She stepped back and took hold of his hands, studied them and said, "Have a seat. Let me get a bag of ice for that."

As she headed to the kitchen Nigel asked, "Where is she?"

"She's in bed, sweetheart. It's been a long day. Poor thing is plumb tuckered out."

Nigel said nothing.

She disappeared into the kitchen. While finding a suitable freezer bag in which to put ice, Gloria was telling Nigel about how she had spoken with Tracy. That she had given her a play-by-play of what happened at the bar. "Tracy said she about fell out when you slapped him off his bar stool. That had to be something." Zipping up the bag of ice, Gloria said, "I sure wish I could have been there to see it."

Walking back towards the living room, Gloria said, "Here you go, sugar. Put this on your…"

Gloria stopped talking to herself and grinned. Nigel wasn't there.

119

While Gloria was in the kitchen talking, Nigel slipped away and opened the door to Candice's room. A nightlight by the bed stand provided enough light that he could see her face. Her eyes were closed, and she looked to be comfortable and sleeping. He walked over and sat on the edge of the bed so he could look at her. He leaned over and kissed her on the lips. She didn't kiss back, but she smiled and said, "I smell you."

Nigel gave a quiet laugh, "Smell me, huh?"

Candice said nothing, eyes still closed, smiling and nodding her head.

"Is that a good thing?"

Candice said, "Very good. You're my favorite smell."

It got quiet in the room. He sat there, watching her rest. After awhile he whispered, "Candice. I'm so sorry. About everything. There is so much I need to talk to you about. There are things..."

She reached up with her finger tips, followed his voice to find his lips and pressed against them. "Shhhh, baby," she said. "Shhh. Not now. Just crawl up here and hold me. Okay?

"Okay," he said.

She heard a smile in his voice and said, "Stay with me all night. Keep me safe."

He kicked off his shoes and crawled up behind her and wrapped his arm around her waist, pulled her in close. He kissed her on the ear and said, "Don't worry. I'll be right here."

"You promise?"

"Promise."

The Accident

He opened his eyes. His pupils exploded wide, to the size of nickels, searching for available light. He was alert; the whole night seemed to go that way. He was exhausted when he crawled into the bed, but he couldn't sleep. From time to time he might doze for twenty to thirty minutes, but his eyes would pop open to a silent alarm in his head. An alarm that was taking cues from the adrenaline that remained in his blood, leftover energy refusing to surrender the body to rest. When overcharged, the body takes a while for all the mental and physiological systems to slow down, to return to some semblance of order. But he didn't mind. Each time he would wake, he could hear her breathing easy, and he could smell her hair which lay scattered about his face.

He eased his head up to take a peek at the nightstand alarm clock. It showed 3:30 a.m. It was early for most, but for others it was the beginning of another very long workday. He decided to join the minority of folks crawling out of bed and starting their daily lives. Feeling a tad bit guilty, he felt obligated to take care of some things. As much as he would have loved to stay there, he needed to get up and get going.

He buried his face into her hair and kissed the back of her head. She gave a squirm indicating approval. He squeezed her tight, and she scrunched her body inward allowing him to squeeze as tight as he wanted. He moved his mouth to her ear and whispered, "I need to go. I have something I need to do."

He eased his grip on her. She grabbed his arm in protest pulling him back in saying, "No, baby. Don't go. Don't leave me."

"I'm not leaving you."

She didn't say anything but liked hearing those words. He couldn't see her face, but she was smiling, eyes still closed.

"I just have something I need to do. I'll tell you about it later this afternoon when I come back to check on you." He kissed her on the head again as she eased her grip.

He had been fully dressed when he crawled on top of the bedspread to hold and comfort her. All he had to do was find his shoes, locate his wallet and phone, and he could slip out the door, leaving her to some much needed rest.

Hearing the twisting of the door knob, she opened her eyes and looked ahead towards the alarm clock, 3:35 a.m. Then she said, "I love you, Nigel Logan."

The words stopped him as he faced the door. With the exception of a glow that bled through the window blinds from a street lamp, it was still very dark, but his eyes had adjusted well. He turned back to look at her. She looked beautiful and at ease. The darkness hid the puffiness, the bruising, and the busted lip and shed no light on what had happened. He said, "I love you more."

Candice winced as sudden light flooded the room. And just as quick, the light was gone and so was he. She pursed her sore lips and closed her eyes and briefly contemplated her next hair color, something he might like better. Then she fell fast asleep.

Nigel got back to his house and found another trophy on his back door steps. This time it was a shrew. He looked around, but the cat was nowhere to be found.

He went in, and after starting a pot of coffee, he disposed of the rodent in a doubled-up plastic grocery bag and placed it in the outdoor trash can.

He ran about the house and gathered all the things he needed. The smell of fresh coffee filled the air, so he poured a quick cup before the pot was done. By the time he had packed himself a bite to eat and threw everything in the truck, the rest of the pot was done. He poured a cup to go and the rest in an old Thermos bottle, premixed with Half & Half.

When he pulled into the parking lot, he was the first to arrive. He got out and checked the gate. It was locked. He would have to wait, but it would only be a matter of time before somebody showed up to unlock everything. The crews would be showing up soon.

Nigel crawled back into his truck and rested, dozing in and out. He was trying to collect what sleep he could. He knew it would be a long and tiring day. His eyes snapped open as he heard knuckles bounce off the driver side window. He turned his head and saw Luther Collins, Little Bit. Nigel got out of his truck.

Little Bit asked, "What are you doing here?"

"I figure somebody won't be showing up for work today," said Nigel. "I can't leave the skipper and crew shorthanded. Not that he's much help to begin with."

Little Bit smiled and shook his head understanding what Nigel was talking about. Little Bit said, "You know he might be out more than just a day?"

"I expect it, but it doesn't matter," said Nigel. "I'll show up for as many mornings as I have to."

Little Bit turned and headed towards the gate saying, "I'm sure Mike will appreciate that."

Nigel grabbed his gear out of the back of the truck and followed. When he caught up with Little Bit the padlock snapped open and the chain ran through the metal gate making one hell of a racket. They both entered and walked down a road towards the seawall where the boats were tied up. When they reached the waterfront Little Bit turned left and said, "Good luck, today."

Nigel stopped and watched him walk away. He paused before saying, "You too. Hope you guys kill it today."

Little Bit said nothing and Nigel turned to the right and walked towards the *Miss Cecelia* which rested easily on her dock lines. Things were quiet, no sign of life anywhere. He jumped on board and walked around to the cabin door. He tossed his gear to the side and tried the door. It was locked.

Knowing sailors and watermen almost never take their keys, he stepped back and surveyed the area thinking, *Okay, Mike. Where do you keep it?* He reached up and ran his fingertips across the top of the door frame and five inches later he felt the key. *Damn. That was too easy.*

He picked up his stuff, went inside, and started flipping on lights. Then he poured himself a big mug of coffee from his own Thermos and started a fresh pot in the galley. He knew folks would be showing up soon and he figured they would appreciate fresh brew waiting for them.

Nigel took a seat at the cabin table and waited as he listened to the coffee maker hiss and gurgle its way to a full pot. A stack of magazines was scattered about. He flipped through them looking for something to read, something to kill the time and fill the mind. He picked up a copy of *Florida Commercial Fisherman* and found an article on policies proposed by the Florida Wildlife Commission to further restrict red snapper fishing in the Gulf of Mexico.

The cabin door opened and Nigel lowered the magazine, looked up, and found himself peering into the barrels of a 16 gauge, double-barrel shotgun. Nigel tossed the magazine aside and said, "Mike! Dammit. What in the hell are you doing?"

Mike Bobo, skipper of the *Miss Cecelia* kept the shotgun trained on Nigel and replied, "What the hell am I doing? What the hell are you doing? Jesus! Nigel, I was prepared to blow your freak'n head off."

"Son of a bitch, Mike. You scared the shit out of me."

"Scared the shit out of you? What about me? I'm walking to my boat and it's lit up like a damn Christmas tree. Somebody's on board doing God knows what, and all I can think of is, 'I'm going to have to shoot someone.'"

"Well, I can damn well tell you," said Nigel, "looking into the barrels of that thing is a hell of a lot scarier than standing behind it with a finger on the trigger. So, why don't you do us both a favor ... and point that fucking thing somewhere else."

Mike realized he was still holding the gun on Nigel. He lowered the red sight so it pointed towards the floor. Then he broke the barrel open and removed the big purple shells from the chambers.

Both of them were out of breath, panting, almost in unison. Then the tension broke. They realized they were arguing about who was more scared than the other. A ridiculous argument. It was Mike Bobo that broke out in a chuckle and said, "Dammit, Nigel. This isn't funny."

"You the one laughing, not me." Then they both were.

With his hands still shaking a little, Nigel poured himself another cup of coffee from what was left in his Thermos and pointed over at the coffee pot with his chin and said, "Fresh pot. It stopped brewing about the time my heart did the same."

Mike poured himself a mug of black coffee and started to walk over to the table. He brought the cup to his lips but stopped short of taking a sip. He looked at Nigel and asked, "Why are you drinking from your Thermos? Why aren't you drinking from this fresh pot?"

"Huh?" replied Nigel. "This is leftover from what I brought from the house. Why?"

"So this coffee is good? It hasn't got like salt and shit in it?"

Mike was being serious and cautious. If Nigel had tainted the coffee, it wouldn't have been the first time. Mike didn't want to gag and puke there on the deck.

Nigel laughed and said, "No. No salt. Promise."

As Mike began his first sip, Nigel said, "Vinegar. I made it with vinegar."

Mike spit what little coffee he had in his mouth out on the floor and Nigel busted out laughing and said, "I'm kidding. I'm kidding. The coffee is fine. Drink it, dammit."

"Damn you," Mike mumbled as he grabbed a few paper towels and threw them on the floor wiping up the spattered coffee with his foot. Then he sat down across from Nigel and said, "So, perhaps now would be a good time for you to tell me why you are on my boat."

"I'm here to work."

"Work? ... What the hell are you talking about? My whole crew should be here any minute."

"So you haven't gotten a call yet? Nobody has called in sick?"

"No," Mike said with a confused look. "What in heaven are you talking about?"

Then a phone rang. It was Mike's. He looked up at Nigel. Nigel looked down at the table. His mouth closed and his cheeks were puffed out, a guilty look of embarrassment. Nigel tilted his head and looked up at Mike nodding his head.

Mike said, "What is going on?"

He took the call. All Nigel heard was, "Yeah, Phil ... Uh huh..." Mike got up and stepped outside to finish the call. Nigel finished his coffee and got up to pour another cup from the pot he made. He sat back down as Mike came back into the cabin. "That was Phil."

"I heard."

"Says he can't make it to work this morning? Said he had an accident. Might be out for a few days."

Nigel was nodding his head and said, "Yup. That's why I'm here, to lend a hand."

"To lend a hand, huh?"

"Uh huh."

"An accident?" Mike said. "Phil had an accident, did he?"

"That's what he said, right?"

"And what is it you know about this accident that compelled you to show up this morning? Out of the blue."

Nigel was about to come up with some lame ass, back-door explanation when the cabin door open and K.C. stepped inside and said, "Chief! What are you doing here?"

K.C. is another one of Mike's deckhands, tall and lanky. He was in the Navy once too. Nigel had helped out around the boat once before and liked working with K.C. Good kid.

It was the perfect distraction. Nigel said, "Hey, shipmate. I'm back to lend a hand. Seems Phil is under the weather. Won't be in for a few days. I'm here to fill in."

"Wow, that's great."

Mike interrupted, "K.C. is Jimmy here yet?"

"Yeah. He was pulling in the parking lot when I was walking through the gate. Should be here any minute."

Moments later a young fella came in the cabin door. He had red curly hair and was shorter than K.C., but what he lacked in height was more than made up for in girth. Nigel thought, SLUFF (Short Little Ugly Fat Fucker). Nigel didn't know Jimmy, but there seemed something familiar about him.

Mike said, "Jimmy, this is Nigel Logan he's going to be..."

At that moment the familiarity between Jimmy and Nigel was reciprocated. Jimmy tilted his head from side to side when he saw Nigel. Then pointed and interrupted Mike saying, "Hey! That's the guy that beat the living shit out of Phil last night. Busted him up good."

Mike said, "What?"

"It was an accident," Nigel said to Jimmy in a sarcastic convincing tone. "Don't you remember?"

Jimmy thought for a moment or two and said, "Oh yeah. It was an accident. That's what everybody told the POPO when they showed up, even Phil."

"The police came? They were called?" asked Mike.

"Oh yeah," said Jimmy. "Phil turned down the ambulance though."

"Ambulance?" asked Mike looking at Nigel.

Nigel shrugged his shoulders and said, "It was an accident. Ambulances get called."

Jimmy said. "You should have seen it, Skip. It was something else. Like a fight scene in a movie or something." Jimmy's smile faded when he saw Nigel's scornful glare. Then Jimmy looked away, coughed to clear his throat and said, "I mean accident."

There was silence in the room. Then Nigel looked at Mike and said, "I'll fill in for as long as it takes."

Mike turned to K.C. and Jimmy and said, "Okay you guys, enough of this. If you want a cup of coffee, grab one. Then get your asses on deck and start getting the boat ready. We still have a job to do."

They declined the coffee and opted for a couple of Mountain Dews from the fridge and ducked out the door.

Mike looked at Nigel and asked, "So what's the story?"

Nigel told him everything. He told him about how Candice went back to Phil. He told him that Phil got drunk and beat her. He explained how Candice's face had been bruised and swollen. Expressing his guilt, Nigel said, "It was my entire fault, Mike. I pushed her away. And because of my own stupidity, she got hurt, bad. I couldn't let things go unanswered." He didn't go into the details of "the accident". He didn't have to. It wasn't necessary.

Mike thought about it and said, "I should fire his ass. The fucker is just mean."

There was silence between the two as they sat drinking their coffee. Then Nigel said, "Naw. Firing him won't do any good. That's just what we need around here, another unemployed asshole. No ... It's best to keep dickheads like him busy during the day."

"So, how long do I get you?" Mike asked. "How long you figure you'll be able to help out around here?"

"As long as you need me. No problem. But only on one condition."

With eyebrows raised, Mike asked, "And that would be?"

"You make sure Phil gets his whole pay while I'm filling in for him."

"Really? You would do that? Give up your pay?"

Nigel said, "Listen, the guy is a class "A" piece of shit. He has a problem, but I'm sure he has bills to pay too, and he needs to eat. I punished him enough last night. I don't need his money too."

Mike shook his head in disbelief, but reached across the table to offer his hand and said, "You got it."

As they shook hands, the cabin door opened. Nigel and Mike turned to look. It was K.C., a crooked grin on his face. He looked at the both of them and said, "You girls going to sit on your asses all morning? Come on, Chief. We got shit to do."

Mike looked at Nigel, smiled and said, "He's in charge."

Nigel finished his coffee and got up. "Coming, boss. I'm coming."

It was late Friday afternoon, the workweek was ending. *Miss Cecelia* eased her way into the channel and headed back to her berth. There was a little extra excitement in the crew; it was payday. It was also the fourth straight day for Nigel to be crewing aboard the *Miss Cecelia*.

Nigel was starting to wonder if Phil would ever come back to work. He didn't mind lending a hand, but he wasn't looking for another career either. But, the days at sea had come at a perfect time. He needed to be on the water and underway, even if it was only coastal, shallow water work. It didn't matter. Regardless of how busy you are, when on the water working a boat, you always find time to think and sort things out.

Most of his thoughts were on Candice. He had seen her over the last few days, but for only brief periods. He made it a point to check on her everyday, but they were unable to spend the kind of quality time that each of them needed. He had photography work waiting for him at the cottage. Plus, he was exhausted. Mike Bobo, K.C., and even the little round fella, Jimmy, put him through the paces. He didn't mind the hard work, but it sure as hell gave him a greater appreciation for getting paid to take pictures of sailboats and to drink beer or bourbon while editing them.

Candice was doing much better. She was back to working the tip trade, swinging her hips and dancing while pulling pints of beer at the bar. All the regulars were glad to see her back, and they all shared with her their own version of what happened the night Phil got his ass handed to him.

All of her swelling and most of her bruising was gone. She told Nigel, "It looks worse than it really is. Nothing a little makeup can't cover." She was in good spirits.

While she wasn't getting to see much of Nigel, she was spending a lot of time with him on the phone. He called her everyday from the boat, at least twice, and he always called her before he went to bed. That was her favorite call. Most of the time she would already be in bed, covers pulled tight to her chin, countering the chill from the ceiling fan that spun wide open, her head deep in a pillow, and the phone pressed tight to her ear. She always imagined Nigel the same way on those calls, both of them in bed, chatting their way towards slumber. Sometimes she was right. It often made her feel silly talking on the phone that way, like she was a kid again, back in high school. Didn't matter though; it made her happy.

The boat crept through the channel, and it was a seagull feeding frenzy. The sky was full and they dove into the sea for an easy meal as K.C. and Jimmy washed down the deck. There was plenty of bi-catch from the last haul of shrimp, so it was a smorgasbord free for the taking. The usual suspects of dolphin also worked the stern wake, grabbing a morsel here and there. And even though they couldn't see them often, they knew the bull and reef sharks followed close behind working the deeper depths.

As the boat cleared under the bridge, Skipper Bobo could see Phil standing at the boat's berth along the seawall. He said aloud, "Great! That's just what I need."

Mike looked back through the pilot house and saw Nigel. He was helping to stow and secure gear. Mike called out, "Nigel! Get your ass up here."

When Nigel came in and approached the helm station, Mike nodded towards the seawall and said, "No trouble. Got it? I don't need this shit."

Nigel looked down and saw Phil looking up at them. He was sure Phil spotted him in the pilothouse. Nigel stepped back and said, "Come on, Mike. I'm not one to look for trouble. It's the last thing I want."

"Well, I think it best that you stay in here until we tie up and I can get a feel for what he wants."

"Not a problem, Mike. Makes perfect sense."

Mike eased the boat towards the seawall and K.C. threw a line to Phil so he could help get *Miss Cecelia* moored. With the boat resting alongside, Mike shut down the engines and said to Nigel, "Stay here."

Nigel said nothing.

Mike Bobo went ashore. He and Phil took a walk down the seawall. When they stopped, Phil looked up towards the pilothouse.

Mike said, "Yeah, he's up there, Phil. I won't stand for any trouble. Understand?"

Phil didn't comment.

Mike looked back up at the pilothouse and Nigel remained out of sight. He turned back to Phil who was holding his paycheck in his hand. He came in earlier and picked it up from the front office. Phil said, "My check, skip. It's full, not a penny missing. They told me at the office you said to make sure I got paid for the time I was out. That's very generous of you. I just wanted to say thanks."

"I appreciate that, Phil. I really do. But you're thanking the wrong guy."

"What do you mean?"

Mike looked at Phil in silence. He held it for a beat or two before turning to look back up towards the pilothouse where he held his gaze.

It took Phil a few seconds to understand, and then the light came on. "You have got to be kidding me. That son of a bitch? That's bullshit."

Nigel was watching the exchange between Mike and Phil through the window, being careful not to be seen. He noticed Phil pacing back and forth, talking with his hands, as Mike stood there. After a minute or so, Phil looked back up at the pilothouse. Nigel ducked back. He was sure Phil didn't see him. When he felt it might be safe, he peeked around the window again. This time he saw Phil walking away and Mike was headed back towards the boat. Nigel moved and stood in the entire window, watching. Mike looked up and saw Nigel standing there looking down at him. Mike shrugged his shoulders as he stepped back on board.

Mike came back into the pilothouse, this time with a couple of cold beers, PBRs that he'd dug out of the fridge in the galley. He handed one to Nigel. The wet, ice-cold bottle felt good against his palm. They both twisted their caps off in unison and clanked the bottles together as Mike said, "Toast!"

Nigel said, "What are we toasting?"

"Your resignation. Phil is ready to come back."

"Well, okay then," said Nigel. "That is something to celebrate, but let's do this right." He held his bottle up again.

Mike thought for a second. Then he held up his bottle and said, "Here's to Nigel Logan. Whose abbreviated career as a commercial shrimp boat deckhand has finally come to an end. May he enjoy his retirement and never board this vessel again..." Mike held those words with a smile. Then he continued, "...under the same or similar circumstances."

Nigel said, "I'll drink to that."

They clanked the bottles together again, this time with a bit more enthusiasm and drank long and deep. The cold beer was good and neither one of them wanted that first drink to end, but they had no choice. They had to come up for air.

Nigel gasped and said, "Man that's good."

Mike nodded his head in agreement and gave a ferocious belch.

Candice pulled an extra tall mug of Coors Light and squeezed in two generous slices of lime and dropped them into the beer. She carried the mug down the bar and sat it down and said, "One Coorsona. What else can I get you?"

She leaned over and placed her elbows on the bar. She put her wrists together and rested her chin in her palms. He did the same. They were only an inch or two away from each other. They were looking into each other's eyes when she said, "You smell like fish."

Nigel said, "I'm sorry. That's what shrimpers smell like. I just got off the boat."

"Is that what you are now, a shrimper?"

"Nope. It seemed like a promising career, but it didn't last. I was fired today. Let go to make room for someone else."

"Really, now. I'm so sorry. I know how much you were looking forward..."

The ridiculous conversation continued on. It was all fun, but Nigel stopped listening and concentrated on her face. Her mouth was moving, but he didn't hear a word. He was looking at her gorgeous eyes and the way they sparkled, even in the dim light of a smoky bar. He liked her mouth, the way it formed smiles as she spoke. While he wasn't paying attention to what was being said, he couldn't help but notice her beautiful, southern, country-girl accent; it's drop-dead sexy. And he noticed her hair. She was back to being a strawberry blond, one of his favorites.

She continued talking and her words started to filter back into Nigel's brain. He was listening again.

"...after all, you have trained so hard and put forth such effort..."

Nigel moved in closer and closer to her. She saw what was coming but continued to talk her nonsense until their lips met. She didn't hesitate being silenced and moved in closer too. He placed his hand behind her head and pulled her in tight. They took occasional small breaths, but continued their passionate public display of affection. They were exploring the inside of each other's mouth, not thinking of the crowd around them until they were interrupted by an eruption of cheers.

They came up for air and looked around. Everybody was laughing and applauding. It embarrassed the both of them, but in a good way. They both started laughing too. Nigel heard a familiar voice and a predictable cliché from across the room, "You kids need to get a room!" Nigel looked around and found Red and Trixie a few feet away.

Nigel gave Candice a wanting look. Disappointment filled her eyes when she said, "I have to close."

Then Candice heard a familiar voice whisper in her ear. "Get out of here, sugar. I got it." It was Tracy, her part-time barkeep. She had already slipped behind the bar and was ready to take over.

Candice turned to look at her, kissed her on the cheek and said, "Thanks."

"No problem," said Tracy. "Just remember, you got to share all the juicy details later."

Candice winked at Tracy and looked back at Nigel. She was thinking of the shrimp boat when she said, "So, it's true? You're really done?"

Nigel looked at her and whispered, "Baby ... I'm just getting started. Let's go find a shower built for two."

They both leaned in for another long and passionate kiss as the nosy patrons erupted again into cheers.

Nigel felt something being slipped into his pants pocket. He turned his head to find a smiling Luke McKenzie standing next to him. Nigel reached into his pocket and pulled out the gift. Nigel cut his eyes at Luke. There was a twinkle in Luke's eyes as he winked and said, "Remember, a couple drops are all it takes."

Nigel smiled as he looked down at his palm and slipped the small vial back into his pocket. He looked at Candice, kissed her again and said, "Come on. We've got to get out of here."

The Howitzer

Nigel finished up the last quarter mile of his Saturday morning run by picking up the pace. He was feeling good and wanted to finish strong. His breathing was under control, only slightly labored. He ran a few calculations in his mind and felt confident he had burnt off enough calories to compensate for the beers he and Red had consumed on the beach the night before.

He made the turn off Woodward Avenue and was heading South down Highway 71. He was thinking, *Yes. Beer calories and then some ... then some.* Then he began to frown. New memories flooded his brain and he said, "Shit!" and really started to push even harder. He had a few more blocks left of his run and decided to sprint, dedicating those last strides to those damn tasty donuts he bought at The Cape Trading Post the morning before.

Using Reid Avenue as a finish line he threw his hands up in the air as he ran through the imaginary victory tape. He broke his stride slowing to a fast walk, fingers laced together behind his head. He strolled his way back to the corner of Reid and Highway 71. The lot there contains a community green space with a large gazebo in the middle.

It was Salt Air Market Saturday in Port St. Joe. It is held every first and third Saturday running from April through November. A guy playing guitar was entertaining from the gazebo as folks milled about. People from all around were peddling their goods to anyone willing to buy. It's a hit with both tourists and locals, and you can get just about anything you want from fresh produce, crafted jewelry, and grass-feed beef to homemade soap and Tupelo Honey.

Nigel was coated in thick, slimy sweat and, in all likelihood, a bit smelly, so he stayed out on the sidewalk away from the crowd. Pacing back and forth, he was catching his breath. His eyes found Joe Crow who had been watching him. Joe threw up a wave. Nigel nodded with a smile and thought, *What the hell.* He walked up on the lawn where Joe was lounged out listening to the music and drinking from a red Solo cup. Nigel plopped down on the grass next to him.

"Did you run a lap for me?"

Nigel held up two fingers with a smile.

"Good," said Joe. "I knew there had to be a reason this beer tasted so good."

Joe opened his cooler and lifted a cold bottle out of the ice, "Want one?"

Still a little out of breath Nigel looked at the beer. He could almost taste it, but decided to be good. He lifted a hand and shook his head no. Then he said, "No beer ... But I'll take a handful of that ice to crunch on."

Joe produced a fresh cup from a bag and was scooping up some ice and melted water as Nigel looked at his watch. It was 1030, a little early to see Joe drinking beer, not that it was a problem. After all, 1000 is Nigel's personal benchmark hour for the acceptable consumption of alcohol.

Joe is a retired tugboat captain. He and his wife Ruby live out on the Cape in a beautiful place that overlooks Pig Island on the bay side. Joe often invites Nigel to the local poker night to play a few hands. The usual suspects sitting at the table love to see Nigel walk through the door because he always sweetens the pot for somebody. Lady Luck doesn't shine on Nigel very often.

"A little early for beer, isn't it, Joe?" Nigel asked.

Joe took a sip. Licking foam off his upper lip, he said, "Trying to get a head start on my afternoon nap."

Nigel smiled and laughed to himself, not because it was funny, but because it was true. There was no doubt; by 1400 Joe Crow would be sawing logs. His own personal daily siesta.

"You seen Red?" asked Nigel.

"At the No Name. Last I saw of him."

"What's he doing there?"

Joe took another sip and shrugged his shoulders. *Beats me.*

Nigel hopped up and patted Joe on the back, "Talk to ya later, Joe. Need to run down Red."

"Come by the house later. Maybe we can get some afternoon fishing in."

"I might just do that."

"Don't come too soon, though. You know..."

"I know. I know. Sweet dreams, Joe."

Nigel started down the sidewalk along Reid Avenue when he came upon Red's Ford Explorer. *Good*, he thought, *he must still be inside.*

Nigel was standing outside the front window of a small cafe and book store. He always wondered why Ms. Barbara, the owner, would leave such a quaint little shop nameless. Perhaps she was thinking that a name would eventually come to her, something catchy and smart, who knows. One day he'd find her when she wasn't so busy and ask, but it wouldn't be today. He could see her behind the counter tending to a line of customers.

Nigel grabbed the door handle and leaned back to read the sign on the front window: **The No Name Café.** He smiled as he walked in.

The place was abuzz with activity as he walked around looking for Red. He kept an eye on Barbara until he got her attention. She read his lips as he silently said, *Red.* Then she rolled her eyes and pointed to the back of the shop.

The No Name Cafe is more than a coffee, sandwich, and book store. The shop has a dedicated area for crafts, meetings, or lectures. It is quite common for the space to be used in one capacity or another: quilting, needlepoint, scrap booking, maybe a local historian speaking on the area's past. You never know.

Red was at the table with three rugged-looking fellas. They were going over maps and charts. Nigel didn't know any of these guys. Except for Red, they looked like they were ready to go hunting. They wore decked out camouflage, outdoor boots, and knives that hung from their belts. One guy had a Rambo knife strapped to his leg.

Nigel didn't want to interrupt, so he stood in the wings figuring Red would notice him sooner or later. Nigel watched with great curiosity. The group looked serious and the discussions secretive as they huddled over the maps, some covert operation in the making. Then something happened to destroy any idea of seriousness, at least in Nigel's mind.

One of the guys noticed Nigel looking in. It appeared he was running the meeting and won the award for best dressed. He was the guy with the knife strapped to his leg. And to match his military camouflage attire; he had the faded remains of face paint about his cheeks. Nigel was thinking, *Captain Camouflage.*

At the immediate sight of Nigel, Captain Camo became overprotective of the information on the table. He reached over and covered as much of it as he could as he sent Nigel a silent message with his eyes. *You're not welcome here. Get the hell out.* The guy locked his gaze at Nigel long enough that he could read the writing on his camouflaged, international orange ball cap. In big bold print was the statement: **HE LIVES**. Underneath that were the words: **The Apalach Sasquatch Society.**

The commotion at the table made Red look up. He smiled seeing Nigel standing there. Nigel smiled back. Red was wearing a yellow T-Shirt that said: **Have You Hugged Your Yeti Today**. Underneath that was a walking silhouette of the elusive beast.

"Red, you've got to be kidding, right? Not this Bigfoot shit again?"

Waving Nigel towards the table Red addressed the group. "Relax y'all. Trust me; this guy isn't your competition. He's not here to get a jump on your discovery. He's what I call a procrastinating believer. He just doesn't realize it, yet."

One of the guys at the table had a spooky look about him. The guy had a scary gaze, a deer-in-the-headlights look and offered a monotone comment, "I was an unbeliever once."

Nigel looked at the guy and said, "Sure. Sure. Whatever you say."

Red interrupted the awkward moment with the formality of introductions, "Everybody, this is my dear friend, Nigel Logan."

"Nigel," Red said pointing to the scary one: Casper the Ghost. "This is Tommy Thompson. Drove over from Carrabelle."

Nigel tilted his head and nodded. *Tommy Thompson*, he thought. *Why did the name sound familiar.*

Red continued, pointing at another guy, "And this is Steve Marsh. He's travelled from Grand Ridge. He's an associate of this man, Jackson Knox," Red said, pointing with an open palm to Captain Camo. "He drove down from Tallahassee and is the chief executive of the Apalach Sasquatch Society, A.S.S. for short."

The irony made Nigel laugh to himself. Jackson continued his stares of suspicion.

Nigel turned to Red and asked, "So, Red. What's this all about? How are you involved here?" Then using a play on the organizations acronym he smiled and asked, "Please don't tell me you are joining this ... this ... ass group."

"Well ... You know I've always had a casual interest in the Yeti phenomenon..."

Nigel interrupted with a grin, "Casual? Have you read your own T-Shirt? Any man that would walk around in something as ridiculous as that has more than a casual interest."

Captain Camo took offense. Now upset, he addressed Red, "What is this, sir? You assured me we would have serious discussions, and now this Mr. Logan arrives and immediately insults our beliefs and mission. Perhaps I made a mistake by coming down here."

"Mr. Knox, please," said Red cutting Nigel a look. "Mr. Logan simply doesn't understand."

Looking at Mr. Knox, Nigel said, "I guess Captain Camo here didn't get his Yeti hug this morning. He seems a bit grouchy."

Jackson Knox stood, "That is enough, sir. You have insulted my honor. I do not have to stand for this. I am leaving."

Red intervened, but with a Freudian slip, "Please ... Captain Camo..." Red clenched his teeth in embarrassment as Nigel snickered. "I'm sorry ... I mean Jackson ... Mr. Knox. Please take your seat. Mr. Logan was just leaving." Red looked at Nigel and spoke through his gritted teeth, "Weren't you, Mr. Logan."

Nigel got up and said, "Hell, Red. You're no fun."

"These are not fun and games," replied Red.

Walking away Nigel said, "Sounds like a joke to me. Come on by the house when you get done. Cold beers on the porch."

Nigel produced a thumbs-up, and through the renewed laments of Captain Camo he heard Red say, "I'll be there in thirty minutes."

Nigel sat on his porch drinking his second beer when he heard the back door open and close. He counted down in his head: *four, three, two, one.* He heard the latched door of his old school refrigerator open. *Snap, Pop.* The selection wouldn't take too long; there was only one kind of beer to choose from: Coors Light. He kept counting down: *three, two, one.* Then he heard the tab of fresh beer get pulled. *Crack, fizz!*

Nigel looked over his left shoulder to find Red standing in the doorway. He had changed from his Bigfoot T-shirt into a T-shirt from the raw bar.

"I see you changed shirts."

"Hell, yeah," said Red. "I may be a casual believer, but I'm not a fanatic."

Nigel took a sip and motioned with his head for Red to take a seat on the swing.

"I'm almost afraid to ask," said Nigel, "but what was that all about?"

"There's been another sighting."

"Oh shit, Red. Come on."

"No, seriously. That guy, Tommy Thompson, he saw it."

"Bullshit, Red."

"Listen. Tommy Thompson is a straight-up guy. We've known each other since grade school. He's a damn local banker for Christ's sake, a pillar of the community. He's just confirming what everybody else has been saying."

Everybody else, Nigel thought. That's a pretty broad term to be used on about three people.

It was true, there had been a handful of folks, four now, if you count Tommy Thompson, claiming to have seen the beast in recent weeks.

Then, Nigel remembered where he had heard the name, Tommy Thompson, before. He heard it on Oyster Radio. The alleged sighting and its sordid details were reported during the local news. Nigel remembered laughing as Michael Allen concluded the news by saying, "Okay, folks, let's return to some good beach tunes. And ah, don't forget to tune in tonight. It's Oyster Radio after Dark, starting at eight. It's great rock and blues like you've never heard before and now with fifty percent more Bigfoot."

Red spilled all the juicy details. Tommy had been looking at some land outside of Sopchoppy, a little town bordering the southern side of the Apalachicola National Forest. It's a remote parcel of land, several hundred acres that bumps up against a generous shoreline of the meandering Ochlockonee River.

Red said, "It was late and after work. Tommy pulled his four-wheeler out there so he could cover as much land as possible. He liked what he saw, and with the sun hanging low in the sky, he took his time enjoying the ride back to his truck and trailer. Tommy said, 'I had just driven by and stirred up a rattlesnake. I took my eyes off the path for maybe a couple of seconds. When I went back to paying attention to what I was doing, there it was.' That's when he threw on the brakes."

"Oh, shit," said Nigel. "Here we go."

"Dammit! Will you let me finish."

Nigel said nothing.

"Tommy said the creature stepped out into an opening. Real casual like, like on a stroll. Tommy froze. He started thinking and figured he needed to call someone. So, he called me. He was whispering. He said, 'Red. You there? You're the only guy I could call. You're the only one I can trust.' I said, 'Tommy, what in the blazes are you talking about?' And that's when he whispered even quieter and said, 'Bigfoot, Red. It's Bigfoot. Right in front of me.'

"At that moment the creature saw Tommy and became furious letting out a horrible, screeching howl. I heard it on the phone. It was awful. I actually got to hear a Yeti on the phone."

Red prefers calling the mythical creature Yeti to Bigfoot. He says Bigfoot trivializes the creature's existence. Nigel thought for a second and without emotion asked, "So, what happened next?"

Red lowered his head and said, "It disappeared back into the woods."

And Nigel said, "Hmmm ... And let me guess. As amazing as all this was, there isn't the first second of video evidence. Not even a picture. Your buddy, Tommy Thompson, instead of doing the logical thing and getting video called you instead."

Red said nothing at first then exclaimed, "But I heard it. I heard it on the phone."

Nigel put up his hand and said, "Red, I love ya, brother. But there has to be something more constructive we can talk about. We've got to change the subject."

There was awkward silence between the two as they sipped their beers. Then Nigel said, "Just the other day, you said there was something you wanted to discuss and ask me. Is that still true?"

Red nodded his head.

"And it has nothing to do with this Yeti nonsense, right?"

Red shook his head, no.

"Perfect then. I think fresh beers are in order."

Red lifted his can and shook it. It sounded near empty. He finished it off, smiled and said, "I'll get em!"

Nigel sat back and listened. Nigel only interrupted Red once or twice with an occasional *You're not serious,* or, *You're kidding me.* But after a career of reading people in the Navy, Nigel could tell Red was telling the truth, or at least Red believed every word that was coming out of his mouth.

Red told Nigel the history of how it all came to be. It was September, 1974, and Red was just starting his junior year at Florida State University, FSU. He and two other classmates had been up all night drinking and contemplating how they would celebrate the opening weeks of the new school year.

Red suggested they do something bold and shocking, something risky, but harmless at the same time. The group liked the concept. The only question was what?

Alcohol consumption often stimulates courage and bravery, and with it comes creativity, especially when conspiring to find something bold and shocking to unveil to the world. They tossed around several ideas, many of which were thrown aside as unimaginative and lame.

"Nigel," Red said, "I can't even remember whose idea it was. It just came out in the discussion as some far-fetched antic. It was offered up more as a joke than something for serious consideration. And for that very reason, it struck me as brilliant. I remember telling the group, 'Yes! Yes! That's it. It's perfect!' We all looked at each other and decided it met all the criteria and we agreed."

Red laughed telling Nigel that once morning arrived, much of the effects of alcohol had worn off, and so had much of the group's motivation and willingness to participate. Red had to browbeat the back-peddlers, but was successful in getting the group to commit.

Red proceeded to tell Nigel what they had done. Nigel sat in comic disbelief, but only for a second or two. Nigel looked at Red and realized he wasn't kidding.

"So, Red, it was you? It was you that started the whole thing? You invented that craze."

"Not just me," he said with a smile. "There were three of us. We had no idea the effect it would have."

"Red," Nigel said laughing, "You guys are a part of American history. What you guys did swept the country by storm."

"I guess. A photographer caught us. He captured the whole thing and sold the prints to the newspaper. It just took off from there. I guess it was a slow news day because it got picked up off the wire."

They both sat on the porch laughing. Red was remembering the event while Nigel was doing a pretty good job of imagining how it all went down. Then Nigel asked, still laughing, "This is great, Red. You never cease to amaze me. But..." Nigel stopped a second to catch his breath. "But, what does this have to do with me. What is it you want?"

Red told him and that's when Nigel stopped laughing and said, "Ah, not just no, but hell no."

"Come on, Nigel. It'll be fun."

Red wanted to exhume the past and relive the glory days. He wanted to reenact the event and he didn't want to do it alone. He wanted Nigel to play along.

"Stop being such a damn tight ass. Sometimes you just got to cut loose."

"No, Red. Forget it. It isn't going to happen."

Red said nothing shaking his head in disappointment.

Nigel said, "When and where do you want to do this? And by the way … you're not getting any younger. You sure you still got the equipment to pull this off?"

"Thanks for reminding me of my age," snapped Red. "And don't you worry about the equipment."

Red disclosed his plan. The annual Song Writers Festival was coming up and he had his sights on pulling off his stunt then. On the final day of the event, hundreds of music lovers would grace the porch and parking lot of everybody's favorite eating and drinking joint, the Forgotten Coast Shrimp and Raw Bar. Lounge chairs and pick-up trucks would be scattered along the street. Each would be occupied with folks listening to some of the finest songwriters Nashville has to offer. They tell their stories and sing their songs. It is an annual tradition and a special treat for anyone in attendance. To Red, it meant a ready-made audience. An assembly positioned to be caught off guard.

On the last day of the Songwriters Festival, it's wise to get to the raw bar early to stake your claim. Nigel got there at 0900 and backed his truck so the bed faced the side of the porch, front row seating to catch all the action. The songwriters would be playing just for him and Candice. He slapped himself a high five for snagging such a coveted parking spot.

Nigel turned the volume up on the Oyster Radio that was playing through the speakers. Then he got out and climbed up into the bed of his truck and sat on the tool box that stretches across the back of the window. He waited. He glanced at his watch and wondered, *Where in hell is he?*

Red was running late, but that's no surprise. He doesn't wear a watch. He operates by his own internal clock. A clock in constant need of winding and not set to any particular time zone. Nigel didn't have to be anywhere in particular, so he waited.

Under normal circumstances Nigel would never partake in drinking beer before 1000, but lyrics coming through his speakers gave him reason to reconsider: *Beer for breakfast. Ain't no sin. Beer for breakfast. Ain't no sin.* He shrugged his shoulders and reached for a cold Coors Light and a wedge of lime. *What the hell.*

As he took a sip the sound of squashed and scattered oyster shells got his attention. By the next sip, Red was hopping up on the toolbox with Nigel opening a beer of his own. They touched cans and Red said, "Morning!"

"Is it, Red? I can't tell. I'm on my third lunar eclipse since sitting here."

Red offered a grunt of indifference then asked, "Are you ready for this?"

"There isn't much for me to get ready for, my friend. What about you? Are you ready?"

"Excited is more like it. I can't wait," said Red as he paused for a second or two. "What about you? Have you changed your mind?"

"No. My mind is pretty well made up. No chance of changing it now. Let's go to The Harbor Inn and get some breakfast to soak up this beer."

By the time Candice and Nigel got to the raw bar, the place was packed. The first group of songwriters was playing and the Gulf County deputies were already hard at work trying to keep people and chairs out of the street. In a matter of hours, it will be a lost cause and the road will be down to a single lane with both law enforcement and drunks attempting to direct traffic.

Red and his wife Trixie were already in the bed of Nigel's truck and the gate was down. Three squatters, cute cowgirls dressed in a variety of plaid blouses, Daisy Duke cutoffs and cowboy boots had parked themselves on the tailgate. Nigel didn't care.

Nigel helped Candice up into the bed of the truck. As she climbed up and sat on the toolbox, one of the three girls asked Nigel, "Who are you?"

Nigel smiled and said, "I'm the guy whose bed you've crawled up into."

She was a little embarrassed, but liked the comment. The girl next to her asked, "So this is your truck?"

Nigel said nothing, nodding.

The first girl asked, "These are awesome seats. Do you mind if we sit here?"

Nigel was a pushover. All three were more than cute. They were sexy little hotties, probably college students from somewhere. It didn't matter. If they wanted to stay, it was alright with him. He said, "Not at all, ladies. You dress up the truck nice. Stay as long as you want."

All three girls jumped off the tailgate. Two of them hugged him, and another kissed him on the cheek. Nigel was grinning from ear to ear when his eyes locked onto a death stare coming from Candice. She maintained her homicidal gaze as he took his seat next to her. Her eyes never left him, even as he reached for a fresh beer and opened it. He could feel her looking at him, so he took a sip, swallowed, adopted an innocent tone and said, "What?"

She tried to maintain an angry disposition, but turned away smiling as she said, "You disgust me."

Nigel reached over and kissed her on the neck, but she slapped him away as she kept her smile and head turned.

With everything back to normal, everyone was enjoying the music. The Nashville songwriters were sharing their stories, and singing the songs they've written for many of country music's best performers. What a collection of talent.

The third round of songwriters was on the porch stage and well into their set when Nigel noticed Red tapping his wrist wanting to know the time. Nigel checked his watch and nodded his head. *It was time.* Red said something to his wife Trixie then jumped off the truck. Did she know? It didn't appear she did.

Nigel lost track of Red but then saw him riding down the road as a passenger in a golf cart. Nigel laughed out loud to which Candice asked, "What's so funny?"

"Nothing, baby. Nothing I can explain now. You'll just have wait and see for yourself."

Candice shrugged her shoulders and Nigel reached over for a kiss. She was receptive. Then he said, "I'll be back. Going to slip inside, get a cold beer and make the rounds." She went back to listening to another of the many number one hits written for George Strait.

After the third round of performers finished their set, Brian Bowen grabbed his microphone. He was serving as master of ceremonies for the event. So before he introduced the next three songwriters, he took time to sell some event swag.

Brian was on the stage holding up and pimping one of the limited edition T-shirts for the event. Then a woman in the crowd stood up, pointed past Brian and screamed, "Oh my God! What's he doing?" Everybody stood to see. Brian turned around and began shaking his head. It was Red. He was buck naked, running down the road towards the event preparing for a flyby.

Trixie stood, up laughed, and then yelled, "Red! You're a crazy ass!"

Trixie turned around to say something to Nigel, but he wasn't there. She asked Candice, who was still laughing and watching Red, "Where did Nigel go?"

Candice was about to answer when her laughter stopped. She covered her mouth and said, "Oh no. Oh dear. It can't be." Candice pointed towards Red and said, "Oh my God, Trixie. Look!"

Red was in full stride running down the road. The crowd was in an uproar. Cheers and laughter filled the air. Even the county deputies couldn't contain themselves. Red was about four or five cars away from the edge of the parking lot when from behind one of the cars Nigel emerged to join him. He too was naked, and both were running like crazy.

Huffing and puffing, Red said, "I didn't think you'd ever show."

Nigel said, "Shut up. I still can't believe I allowed you to talk me into this."

The event had turned into total chaos. Brian Bowen used his microphone to speak to the both of them as they ran by, "Hey, Fellas! I'm trying to sell some damn T-shirts here. You're stealing my thunder!"

Through the jeers and whistles Red asked, "So what made you change your mind?"

Nigel laughed and said, "How often does someone get to run naked with the guy that invented streaking?"

"Glad to have you along comrade, but..." Red huffed and puffed some more so he could finish his thought. "But ... had I known you were bringing a Howitzer to the party" ... huff, puff ... huff puff... "I wouldn't have asked."

"Just keep running, Pee Wee. Keep running."

In the bed of Nigel's truck Candice was standing on the toolbox watching, still with her hands over her mouth. Nigel saw her and blew her a kiss. Candice dropped her fingers below her lower lip and mouthed the words, *I love you*. Nigel winked and went about his running.

In her husky voice, Trixie was screaming, "Run, Red! Ruuuun!"

Red replied with a sign of victory, pumping his fists in the air.

One of the girls from the tailgate looked up at Candice and asked, "Isn't that one your boyfriend?"

Candice smiled and nodded her head.

The tailgate girl said, "Well, it doesn't suck to be you."

And as Candice replied, "No, it doesn't," one of the deputies jumped into his squad car and pulled out onto the street behind Red and Nigel. He turned on the flashing lights, hit the siren a couple of time, and laughed as he addressed them through the PA system, "Pull over you two and keep your hands where I can see them."

Red turned to Nigel and said in a serious tone, "It's just a show of force. A formality. Don't stop. Follow me; just be mindful of the rattlesnakes."

Red made a sudden, sharp turn to the right. Off the road he went. Nigel was right behind him but made sure to maintain a safe distance. The deputy laughed and watched as the two of them disappeared into the woods.

The Article

The two guys weren't particularly interested in the news, local or otherwise. They were smoking a big, fat joint of cheap, stinky weed and passing a quart bottle of Old English Malt Liquor back and forth. The dope got them high enough, but the smoke was rough and harsh to the throat. The malt liquor helped ease the burn between tokes.

They were sitting on an old smelly sofa, stuffing and padding poured out of rips on both arms. One guy was big and overweight, unable to climb a flight of stairs without stopping to catch his breath. He was bald and had no neck, which gave the appearance that his head was too small for his body. Perhaps it was. He sweats a lot, and always bitches about the air conditioner not working, even though it was.

The other guy was much thinner, downright lean. His body fat was near three or four percent. His muscles were firm and well defined, wiry-looking absent of bulk. He appeared fit but had never put a day's worth of effort into it. Never once has he ever entered a gym or lifted a weight. He was by all accounts, a product of genetics. The only effort he put into his appearance was the cornrow braids, the scattering of cheap strip mall tattoos about his arms, back and neck, and the fake gold teeth that covered his incisors and bicuspids, not that any of it was much of an improvement.

The fat, bald one sat in a slow stupor holding the joint, forgetting to offer it to his partner. The skinny one was watching one of those courtroom judge shows: Judge Judy, Judge Joe, Judge Wapner ... he didn't know. He became inpatient and uninterested with the case being argued. It was one of those roommate disputes, something to do with free-flying parakeets and excrement landing into a bowl of Cheerios and other areas of the apartment. "This is bullshit," he said.

He looked over at his partner and saw the joint burning between his fingers. He reached over and snatched it saying, "Give me that ... and give me that damn remote."

Unexcited and abandoned of motivation, the fat, bald one said, "Screw you, Willie Bee." The fat, bald one picked up the malt liquor and took a drink, sat it down and resumed staring at the wall saying, "Get the remote your damn self."

Willie Bee, the lean one, mumbled obscenities and other unintelligible words as he reached across the vast real estate which was the fat, bald guy's lap. He grabbed the remote. While he pulled hard and long on the joint with his left hand, he used his right hand to point the remote at the TV screen to surf channels. His lungs were full of smoke, a painful looking grimace stretched across his face as he held the smoke in his lungs. Then he saw a familiar face on the screen. His eyes grew wide as he studied the picture being displayed in the corner of the screen. When he made the connection, he exhaled, coughing and hacking the words, "There he is, Cornbread! There he is. That's him!"

The picture being shown on the afternoon newscast changed to another face, a more familiar face. That's when Cornbread, the fat, bald one, said with little excitement, "Hey ... It's T-Daddy."

"Yeah, and that other one be the one that killed him."

Willie Boyd Anderson, otherwise known as Willie Bee, and Cornbread, who is never known by his real name, went quiet as they watched and focused on the TV. Alternating images of Nigel Logan and T-Daddy Lundsford, their old band leader, flashed across the screen as Sherry Stone promoted her upcoming special segment about her up close and personal interview with Nigel Logan.

The news anchor looked across the big studio floor where Ms. Stone stood beside a huge screen displaying a split image of Nigel and T-Daddy. The anchor asked, "So you were actually able to run down and find Mr. Logan after all this time?"

"Yes. He lives in a sleepy coastal town on the panhandle of Florida called Port St. Joe. He has a quiet existence there and seems to have laid down some new roots."

"So, without giving away too much, why did you decide to hunt down the man that some argue is the guy that got away with murder?"

"Good question. I had both business and personal reasons for wanting to find Chief Logan. Our meeting was emotional and interesting, both in what he shared with me and I with him."

"So Sherry, after spending time with Mr. Logan, do you think he is guilty of the Terrance Lundsford murder?"

Sherry got quiet, but she knew she couldn't take her time. Dead air time was destructive to the viewing experience, a taboo in the world of television and radio, so she let it sit for a beat or two before saying, "I guess you'll have to tune in later and make up your own mind."

"With a forced but natural sound, the anchor laughed and said, "I guess we will. What time does it air?"

"Tonight during the ten o'clock newscast, plus I have written about it as a guest columnist with the *Virginian-Pilot*. You can read about it there in the morning edition."

Willie Bee pointed the remote at the TV and killed the power. He took a hard hit from the big roach but there was nothing. The fire was gone, so he brought it back to life with a Bic lighter. He held the smoke as he offered the joint to his partner, but Cornbread declined. *Enough is enough.*

Willie Bee finally exhaled, took a swig off the malt liquor and said, "Where did she say he was?"

"Who?"

"The guy that killed T-Daddy, Cornbread. Dammit, were you not paying any attention at all?"

"Nope. We got anything to eat?"

"It was Saint Port something..."

"I told you. I don't know. What's in the fridge?"

There was a break in the weather. The temps were not off by much, but the humidity was way down. That made all the difference in the world. Not that Nigel ever complains about the heat and humidity. No, never. After years of standing hours upon hours of sea and anchor detail in the Chesapeake Bay, in the middle of winter, where the cold, the wet, and the wind always found a way into the depth of his bones, he swore that given the chance, he would never, ever cuss or complain about the heat again. He has pretty much kept to his word, but appreciated the change in climate.

The weather was too nice to waste inside. He grabbed a large Tervis tumbler, filled it with ice and topped it off with sweet tea. He went outside and plopped down in an Adirondack chair that held the shade of one of his huge crepe myrtle trees which lined his side yard. He took a sip of tea, closed his eyes, and laid his head back to allow his face to be surrounded by the dry warmth. He thought to himself, *If I had a good pillow, I could sleep here for hours.*

Moments later those thoughts were set aside by something bumping up against his ankle. Nigel's eyes opened and he looked down to see the cat. It was the same big, grey tabby that hangs around leaving gifts of rats and other varmints on his back steps. Nigel looked down on the big male, still no collar. He reached down to rub his head. The cat met him halfway pushing his ears across his fingers, "I'm guessing you're one hell of a lady's man. Aren't you?"

The cat jumped up onto his lap. "Uh huh ... That's what I thought. A big carousing Tom you are. A girl in every port. That's what I'm willing to bet."

The big cat circled around in his lap before beginning to knead a spot on his thigh. Nigel winced a bit at the sharp prickle of the cat's claws. He was about to shoo it away when it fell into his lap and rolled on its back.

Nigel continued, drinking his tea, petting the cat, and enjoying his afternoon. The cat seemed to doze off, eyes closed with methodical breathing. After awhile he saw his neighbor, the widow Marge, out for a stroll down the street. Nigel called to her. "Afternoon, Marge. Done with work today?" She works part-time at the Piggly Wiggly.

"No work today," she said. "Took the day off."

"Well, you picked a good one to do that."

Marge was looking at Nigel in the chair. She took on a curious look before asking, "What have you got there, Nigel?"

"Oh yeah. I was going to ask you. Do you have any idea who this cat belongs to? It's the friendliest thing."

Marge started to walk into the yard for a better look. She stopped just a few feet away and said, "Well, I'll be...."

"What?"

"If I wasn't seeing it with my own eyes, I would have sworn..."

The cat's eyes opened, his head made a quick turn and he saw the lady, the lady that chases him with a stick. In one singular move, the cat dug his claws into Nigel's thighs and launched himself off his lap. "Dammit!" Nigel protested as he looked down at the thin lines of fresh blood that streaked across his legs.

"I'm so sorry, Nigel," Marge said. "I didn't mean to spook him like that."

Nigel took his hand and rubbed his legs, rubbing the blood back into his skin saying, "That's okay, Marge. You wouldn't have known he would act that way."

"That's just it, Nigel. Yes, I did. That cat's as wild as they come. A nasty, feral tomcat that's always trying to sire my little Sissy."

"So you're saying the cat doesn't belong to anyone?"

Marge laughed and looked down at the end of the yard where the cat stood watching them. She smiled and said, "No ... I wouldn't say that. Not now anyway." She laughed again and said, "That cat either belongs to you now, or you belong to that cat. It's one of the two."

Nigel looked down the yard at the cat. It sat stiff with excellent posture as it watched. Nigel turned back to Marge as she was turning to walk away. Again she was talking to herself, "I would have never believed it had I not seen it with my own two eyes." When she got back to the pavement she turned to Nigel and said, "Keep that damn cat away from my Sissy, now. You hear me?"

Nigel said, "Yeah but..." The rest he let fall away.

He turned back to look at the cat, but it was gone. He shook his head in disbelief when he heard the sound of the mail truck on the adjacent street. It slowed and stopped at his box. He watched as the cute girl in tight, booty-shorts stuffed something in his mailbox.

The sweet mail girl offered a smile and a wave as she drove off. He finished his tea and stood up, headed to the mailbox.

There was no junk mail, but there was a big yellow envelope he pulled out into the sunshine, no return address. It wasn't needed. The postmark indicated Virginia Beach, Virginia, plus there was a familiar signature fragrance that he knew belonged to Sherry Stone. He often wondered when he would hear from her again.

He stood looking at the package. He hadn't even opened it yet, but was pleased to have it in his hand. He knew if she had written something he wouldn't have approved of, she wouldn't have sent it. She cared too much to send something he would find upsetting. Or at least he hoped.

He brought the envelope up to his nose and found the spot where she had sprayed the envelope. He took in the scent. It stirred memories of their last encounter, that last night in her hotel room. They were memories of things that could have been but were not allowed to materialize. He might one day regret the way things turned out that night. He might regret stopping her and himself from enjoying each other, a bed, and a lazy morning between the sheets. But not today. He was in a good place; he had Candice. And for now, she was all he needed. He laughed at himself. Candice wasn't just all he needed; she was all he could handle.

He went back into the house and recharged his glass of tea before returning to his chair and the shade. He took a sip and set the glass down on the ground. Then he pulled his dollar store readers out of his pocket, left lens poked out because it isn't needed, and put them on. He smelled the envelope one last time and smiled. He liked the way she smelled. There was no doubt about that.

He took his right index finger and worked it between the gap of the glued envelope flap. He wiggled his finger into the package until it would progress no further. Then he used his finger like a letter opener and ripped it open.

"Son of a bitch! That hurt!" he barked out loud to himself.

A long, deep paper cut produced bright red, oxygenated blood on the inside of his finger. "Son of a bitch." he said again, this time not as loud. He put the side of his finger in his mouth and sucked on the silly, painful wound.

Always with him in spirit, he was sure it was Candice's way of punishing him for taking in that last sniff and memory. "Logan ... You're an idiot," he said to himself.

He looked inside the big manila envelope. It contained a newspaper. He pulled it out. It was already opened to the page he would be interested in. A note was paper-clipped at the top of the page. It was a simple note that made him smile. It read, *No regrets ... Okay, maybe one. Love always, Sherry.* A winking smiley face was drawn at the end of her name.

The special commentary made page three of the first section. It was titled: *Who really killed T-Daddy Lundsford?* Nigel read the title to himself several more times before proceeding with the article. *What was her angle going to be?*

He began to read.

The Scales of Justice illustrate the weight of evidence against an accused. At the beginning of every case, the scale held by Lady Justice tilts in favor of the defendant. One is always presumed innocent before proven guilty. It is the job of the prosecution to build their case and supply enough evidence to tip the scales of justice towards a conviction.

The elaborate protections built into our judicial system serve not only to protect society and punish those that choose to violate its laws; it also provides protections for the accused as well. Any civilized system would. It is a balanced system by design, orchestrated like no other justice system in the free world. It is a system I believe in, every time ... until it falls short on its promise to society, and, more importantly, the faces of the victims.

Grace Matthews is one such victim. Perhaps you remember her; I'm betting you don't, so allow me to remind you. She was beaten and raped in connection with a carjacking incident. She never got to see the scales of justice tilt in her favor. Because of the mishandling of DNA, the cornerstone evidence in the prosecution's case, the case never went to trial. And the accused, Terrance Lundsford, otherwise known as T-Daddy, was set free to roam the streets of Norfolk.

The system failed Grace Matthews. It failed society and the community it is designed to protect. It failed us all. On a more personal note, in turn ... it failed me. Once a silent victim who carried internal shame, embarrassment, and often self-doubt, I refuse to remain reticent. Terrance Lundsford raped me too.

She went on to describe, much as she had with Nigel, the details about her own personal nightmare with Terrance Lundsford. She answered questions about why she never said anything and about why she never sought to press charges. She described the personal humiliation, and guilt she felt for letting herself and her family down. She explained her rationale for handling the situation as juvenile and immature.

I was so young and stupid. I figured if I didn't say anything, if I acted like it never happened, then maybe it would all go away. But it didn't. It stayed there in the back of my mind, haunting me ... until now.

Nigel grabbed his tea and took a sip. He took a deep breath and continued reading.

A little more than two years ago a man entered my life. He was someone I had never met until recently. In an instant, he made his way to the center of the local news as the primary suspect in the murder of Terrance Lundsford. I'm speaking of Chief Petty Officer Nigel Logan.

152

Nigel read on as she recounted the circumstances and police suspicion of his involvement. She mentioned the murder weapon, Nigel's own hand gun. She mentioned his connection to Grace and the entire Matthews family, particularly Grace's father, Captain Charlie Matthews. She described the naval connection. Nigel had served, on many occasions, with and under the command of Grace's father. She painted the picture of family.

It was the same family picture the prosecution had planned to paint for a jury. Such a vivid image would establish motive. The kind of motive the prosecution planned to use to argue that Nigel Logan was a dangerous man, a rogue vigilante. That he had decided to take the law into his own hands and punish Terrance Lundsford himself in an execution style killing. A killing to avenge Grace Matthews. But despite the overwhelming evidence against Nigel Logan, the Grand Jury refused to give the district attorney the indictment he sought.

Nigel read on.

Perhaps, it was poetic justice. Grace Matthews never got her day in court. She never got to see her attacker stand trial for the crimes against her. Meanwhile, a frustrated district attorney continues to stand on the sidelines as his prime suspect in the Lundsford murder runs free.

I called the DA's office for comment and a spokesperson for the office confirmed the Lundsford murder was an "active case still under investigation" and that "new developments were surfacing regularly." When asked if the district attorney was planning on seeking a new indictment from the Grand Jury, I was told, "The office was not prepared to comment on what it may or may not have planned."

In addition to having a personal interest in the Lundsford murder, I am still a news reporter. The professional journalist in me wanted to seek out Nigel Logan. This reporter wanted to sit down with him, ask questions, get a feel for and understand a few things about the man. The man many believe got away with murder.

After some research and rummaging for local intelligence, I caught up with Chief Logan in the sleepy coastal town of Port St. Joe, Florida. I found him at a neighborhood raw bar with friends, beer, and conversation. He was surprised by my presence, but he did not run or hide from my desire to interview him. He welcomed me into his simple existence and treated me with kindness and respect.

Nigel read on as Sherry Stone recounted their conversation about Lundsford, himself, and Grace Matthews. She made it a point to include her question about whether he had killed Terrance

Lundsford. She was accurate in describing his sidestepping of the question and how he turned the conversation around to focus on the victim, Grace Matthews.

She went on to describe her own secret, how she and Grace had much in common. They had both been attacked by Terrance Lundsford. She had never told anyone until that day. Nigel had been the first to hear those words. Now she was telling the world. Nigel thought, *Brave woman.* Then he read her closing remarks.

So the question remains: Who really killed Terrance Lundsford? For me, the killer is Nigel Logan. Not because I have proof or damning evidence, but because I don't want it to be anybody else but him. The very idea that he killed Lundsford to avenge the rape of Grace Matthews gives me peace. Now that I have met the man, and looked into his good heart, I can transfer what he did for Grace as an act to avenge the crimes against me as well. He didn't just kill Lundsford for Grace Matthews; he did it for me too. For that reason alone, justice has been served.

"So what do you think?" asked Willie Bee.

The Big Man was just that ... big, not obese, but he hadn't missed any meals either. Everybody calls him Big Man, first for his size and second because of his first name, Manchester. He was well dressed, far overdressed for the sleazy, shithole of a bar they were sitting in, a bar he owns. He has several just like it. All of them located in the most depressed slums and crime-riddled ghettoes of Norfolk. They are bars designed to exploit the weaknesses and extract the last flowing dollars of a people already pinned down by a lack of means. Everyone looks up to him, but, in reality, he is nothing more than a polished disease nobody can diagnose, a powerful man in a wide net of poverty.

They were sitting at a table in the back corner, Big Man sat with his back to the wall so he could keep an eye on the front door. He put the newspaper down and barked for another cognac. The bartender reached under the bar and grabbed a bottle of Remy Martin. An identical bottle sat up on the shelf, but it was full of cheap brandy for which his customers paid a premium. It was that way for almost every bottle on the shelf.

Big Man took a sip and asked, "We know where this place is? This Port St. Joe."

Cornbread spoke up trying to sound informed, "It sounds tropical. I think it's around Miami."

"Shut up, Cornbread," demanded Willie Bee with a look. He paused and spoke to the big man. "No, boss. It's not down around Miami. It's right here."

Willie Bee pulled out a map and pointed to a spot on the panhandle. Big Man studied the map and said, "Looks like a small town. Not much around it." Then he pulled out his phone and pulled the area up on Google Maps. "Yeah, nothing down there much. A guy could get lost real easy down there. Never get found."

"So, what cha think, boss?" asked Willie Bee.

Smiling, showing off his gold-capped teeth, Big Man looked around the room and said, "I think it's time we pay Mr. Logan a little visit."

"Yeah!" said Willie Bee. "Go get that motherfucker."

"Can you two handle this? Go down there and make this guy pay for what he did to T-Daddy?"

Willie Bee said, "Hell, yes. We'll go down there and take care of his ass."

"Are you sure you can handle it? Maybe I should send someone down with you. Someone like Jimbo."

James Waters, otherwise known as Jimbo, is a nasty fellow. His freedom to prisoner ratio runs at about fifty-fifty. Let's just say he's comfortable on both side of the bars. Most of his time served has been because of several battery and aggravated assault convictions, but he's capable of worse and has done so. While on a work detail, he knocked out and stabbed another inmate with a homemade shank, left the guy to die in his own pool of blood. He was never connected with the death. The rumor is it was an inside job. Jimbo was paid to do it, to make the guy go away.

Big Man looked at Willie Bee, then at Cornbread. He shook his head. The more he looked at Cornbread, the more he knew he was worthless. The mere sight of Cornbread made the idea of Jimbo going more sensible. It would be insurance.

Willie Bee said, "I know what you're thinking, boss. It's okay. We got this. We don't need Jimbo Waters. Not really."

Truth is Willie Bee is scared to death of Jimbo. He doesn't want anything to do with him. Jimbo was dangerous and Willie Bee knew it.

Big Man sat and stared at Willie Bee. He could see the fear in his eyes. And for Big Man that was all the convincing he needed. He looked at Cornbread and said, "Your fat ass is staying here."

Cornbread didn't protest.

Willie Bee sensed what was about to happen, and the idea of going to this place, Port St. Joe, was no longer appealing. He tried to plant a seed to stay in Virginia too. "What about me, boss? I guess I'll be staying behind too?"

"No. You're going."

"But, Big Man. Jimbo don't need no help. He's…"

"Shut up, Willie Bee. You're going and you'll do whatever Jimbo says."

"Okay, boss. Whatever you say."

Big Man picked up his phone and dialed a number. It rang three times before it was answered.

"Jimbo. It's Manchester."

Willie Bee watched as Big Man got up to excuse himself, to talk in private with Jimbo Waters. He watched with anxiety and anticipation as Big Man stood across the room. He couldn't hear what was being said, but he did see Big Man look back across the room at him, making eye contact each time. Willie Bee was getting nervous.

Big Man ended the call and walked back over to take his seat. He studied his drink, took a sip and said, "You leave this weekend."

Willie Bee was desperate. He wanted to get out of going. He didn't have much to go on but felt like he had to try so he said, "This weekend, boss?" He paused to think. And think he did, thinking hard for anything to say. However, the brain didn't answer and the words never came, so he said the first thing that came to mind, "I don't know boss. This weekend might not be good for me."

Big Man never stopped looking at his cognac. He took another sip then repeated, "You leave this weekend."

Willie Bee's soul sank, but he said, "Yes, boss. This weekend, boss. I got it, boss."

Big Man smiled. He likes being called boss. Because of his position and control in the hood, he is considered by many to be sort of a black Godfather. He was capable of delivering on favors that met the needs of the community and individuals. Favors that came with certain expectations and promises of reciprocity.

Things were complex with Big Man. He had done much to help promote T-Daddy and the band. He had gotten them many gigs. He didn't even like T-Daddy's music. Big Man likes the blues. He's a Mississippi Delta blues man. The lack of melody, and disjointed rhythm and beat of rap just wasn't his style. He hated it. But despite that, he had gotten T-Daddy and his band into places that otherwise would have slammed the door in their faces.

There was the other thing too. Big Man's interest in T-Daddy's death was personal. Big Man was more than just some second-rate neighborhood Godfather thug. He was Manchester Lundsford, the brother of T-Daddy's late father. Big Man was T-Daddy's uncle.

Tate's Hell

The ride in the car was quiet and slow, no radio and no talking.
It was forbidden. They were heading south on Interstate 95. And
while many travelers think 95 also doubles as the speed limit, the old,
purple, metal-flake Buick 225 cruised at a steady sixty miles per hour,
never getting out of the passing lane. Traffic had to dodge the
sparkling deuce and a quarter, often adding prolonged horn blowing
in protest. But it didn't matter, the driver was unfazed. He was happy
to clog the fast lane and ignore the displeasure of the drivers around
him. Jimbo didn't care.

Before they left Virginia, Jimbo made it clear; there would be no
talking. He needed time to think things through. They were on the
road maybe ten minutes when Willie Bee reached over to turn on the
radio. His fingers were only inches away from the dial when Jimbo's
knuckles came off the steering wheel and hit the top of Willie Bee's
hand.

Willie Bee wailed, "Son of a bitch!" as he pulled his hand back
flopping his wrist back and forth. "That hurt!"

Jimbo said nothing but in rapid fashion turned to burn a look
towards his partner. The non-verbal message was delivered: *Shut up!
Don't say another word.* Willie Bee turned away and looked out the
passenger side window. He was rubbing his hand thinking, *this son of a
bitch is crazier than I thought.*

The slow ride, the constant horn blowing, and the obnoxious
silence inside the car began to take its toll on Willie Bee. It made him
a nervous wreck. He turned to look at the huge man behind the
wheel, but his profile never changed. Jimbo maintained a stoic,
distant expression, as if he was the only one in the car. Not that
Willie Bee was looking for any attention. The first acknowledgement
that Willie Bee was even in the car came when they pulled off the
interstate for gas. Jimbo broke the silence and said, "Get out. Fill her
up and get me a quart of Budweiser."

Willie Bee didn't hesitate.

Minutes later they were back on the interstate. Willie Bee had never tasted a Budweiser before. He always thought of it as some redneck beer for white boys. But, if Jimbo was going to drink one, it might be smart to drink one too. He could use it as a good ice breaker, make it seem like they have something in common. Willie Bee took a sip and smiled. He held up the bottle looking at the label and said, "Damn. This shit is pretty good."

Jimbo said nothing but glared another silent message. Minutes later Jimbo said, "Roll a joint. The first aid kit is in the glove box."

Willie Bee opened the box and found the stash, a white box with a red cross printed on top. He opened it and found the sandwich bag of dope. He unrolled and opened the bag bringing it up to his nose. It was rich and aromatic, not like that backyard crap he and Cornbread smoke.

Jimbo glanced over at Willie Bee and saw him loading up a big fat joint. "Not so big, goddammit!" said Jimbo. "That ain't no shit-weed, dammit."

Willie Bee put half the weed back in the bag and held up the new load for Jimbo to see. "Still too much, but it will do," Jimbo replied.

Willie Bee raked a little more back in the bag and finished rolling the joint. The leaves were sticky with resin. He couldn't wait to smoke it. Jimbo said, "Give me that. And the lighter too."

Willie Bee watched as Jimbo fired up the joint. The smell of the smoke was like heaven. He thought about reaching for the joint but thought better of it. He figured he'd wait until Jimbo offered it back. But he didn't. Not at first anyway. Willie Bee waited and thought, *What an asshole. He isn't even going to share.*

Jimbo had no intention of sharing, but the joint was big enough that when he had his fill, he offered the rest to Willie Bee. "Here. Finish this."

Willie Bee took the roach and hit it like a starving dog. It was good. As he held the smoke in his lungs, he looked in the first aid kit for a roach clip and found a pair of hemostats. He clipped it on. Then he exhaled thinking, *it was the best ever.* There wasn't much left, so he added a little fire to the end and brought the roach to his lips and pulled hard until the fire was out. He held the smoke again for as long as he could. It was nice to exhale and not cough the smoke out of his lungs. He looked at what was left of the roach, popped it into his mouth and washed it down with beer thinking. *Damn that was sweet.*

It didn't take long before Willie Bee started to feel the effects. He gazed out the window in quiet euphoria and watched as the southern countryside slipped by at what seemed a snail's pace. He even forgot where he was and why he was in the car. But a quick glance at Jimbo behind the wheel brought the eerie reality back into perspective. As he remembered the mission, to hunt down and kill Nigel Logan, he was shouldered with a haunting sense of paranoia. As the other drivers flew by, laying on the horn, he was certain they knew what they were up to. He shrunk down in the seat as he looked out the window.

Willie Bee's mind shifted back and forth between paranoia and euphoria, but now he was thinking of food. It had been awhile since either one had eaten anything. He salivated over the various billboards that flew by but found others confusing. Some left him wondering where in the hell Jimbo was going. Willie Bee had never been to South Carolina before, and the signs and billboards that increased in frequency left him dazed. By the time they were only four or five miles from the border, Willie Bee was being inundated with visions of Mexico. The signage and billboards were promoting *South of the Border*, the state line rest stop and roadside attraction famous for its Mexican influence, architectural style and décor.

For most vacationers and travelers on Interstate 95, a brief sojourn at *South of the Border* is a tradition. It serves as the perfect break from the endless miles to points further south. Many fathers have, at least on a temporary basis, lost the enduring love of their children by ignoring the allure and driving past without stopping, an almost unforgivable act in the mind of a little boy or girl.

For Willie Bee, the constant barrage of signage left him in a tizzy. Frustrated and forgetting his place, he spoke in a sarcastic tone as he looked at one of the billboards. "Where in the hell are you going, Jimbo? And who is this Pedro?"

In an instant, Willie Bee realized his mistake, and he turned just in time to see Jimbo's fist connect with the side of his face. As his head bounced off the passenger side window, he heard Jimbo say, "Shut up! Dammit ... I said, 'no talking,' remember? All you've done since leaving Virginia is run your mouth."

Willie Bee cowered as he rubbed his face and head.

Jimbo said, "I'm hungry," as he pulled off the exit to visit with Pedro.

In aggravation Jimbo asked, "What the hell are these people looking at?"

Now allowed to talk, somewhat, Willie Bee answered, "Us, they're all staring at us."

"No shit. I know they're staring at us, Jackass. But, why?"

Willie didn't want to push his luck on speaking, so he just shrugged his shoulders.

They were arriving in Port St. Joe. It was late in the afternoon. The big, sparkly, purple Buick was rolling into town after traveling all day and night. To Jimbo his ride seemed normal, as it did to his passenger. Around the neighborhoods of Norfolk, the big Buick drew its share of attention, but nothing like this. Such a customized ride was commonplace back home, but not so much in the new town they found themselves in. The vehicle was seen as a strange novelty. It caught frequent stares, pointing, scowls, even laughter as it cruised down Reid Avenue.

Residents of any rural, southern town, especially one made up of fishermen and hunters, are always going to find interest and humor in a vehicle which appears to belong in a circus parade. The shiny, purple Buick stuck out like a sore thumb. Its suspension was lifted and set to a Carolina squat. The wheels and low profile tires were oversized leaving just enough clearance in the rear wheel well. Gold fringe dressed up the top of both the forward and back windshield. Handcuffs and large stuffed dice hung from the rearview mirror as the heads of two dog statues bobbled on the rear dash. If they had hoped to roll into town incognito, they were shit out of luck.

In a town with only two stop lights, it doesn't take long to have driven all the streets. Before long, they were on the outskirts of town and had discovered the more prominent black side of town. They needed a drink and a couple of rooms to rent, so they decided to ask around. Jimbo said, "Ask these cats."

The car rolled to a stop in front of a small house. The house had seen better days, the whitewashed paint had worn through to bare wood in several places, but, all in all, it was well kept. On the porch sat three older gentlemen. They were drinking beer and playing checkers.

Willie Bee raised his voice as he called through the passenger window of the car, "Hey! Where can a brother find a drink and a room to rent?"

The two playing checkers ignored Willie Bee, never even looked up. The one gentleman not playing checkers came off the porch and walked down to the street. Without answering he walked along and around the car. He was checking it out, from the fancy paint job to the big, low-profile tires. He shook his head in amazement and said aloud, "Ooooo Weee! Damn!" Then he looked back up to the porch and said, "Hey, Joe. You got to see this."

Joe, one of the checker players, looked up. Then he stood and came off the porch.

The other guy said, "It's like your old car, Joe. Check it out."

Joe made it out to the sidewalk and stared, giving the car a good examination.

Willie Bee could see Jimbo getting impatient so he said, "We need a place to stay, old man. And a drink."

Joe continued to check out the car while the other one said, "Old man! Who you calling an old man, punk?"

Willie Bee laughed and said, "You. You the old man..."

Joe walked over to Willie Bee's window and said, "Shut up, son." Then Joe looked over at Jimbo and asked, "This your car, boy?"

Jimbo said nothing.

Joe said, "Looks like a '73 model."

Jimbo still said nothing.

"I used to have a '73, two twenty-five. It was black, the sweetest deuce and a quarter that ever rolled off the assembly line. I bought her new, she was perfect."

Jimbo still wasn't joining in the conversation. He wasn't even acknowledging the old man. Jimbo kept his head looking forward, but Joe didn't mind. Joe shook his head as he looked in at Jimbo. Then he said, "Yeah, I miss that old car. I often wonder where she is today. You know what I mean?"

Joe waited for an answer, but Jimbo said nothing. The silence was even starting to make Willie Bee a little nervous.

Then Joe said, "I guess not. Well ... I'll tell you one thing. I don't know where that old car is, but, wherever she is ... whoever has it ... I hope they haven't screwed it up like you have this one. This piece of shit looks like a purple people eater. It's a damn disgrace to the memory of a once fine car."

The other gentleman on the sidewalk and the other checker player on the porch busted out laughing. The guy on the porch said, "Purple people eater! Damn, Joe. That's what I was thinking."

The other guy, the one that wasn't playing checkers said, "Uh huh! They done mucked this ride up good. Looks like one of those clown cars the Shriners drive in Panama City."

Willie Bee looked over at Jimbo who was now furious. The second Willie Bee saw Jimbo grab the door handle, he said, "No trouble, Jimbo. Remember what Big Man said, 'No trouble.'"

Jimbo didn't listen. He slammed the door and walked around the front of the car. Joe stood his ground as Jimbo approached. That's when the shotgun appeared on the porch. The guy on the porch said, "Hold it right there, mister."

Jimbo didn't pay any mind to the guy with the gun until he fired a round in the sky. Jimbo stopped in his tracks. He looked up to see the guy on the porch pump another round into the chamber and pointed it towards the street. "That's better," said the guy on the porch.

Willie Bee got nervous and sunk down below the window and said, "Hey! You shoot that thing you'll take out your buddy too."

The guy on the porch said, "I don't give a shit. Don't like him much either. Beats me at checkers every time."

Joe looked back at his checkers partner with a look of astonishment. Then the checker player with the shotgun said, "Just kidding, Joe. Step to the side."

Joe and the other older gentleman made their way up to the porch while the shotgun was trained on Jimbo. That's when Jimbo finally spoke. He said, "Old man, that birdshot will hurt, but it won't kill me."

"That's the funny thing, son," said the man with the gun. "I can't remember if it's the second or the third round that has the slug in it. I'm guessing you don't want to find out."

Jimbo said nothing.

That's when Joe said, "Boys, I'm not sure where you are coming from..."

The one that wasn't playing checkers said, "Virginia, Joe. The tag says they're from Virginia."

Joe continued, "Virginia, huh? Well, you Yankee boys are a long way from home. Didn't your momma teach you any manners? Perhaps you tell us your business here."

"Willie Bee said, "We're looking for somebody."

"Like who?" Joe asked.

Jimbo said, "None of your goddamn business, old man."

Now the sounds of sirens were starting to fill the air. Jimbo and Willie Bee exchanged looks. That's when the one not playing checkers said, "Well, unless you want to explain things to the police, you better get your asses out of here."

That's when Jimbo turned to rush back to the car.

As Jimbo was hurrying away, Joe said, "And don't you ever bring that ugly piece of purple shit down this road again. You hear me, boy?"

The three old gentlemen laughed as Jimbo and Willie Bee tore off down the road.

The two that were playing checkers went back to their game. Joe said, "It's your move, Charles."

The two men went back to staring at the board, then Charles said chuckling, "Shriner clown car ... That was funny, Clyde."

Jimbo and Willie Bee found a small motor lodge on the side of Highway 98. It's run by an older couple that bought the place several years ago as a sleepy retirement business. The rooms are clean and come at a reasonable rate. They like to keep things inexpensive for the fishermen that pull their boats from all over the country to wet their lines in St. Joe Bay. Their generosity in room rates has often come back to bite them. They rely on return business, but they've had their fair share of ungrateful visitors who are loud, trash rooms, and don't follow the rules. They've seen visitors come and go, and they've had to learn to profile people looking to get a room, especially those without reservations.

Willie Bee strolled to the reception counter with his hat sideways and his trousers hanging low. His belt was pulled tight below the cheeks of his ass, so he walked with his knees spread wider than his shoulders to keep his trousers from dropping to the ground. He resembled a drunken penguin when he walked. He had on a tight-fitting white tank top which was garnished with fake gold chains and other assorted bling bought at a Kmart.

The owner of the hotel came close to illuminating the "No Vacancy" sign.

"How much for a room?" Willie Bee demanded.

The owner looked out the window and checked out the car in front of the office. He saw the driver behind the wheel and their eyes met. The owner wasn't impressed. The only thing that came to mind was *trouble*.

With hesitation the owner said, "The rate is seventy-nine dollars a night with a two hundred and fifty dollar deposit. How long are you expecting to stay?"

Willie Bee put his hands palm down on the counter and tilted his head from side to side with each syllable as he said, "How am I supposed to know how long we'll stay?" Then he took a step back from the counter and said, "Did you say a two hundred and fifty dollar deposit?"

The owner maintained eye contact with Willie Bee before saying, "Oh! Did I say two fifty? I'm sorry. I meant three hundred. Do you want a room or not?"

Willie Bee, tired and aggravated, spun around in amazement trying to think of what to do. He paid no attention when the phone rang and the owner said, "Excuse me while I take this."

Willie Bee was thinking, tapping his fingers on the counter, his head was bobbing as he looked from side to side. He looked out towards the car where he knew a tired and impatient Jimbo sat waiting. Their eyes met. Frustrated that things weren't moving fast enough, Jimbo gestured with his hands, *what's taking so damn long*.

Willie Bee turned around and the hotel owner was holding his palm over the mouth piece of the phone. He asked, "Do you want a room, or not?"

"Don't rush me, dammit. You hear me?"

Willie Bee looked back at Jimbo and caught a cold and angry stare. *Okay*, he thought. He'd get the room. He turned back to the owner who was finishing up his call. When he hung up, Willie Bee said, "I'll take it."

The owner said nothing at first, but he reached under the counter and flipped a switch. Then he pointed out towards the sign by the highway. Willie Bee turned to look. The "No Vacancy" light was now flashing. He turned back towards the owner and said, "What?"

"It's too late," said the owner. "You waited too long. I gave you a chance. That call ... They made reservations for my last room."

"Now, all of a sudden, you don't have a room?"

"Nope," the owner lied. "I'm all booked up."

Willie Bee was showing his teeth as he spun around and jumped in the air. He came down, slapped the counter and said, "What do you mean, all booked up?" He went into a furious rant calling the owner every name in the book. He meandered and ranted around the small lobby. His left hand was flinging in the air as his right hand had a grip on his britches.

The owner watched with bland enthusiasm but maintained a grip on the .38 caliber Saturday Night Special under the counter. He didn't expect to need it, but he'd rather be safe than sorry. The rant was getting old, and the owner was finding it harder and harder to appear stoic and patient. At his first opportunity he asked, "Are you through yelling, young man?"

Willie Bee spoke through clenched teeth saying, "You're a racist. That's what you are. It's cause we're black, isn't it?"

At that moment the front door opened. Both men looked to see Jimbo standing in the doorway. Willie Bee looked back at the motel owner and smiled.

"It has nothing to do with you being black. It has everything to do with your being an asshole. And the fine print in the contract clearly says, 'Assholes not welcome.'" That's when he placed the revolver on the counter and said, "Now, get out."

Unexcited, Jimbo said, "Come on. Let's go," and turned to walk out the door.

Willie Bee was biting his lower lip and showing his gold teeth as he backed away with great care. In a final defiant tantrum, he jumped high in the air and pounded his feet onto the floor. His right hand lost its grip on his pants and the trousers fell straight to his feet. Willie Bee almost tripped over himself as he tried to pull his britches back up.

Jimbo stopped the car at the next roach motel they came to as the sun started to put itself to bed for the night. He didn't want any more screw-ups, so he left Willie Bee in the car as he went into the office. Willie Bee didn't mind since he was sporting a fresh, swollen lip that was still bleeding. A few minutes later they were standing outside their room. Jimbo opened the door and walked in switching on the light.

Willie Bee followed and noticed only one king size bed in the middle of the room. He knew better than to say anything, so he dropped his bag on the floor and plopped down on the armchair in the corner. Besides, he was too tired to care. He was asleep in about thirty seconds.

Jimbo didn't waste any time either. He had been driving straight for more than eighteen hours and was ready to catch some sleep. He could worry about finding Nigel Logan in the morning.

Willie Bee was curled up and contorted in the chair while Jimbo's entire mass was sprawled out taking up almost every inch of the mattress. They had been asleep for only an hour or so when the dog started barking. Both did their best to ignore it in hopes that it would stop. It didn't. It was a high-pitched, yapping bark. Any barking is bad, but it's worse when it comes from a little mutt that thinks it weighs 120 pounds.

Willie Bee squinted his eyes tight to shut out the noise. It didn't work. Jimbo wasn't as patient and jumped from the bed. Willie Bee stayed still but opened one eye to watch. Jimbo walked over and opened the door and the barking grew louder. Jimbo stood in the doorway looking around for a bit then stepped out and shut the door. Willie Bee got up and pulled back the drawn curtains to take a look. He only heard the dog. He saw nothing.

Jimbo didn't know what kind of dog it was. It was small and furry. He saw the rhinestones that lined the collar around its neck. It was no stray, but Jimbo didn't care.

The little dog had no idea that someone was behind it. It was too busy concentrating on the raccoon pacing the closed lid of the dumpster. The raccoon would stand on its back two feet and hiss and snarl at the dog. This only intensified the barking.

Jimbo stepped behind the dog and reached down with both hands grabbing it around the neck. The application of pressure was firm, enough to stop breathing and noise. Except for a small initial yelp, the barking stopped. Jimbo squeezed harder and harder. The dog clawed and squirmed, trying its best to get away, but it couldn't. The movements of the dog started to slow until it no longer struggled at all. The little dog went limp in the firm grip of Jimbo Waters.

Jimbo walked over to the dumpster where the only witness to the dog's last living moments stood prepared to fight. The raccoon once again rose on its back two legs and showed all its teeth in a defiant growl. Raccoons are common carriers of rabies, and if Jimbo knew this, he didn't care. He looked at the raccoon and gave it a swift backhand knocking it off the dumpster. Then he opened the dumpster and tossed the dog in and let the lid slam shut.

When Willie Bee heard the barking stop, he strained his neck and eyes trying to see around the edges of the big motel room window. He saw nothing, so he closed the curtain and crawled back into his chair and pretended to be asleep. Moments later the door opened and Jimbo came back in the room. Willie Bee squinted and watched his big partner fall back onto the bed and return to his snoring.

The next morning Willie Bee and Jimbo sat in a cafe booth having coffee. They were waiting for a phone call from Big Man, Manchester Lundsford. Big Man didn't want Jimbo and Willie Bee to go around town asking questions, so he promised to do some research to come up with an address for Logan. Big Man knew that in cautious small towns, word travels fast. If his crew turned over every leaf in town, it wouldn't take long before it would get back to Logan. Things had to be done off the radar.

But there was a problem; Big Man was having a difficult time rounding up any information on Logan. The Internet is a great resource for finding folks, but Logan was invisible on the Internet. His electronic footprint was minimal. What little he could find only pointed to his long-established existence in Virginia, his Navy years, but nothing in Port St. Joe.

Big Man found Logan's sailing photography gallery, SailPixs.com, but it gave no location. Yet, it did list a contact phone number. Big Man picked up his phone and decided to give the number a try.

Nigel was at the Reid Avenue Bar and Bottle Shop sitting on stool seventeen. He was having lunch and a beer with Candice, the bar's manager and his steady girl. It has become part of the P.O.D, Plan of the Day, that Nigel drops by and brings lunch. He surprised her with a plate of Paul Gant barbecue.

Paul Gant has a small roadside barbecue joint just on the outside of town. There is nothing fancy about it. It's better described as a permanent food truck with cookers and smokers out back. It has been there for years and for good reason. It's the best damn barbecue around. Folks come from all over to load up on Paul's fabulous cooking.

Several weeks ago, Nigel and Red stopped to grab a few plates for themselves and Trixie. There was a fella standing at the window waiting for his food, not just any food ... all the food. As Red and Nigel were waiting, a girl behind the window leaned out and said, "Sorry, we'll be closing early today. We're out of food."

Nigel looked at his watch. It said 1503. He looked up, "Out of food? What do you mean, out of food?"

The guy in line turned around and said, "I'm sorry fellas. I just bought everything they have cooked and everything else that is still in the cooker."

"Everything?" asked Red. "You got to be shitting me."

"I'm sorry," said the guy. "We're having a big party."

"Are we invited?" asked Red.

The guy returned a sheepish smile. *No, you're not.*

Nigel had a mouthful of pork when his phone rang. He chewed faster as he reached for his phone. He looked at the screen and stopped chewing. It was a Virginia area code, and he didn't recognize the number. He started his chewing back when Candice asked, "Well, are you going to answer it?"

Nigel swallowed and set the phone down on the bar. "Naw. They can leave a message if it's important."

Nigel watched the phone as it continued to ring. Then it stopped, went to voicemail. Nigel kept an eye on the phone. He wanted to see if the message light would come on. It didn't. He picked up the phone and added the number into his contacts: *??Virginia Caller??*

Several hundred miles away Big Man ended his impromptu call to Logan the second he heard the voicemail message start. He set the phone down to think. He got up and went to the bar and poured himself a cognac. He always feels smarter when he's drinking cognac. While feeling the burn of the sweet and aromatic liquor, something dawned on him.

He was reluctant to pull someone else in, but Big Man needed information. The person he felt might be able to help was also a fan of the late T-Daddy Lundsford. He walked back over, picked up the phone and dialed.

Jeffery Wheeler works as a mail handler at the Virginia Beach post office. Big Man didn't provide any details about what he was up to, but he didn't have to. The second Big Man mentioned the name Nigel Logan, Jeffery Wheeler didn't want or need to hear more. He was all in and supportive of whatever Big Man had planned. Wheeler said, "Port St. Joe, Florida, huh? Let me see what I can do. I'll call you back."

After a long wait, Jimbo's phone rang. He looked at the screen, then to Willie Bee and said, "This is it. It's Manchester." Jimbo answered the call, "What you got, Big Man?"

Jimbo held the phone to his ear for several minutes and said nothing, just listened until he ended the call with a smile. "McClelland Avenue," he said. "He lives on McClelland Avenue. We don't have a house number, but Big Man says it's not a long street, just a few blocks." Jimbo told Willie Bee to settle up with the waitress. They finished their coffees and headed for the door.

They gave the street one slow careful pass, checking out the houses. There were several they could ignore. They were confident he lived alone, so they wouldn't expect to see a yard or driveway full of cars. He had no children, so the appearance of toys around the house would help cancel out possibilities. They noticed three elderly residents, one male and two females standing by their mailboxes. They were drinking coffee and gossiping about lord knows what. They stopped their chatter to take a good look and snicker at the purple Buick as it rolled by.

Jimbo and Willie Bee wanted to take another pass along the street but decided to wait. They didn't want to draw anymore attention to themselves than they already had. After several minutes they decided to approach McClelland Avenue via an adjacent street. From Long Avenue they hung a slow left on 13th Street, a short block. Jimbo stopped in front of a detached garage facing the street. It belonged to a little house on the corner lot. Parked out in front of the garage sat a center console powerboat. Jimbo asked, "What did Manchester say Logan's business was?"

"He takes pictures. Some kind of photographer. Boats or something," replied Willie Bee.

Jimbo grunted, "This is too easy," as he pointed to the graphics on the side of the boat: SailPixs.com. He took his foot off the brakes and eased on down the road and stopped in front of the drive that separated the garage and the back of the house. He slapped Willie Bee on the leg and said, "Look, fool."

He did and Jimbo let the car creep on down the road. Willie Bee said, "Oh ... This is way too easy. Did he see us?"

"I don't think so."

Jimbo and Willie Bee crossed over McClelland Avenue and drove another block before turning around. They stopped the car on the side of the road to watch.

Willie Bee said, "He's either just got home, or he's about to leave."

Reaching over and backhanding his partner, Jimbo said, "Shut up and watch, dammit."

Ten seconds later they were tailing Logan's pickup truck, at first from a safe distance. But with slow traffic and only two stoplights, the purple Buick found itself closing ranks. By the time they were at the second stoplight, they were right behind Logan. They were in a turning lane waiting for a green arrow. Jimbo saw Logan's eyes in the Ford's rearview mirror.

Nigel didn't notice the purple Buick until it was behind him in the turning lane. He gave the two occupants a glancing look but focused most on what he considered a bastardized classic. *Who could do such to a car and think it actually looks good?* "That's some ridiculous shit right there," he said aloud.

The light turned green and Jimbo followed and watched as Logan was shaking his head and laughing. When Logan's pickup turned left into the City Marina, Jimbo continued on straight and turned around at the end of the street. They pulled off onto the side of the road to wait and watch.

Willie Bee pointed and said, "There he is, walking down the dock. Where do you think he's going?"

"Don't ask stupid questions. Less talking more watching, dammit," replied Jimbo.

They sat and watched as Logan strolled along. He stopped a couple of times to chat with a few folks, but not for long. They kept an eye on him and watched as he stepped onto a sailboat. They could see the name on the stern: *MisChief*. Minutes later they saw Logan letting loose the dock lines and pulling out of the slip. As the boat slipped through the water, Logan started to remove the cover from his mainsail. He looked up and again saw the purple Buick but thought nothing of it as he went back to the task at hand.

"There's your answer," said Jimbo. "He's going for a boat ride." He pulled the shifter back into drive and eased away.

Jimbo parked the car at a house at the end of Logan's street. It looked empty and abandoned. The grass was knee high, and it had an old and faded "For Sale by Owner" sign out by the street. The phone number was bleached by the sun, but Jimbo could see the 404 area code and knew that meant Georgia, probably Atlanta. "These people haven't been here for years," he commented, "Get out and snoop around."

"In broad daylight?" protested Willie Bee.

Jimbo pulled his hand back and Willie Bee lifted his hands and arms to protect his head. Jimbo stopped and withdrew his attack and said, "Just do it, dammit. I want to see if it's safe to leave the car here or not."

After a few minutes, Willie Bee tapped on the driver's side window and gave a thumbs up. Jimbo rolled the window down and Willie Bee said, "Nobody's here. Like some ghost town shit or something."

Jimbo pulled deep into the drive and parked under a carport that looked as if it would collapse in a strong wind.

Jimbo and Willie Bee walked around the block to get to Logan's place. As they walked, Willie Bee started to think about the way he'd been treated the entire trip. Jimbo scared him. Hell, he scared everybody. But he was sick of getting slapped around and talked down to. The more he thought about it, the more it bothered him. He hated the silent treatment and not knowing what was going on. He'd had enough. Forgetting his place he stopped walking and said, "So, Jimbo, what the fuck are we doing? Do you plan to share your ideas? I don't like being left in the dark."

Jimbo stopped and turned around in the middle of the street. He gazed at Willie Bee with contempt. Willie Bee wished he hadn't said anything now, but he was frustrated. It just came out. Willie Bee stood his ground as Jimbo approached. Scared shitless, he faced Jimbo and awaited the worst.

Jimbo poked his finger into Willie Bee's chest and with the slightest hint of a smile said, "I was wondering how long it was going to take you to man up. I thought I was going to have to leave you for dead and do this all myself."

Leave me for dead? The thought left Willie Bee with an internal shiver. He wasn't expecting to hear those words, but he maintained eye contact and replied, "That doesn't sound like much of a plan now does it? So let's have it. What the hell are we planning to do?"

Jimbo's hint of friendliness retreated to a frown and was followed up by a quick smack to the face. "Don't try and get cute with me. We're working together, that's all. It doesn't mean we're pals. Got it?"

Willie Bee held the side of his face and looked up at Jimbo and offered a wince and nod of affirmation.

"Good," Jimbo said. "Now, let's go get this guy. We're breaking into his place to wait him out."

"What if somebody sees us snooping around?" asked Willie Bee.

"They won't."

"How can you be so sure?"

"Because you're going to be damn careful. That's why. Find a way in, a window maybe. Then unlock the back door."

"That sounds dangerous."

"Everything we are doing here is dangerous."

They cased the place from a distance. The truck was still gone and everything looked quiet. Jimbo said, "Get going."

Willie Bee disappeared around the corner of the garage, but he wasn't alone. He was being watched. Every move Willie Bee made was tracked from the shadows of some low-hanging palm fronds. He was under careful surveillance by the unblinking eyes of the cat; the mysterious gray tabby Logan calls Tom.

Willie Bee made his way to the back door. For shits and giggles, he grabbed the knob for a quick test. He grinned, then slipped into the small kitchen and shut the door. He stood still for a minute or two. He was listening for any sign of presence. All he heard was the creaking sounds of an old, empty house. He looked in the refrigerator and pulled out two Coors Lights.

The vivid yellow eyes of the cat gave way to black pupils the size of dimes. He was taking everything in and was on full alert as Willie Bee came out the back door. The cat shifted around another frond, but he never took his eyes off the intruder. And he watched as he slipped around the corner of the garage.

Willie Bee handed Jimbo a beer and said, "This is easier than we thought. The place is wide open."

Jimbo grunted and said, "Don't be an idiot. Nothing in this business is easy. Don't forget that. Let's go."

Jimbo slipped into the back door and Willie Bee followed. Like Willie Bee had done before, they stood still to listen. Then Jimbo said, "Let's search the place, get a lay of the land."

They made their way around the small cottage and took their time memorizing the tiny floor plan.

Meanwhile, the gray tabby remained under the palm. He was watching the back door they had left cracked open. Stalking, the cat took a couple low cautious steps and stopped. Then it dashed in a flurry of stealth and speed. It darted towards the door and slipped through the crack. Once inside he made two explosive leaps, one off the floor and the other off the kitchen counter. He landed on top of the refrigerator. The two-part move was fast and smooth, but to the naked eye could have been mistaken as one fluid motion. The cat positioned himself at the back of the fridge and gave himself a bird's-eye view.

Jimbo and Willie Bee searched the house for weapons and valuables. They found none. They were just about to settle in for the wait when Jimbo noticed an odd-looking piece of the wall behind the television stand. He pulled the cabinet away and discovered the tongue and grove patchwork that now covered the original fireplace. Jimbo played with the boards and discovered they could be removed. As he pulled the boards away, he smiled. He found Nigel's safe. It contains everything, most important of all Nigel's available cash, an excess of some one hundred fifty thousand dollars.

Since his arrival in Port St. Joe, Nigel has paid cash for everything. He never pays with a credit card or his Navy Federal Credit Union debit card where his monthly pension retainer is sent. The idea being, the authorities still investigating the Lundsford murder would be monitoring his account activity. And the last thing he wanted to do was to leave a financial trail that would be easy to follow. All that worked fine, until the Sherry Stone story broke. Now, it was no secret, but Nigel didn't care.

Jimbo fiddled with the latch of the safe, but it was locked tight. He shook the box and listened. He couldn't hear much, but felt the shifting of items which could be anything. He tossed the safe to Willie Bee and said, "We'll take this with us. We can break into it later. Now we wait."

Jimbo went back towards the kitchen and looked around. That's when he noticed the backdoor. "You idiot!" he said. "You left the door open."

It wasn't Willie Bee's fault. The door doesn't close well on its own. You have to make sure it latches, otherwise it will pop open. It's just one of the personality traits of an old house built in the forties.

Jimbo shut the door, but he didn't see the two eyes watching him from above until he turned around and took a couple steps. He stopped and tilted his head. The cat was so quiet and still, it didn't look real. But it got real when it opened his mouth and gave an angry hiss. Jimbo got a full view of its sharp and well-used teeth. Then it was game on.

Before Jimbo knew what had happened, the cat launched itself off the refrigerator and wrapped himself around his face and head. Jimbo stumbled back as the cat dug his claws and teeth into whatever flesh it could find. In unexpected pain and agony, Jimbo yelled out, "What the...", but that was all he could get out. Jimbo grabbed the cat and tried to pull it off his face. But its claws were dug in so deep, it hurt even worse. "Willie Bee! Goddammit! Get it off of me."

By the time Willie Bee got to the kitchen, Jimbo had ripped the cat off his face. The cat was as wild as anything in the jungle. He was biting and scratching his way along Jimbo's hands and arms. Jimbo slung the cat across the kitchen and out of the room. Willie Bee had to duck as it flew by.

Blood was streaking down Jimbo's face and arms. He held his face in his hands. He pulled his hands away to look at them, but the cat wasn't done. The cat shot across the floor and took flight, latching back onto Jimbo's face. The fight was back on, and the cat was fast with the claws and teeth. He seemed to be winning until Jimbo got his hand around the cat's neck and began to squeeze. Like the small dog the night before, the cat tried to scream and hiss but

Jimbo had cut off all its breathing. The cat's grip around Jimbo's face started to relax and he was able to peel the cat away. Jimbo shook the cat with rage and held it out away from his body so their eyes could meet. Jimbo walked the cat out of the kitchen and into the living room. He squeezed harder and harder, and the cat began to succumb to Jimbo's offensive. Before long, the strong gray tabby, the cat that had chosen to befriend Nigel Logan, the cat that had decided to attack and protect, was hanging limp in the fists of Jimbo Walters. When it was obvious the cat was dead, Jimbo pulled the cat back into a windup and threw him against the wall as hard as he could. He watched as the cat slid down the wall to where it lay motionless on the floor. In a cold, emotionless tone Jimbo said, "Take that, motherfucker."

When Nigel pulled the truck into his drive the sun was just setting. From the east moving west across the landscape, darkness replaced what was once daylight. He removed his sailing gear and walked to the back door where he saw the prize of the day. It wasn't just one shrew, it was two. They were both on the steps side by side. Nigel tilted his head as he studied one of them. It looked different than the other, more distorted. One looked as if it could spring to life and dash away, the other looked molested, as if it had been stepped on or something.

Nigel shrugged his shoulders and looked around for the cat. It rarely missed an opportunity to welcome Nigel home, especially after such an impressive kill. He looked along the fence line. He bent over to peek under the palm. He took a quick glance behind the boxwoods. Nothing. Walking to the garage for his shovel Nigel spoke into the trees, "Thanks, Tom. You outdid yourself this time."

After disposing of the rodents, Nigel went into the house. He shut the door and stopped. Something was amiss. The kitchen was a mess and there was a new smell in the house, a faint hint of cologne perhaps. He took a few steps and observed the chairs around his small dining room off the kitchen. He asked himself, *Is that how the chairs were left?* "No. They weren't," he said aloud.

Nigel took two more steps and entered the little dining room.

Jimbo was fast and came around the corner before Nigel could get his guard up. Jimbo struck Nigel with a mighty blow to the nose. Nigel fell back stunned and dazed. He landed against the wall, stunned, his eyes now flooded with tears. He felt the blood begin to flow down across his lips.

Nigel, unable to see well, looked up and saw his attacker as a blur, but that was enough. Nigel lunged but was hit hard again. Nigel went down on one knee. Vulnerable, Jimbo hit him a third time in the jaw and watched as Nigel hit the floor face down.

Nigel wasn't prepared to give up. He began to get up on his hands and knees and crawl towards the living room. Jimbo followed him. As Nigel began to stand, Jimbo sucker punched him in the back of the head with another devastating blow sending him back to the floor.

Nigel tried to catch his breath. He was dazed, not sure of what was happening. He felt himself drifting away as he stared across the floor. A brief moment of focus was restored and he began to see the cat through his bloodshot eyes. It was motionless on the floor: eyes and mouth left wide open from its last moments of life. Nigel's heart was torn and filled with anger. He slid his hand across the floor trying to reach the cat. In an exhausted whisper Nigel begged, "Tom. Please ... Tom... No…"

Jimbo blindsided Nigel with another hit to the head, bouncing it off the hardwood floor. He was motionless on the floor as he looked across at Tom. He wanted to call out to the cat again, but he couldn't. His eyes closed. Everything went quiet and dark.

Jimbo and Willie Bee were easing the big Buick out onto Highway 98. The headlights were shining a path back toward Apalachicola. Willie Bee stared out the passenger side window looking out over the dark bay. His mind was racing as he relived the past twenty-four hours and wondered what the next twenty-four would bring. *What the hell have I gotten myself into*, he thought. He turned his head to look at Jimbo when he heard the tones of a phone being dialed.

Willie Bee watched Jimbo hold the phone to his head. When there was an answer on the other end, there wasn't much conversation. "We got him," Jimbo said. "He's alive and packed tight in the trunk. What now, Manchester?"

Willie Bee watched as Jimbo listened on the phone. Big Man did all the talking, and Jimbo gave no expression or hint about what he was being told. After a while, Jimbo ended the call and threw the phone on the seat next to him and continued driving. Willie Bee asked, "Well?"

"We're going to Eastpoint," Jimbo answered, "to meet somebody."

"Who we gonna meet?" asked Willie Bee.

"Don't know his name and he doesn't know ours. And that's the way we're going to keep it too."

"Well, how in the hell are we going to..."

"Shut up, Willie Bee," Jimbo snapped, "you're starting to talk too much again."

Willie Bee became frustrated once more. He was being left in the dark, and he didn't like it. He wanted to know. He wanted to prepare mentally. This was a first for him. Willie Bee has done a lot of bad and terrible things in his life, but killing somebody wasn't one of them. He turned his head and gazed towards the back seat. Just behind the crushed velvet seat and in the trunk was Logan. They hadn't heard a peep from the trunk since they dumped him in there. It was quiet and there was no sign of movement. Willie Bee wondered if he was already dead.

Willie Bee turned and gave Jimbo a brief glance. Then he turned back to watch the darkness outside his window. He had never seen such darkness. Jimbo knows, but only from the confines of solitary confinement. Little did either of them know, it was about to get a lot darker where they were going.

Nigel couldn't remember anything at first. He was confused, disoriented, and unaware of his whereabouts. The only thing he knew for sure was his brain was pounding with a powerful headache. The pain resonated from deep inside his gray matter and exited through his eyes which were still closed. He remained quiet, listening to the strange noises and the odd movements of his body. *What is going on?*

Then he heard what he thought were voices, muffled but voices. *Who is that? What the hell is happening?* He wanted to hold his head, squeeze the pain away, but he couldn't. His hands were somehow restrained behind his back. Mild panic was starting to set in, and then a vision came. He was starting to remember. Nigel opened his eyes and the memory of the struggle started to come back. Then, in the memory, he saw the cat.

Tom was on the floor. He was dead. It was a still picture, an image frozen in his mind. Nigel closed his eyes again to study the memory. He could see the cat's last struggle for breath, its mouth open. Blood had dried and hardened on the floor. It had matted his fur having oozed from his nose and ears. He had been dead for a while. He was motionless. In a soft voice of mourning he said, "They killed him. The bastards killed him."

Nigel opened his eyes. His head still hurt worse than anything, but it was all coming back to him. He looked around the tight space, a slight red glow from the taillights bled inside; the motion of movement was realized along with the slight smell of exhaust. He was in the trunk of a car. *What did they want with him?*

In the back of his mind, he knew. But he tried not to think about it. His thoughts ran from Tom to Candice. He closed his eyes again. He saw her sweet face and wanting smile. She was wearing a hair color he hadn't seen yet, perhaps a color his subconscious wanted to see on her. He didn't know. He allowed his imagination to kiss her, perhaps for one last time. She spoke to him, and he heard her. It was as if she was actually there. He saw her face and she was pouting, her bottom lip stuck out all sexy like as she begged, "Don't go, baby. Stay with me."

She faded away from his mind as he opened his eyes wide and whispered, "Okay."

He assessed his situation. His hands were behind his back. *Were they tied together?* He twisted his hands from side to side and the hairs around his wrists were being pulled. *No ... It wasn't rope*, he thought. *It was tape, probably duct tape.* His ankles were in the same condition, taped together, but freeing his hands was the top priority.

Lucky for him it was a big trunk, bigger than anything made for the current models of today, so it gave him a little room to move around. It was also hot in there and Nigel was already sweating profusely. He figured he might be able to use that to his advantage, so he began to work his hands and wrists back and forth, round and round in every direction. He was trying to let the sweat work against the adhesives that were bound to his skin and hair.

Back up in the cab things were still quiet. Jimbo continued his slow roll down Highway 98. Willie Bee kept his mouth shut and continued his aggravated stare out the window. Then, to Willie Bee's surprise, Jimbo spoke. "I don't like it. Don't like it one bit, dammit."

"You don't like what?" asked Willie Bee.

"I don't like bringing someone else into this, that's what."

"What is it Big Man wants us to do?"

Jimbo drove on for a few beats then said, "Big Man made a few calls to Tallahassee. He found a friend of a friend who turned him on to somebody in the area. Somebody that knows the area real good. He's going to take us somewhere so we can finish this business. Somewhere off in the woods, or something."

Willie Bee said nothing.

"Friend of a friend," Jimbo said frustrated. "What kind of bullshit is that?" He drove on down the road a mile or two and added, "We have no idea who these friends of friends are. Too many people in on this now ... Dammit Manchester!"

Willie Bee said, "Jimbo ... I'm with you. Why do we need someone else? Shit! With the way you pounded and punished Logan back there, he's probably already dead."

Jimbo turned his head to look at Willie Bee who was pointing over his left shoulder with his thumb adding, "We ain't heard a peep from him since we left. We just need to find a road and dump his ass."

Willie Bee took a little comfort in seeing his idea being bounced around in Jimbo's head. It was being considered. After about a minute, Jimbo shook his head and said, "No. This is Big Man's job. And if Manchester wants it done this way, then that's how we will deliver."

Willie Bee was about to say something else but was interrupted by the squealing of tires and the impact of his shoulder and head being slammed into the windshield. Not wearing a seatbelt, he was thrown into the glass as Jimbo stood on the brake pedal bringing the big Buick to a stop. "What the..." Willie Bee protested, but when he looked at his partner, Jimbo was staring out into the street and the glow of the headlights.

In the trunk, Logan was slung and rolled forward hitting his head. He was tempted to call out, but kept his tongue. He didn't want them to know he was conscious.

The big black bear, a huge male, took up most of the street as it walked out and into traffic. The bear wasn't afraid of the big Buick. It turned towards the car and stood on its back legs raising its huge front paws in the air. It roared in anger and took a few steps towards the car.

"Jesus!" screamed Willie Bee. "What the hell is that?"

The bear got to the front of the car and slapped the hood with a paw as he came down on all fours. Paint was flying everywhere as the huge claws were dragged across the hood. Jimbo yelled, "Son of a bitch!" as he put the car in reverse and backed away several feet. The big bear stood and roared again before dashing off across the street and disappearing into the woods.

Jimbo yelled at Willie Bee, "Get out and check on my car!"

"Screw you! You get out!"

Nothing was said for a moment or two. Then Jimbo put the car back in drive and started back down the highway. They rode in silence, each keeping an eagle eye on the road. Jimbo asked a question neither one of them could answer, "What kind of goddamn place is this anyway?"

When they rolled into Eastpoint Jimbo found the assigned rendezvous spot, a bank parking lot on the corner of Hwy 98 and Jefferson street. They pulled in and parked off to the side, out of the light. A guy in a pickup truck got out and approached the car. When he got to the driver's side window, he made a motion to roll down the window. Jimbo did.

The guy chuckled and said, "Well, they weren't kidding when they said I couldn't miss the car. That you'd be driving a big purple Buick."

Jimbo offered nothing but a stare.

"I understand you boys need a little help."

"Could be."

"Well," the guy said, "follow me." Then he walked back over to his truck, started it up and began to back out of his parking spot.

Jimbo looked at Willie Bee who offered nothing more than a shrug of his shoulders. Jimbo started the car and fell in behind the truck that pulled out onto highway 98 and continued east.

They rode for awhile until they came into another small town, Carrabelle. The truck pulled off the road and into a vacant parking lot. The guy got out and walked back over to the Buick. Jimbo looked at Willie Bee and said, "Stay here." And he got out of the car and met the guy behind the Buick.

"This is where I ride with you," the guy said. He stepped back and looked at the Buick and continued, "I guess this should be alright. We're in a drought. Been dry as hell, so there won't be any mud."

"Mud?" Jimbo asked. "Where we going? I don't want any mud on my car."

The guy laughed looking at Jimbo's ride and said, "Shit, Buddy. A little mud might do this heap some good."

Jimbo bit his lower lip and said, "I ain't your Buddy."

Logan got quiet and still when he felt the car come to a stop. He heard the car door open and slam. Then he began to hear voices coming from outside the car. They were only a few feet away, but the conversation was muffled. He made out some of the broken details, something about the perfect place, a secluded area, nobody around for miles, several days before ... Then Logan heard two words that came through without any misunderstanding: Tate's Hell.

Logan worked with even more determination to free himself. He could move and twist, but the tape was too tight around his wrists. And with his hands behind his back, it made it even more difficult. He couldn't squeeze them out, so he tried to work his arms and hands over his butt. At least then he could get his hands out in front where he could work more effectively. He tried and tried, yet, despite his best efforts, he was unsuccessful.

He was getting tired. The heat in the trunk was overwhelming and he was becoming dehydrated. Each additional effort seemed to have less strength behind it, less determination. He needed time: Time to rest, to think, time to rebuild his power and stamina. But time was something he didn't have. He understood his own fate if he didn't get free, so giving up wasn't an option. He had to keep trying.

The area known as Tate's Hell covers over 202,000 acres of wilderness outside Carrabelle, Florida. Prior to the 1950's, before the timber industry took an interest in the region, the area was a contained ecosystem of hydrologic importance. Its vast swamp lands and network of creeks fed a critical freshwater supply into the upper Apalachicola Bay which supported the healthy production of oysters in the region.

TALES FROM STOOL 17 – TROUBLE IN TATE'S HELL

From the 1960s through the 1970s, much of the area was disturbed and altered to make way for the creation of pine plantations to support an eager timber industry. The alterations included a vast network of built up roads and ditches which disrupted the fragile ecosystem. The area was further damaged when the pine crops were planted and heavily treated with hazardous fertilizers to support their growth.

The Florida Department of Forestry acquired the property in 1994 for its protection. The goal is to reverse much of the damage caused by the timber industry. This restoration project involves removing much of the roadbeds and ditches so the network of streams and creeks can return to some sense of normal flow. Turning the tide on the damage will take time and there's so much more work to do.

The area gets its name from a popular legend. Back in the 1870s, Cebe Tate was a cattle farmer from Sumatra, Florida. His livestock would often fall prey to the attacks of a local panther that roamed the area. Fed up with the big cat's assaults, Cebe set out with a shotgun and his hunting dogs to track down and kill the panther responsible for killing his cattle. In short order, he became lost, disoriented, and separated from his dogs. He meandered and wandered for over a week drinking the black, murky waters of the swamp and eating God knows what to survive. He became prey to the heavy mosquitoes and other flying insects. In the end, he would succumb to the venom of several snake bites, but not before wandering into a clearing around Carrabelle where he uttered his final words: "My name is Cebe Tate, and I just came from Hell."

The guy kept talking, but Jimbo had heard enough. He looked at his watch and noted the time. It was going on 9:30 p.m. "Shut up," Jimbo barked. "Get in the back. We're wasting time."

The guy told Jimbo where to go from the back seat. They backtracked a bit and pulled off Highway 98 and onto a road that disappeared back into the woods. The guy had Jimbo going every which way. The network of dirt roads was like a maze. In places, the dirt roads would narrow to a point that brush would sweep the sides of the wide Buick. This didn't make Jimbo happy at all. "Where in the fuck are we going, dammit?" Jimbo demanded.

"Just a few more miles," the guy said. "It opens up a bit around this next corner."

Jimbo said nothing, but stewed over the scratches he knew he would have to buff out or repaint.

"Turn right at the next road," the guy said. "Then we'll go about another mile and hang a left. We're almost there."

Jimbo didn't like being told what to do, but he did it anyway. He didn't have much choice. Manchester had sent this guy to help, so he would do as he was told. What else could he do?

When Jimbo made that last left turn, he said, "What the..." The headlights shone on a big Florida panther that was standing in the middle of the road. Both Jimbo and Willie Bee looked at each other, but by the time they turned to look again, it was gone. Jimbo looked back at the guy in the back seat who shrugged his shoulders and said, "Critters. We got critters."

Jimbo noticed the road was getting moist and soft, not as dry as before. It ended in a clearing next to a body of water. The headlights shone across a motionless swamp and through a stand of cypress, Spanish moss hanging from the tree limbs.

The guy patted Jimbo on the back and said, "We're here."

Willie Bee asked, "Where the hell is here?"

The guy just smiled.

Jimbo shut the car off and turned off the lights. It was pitch black. They couldn't see a thing, including each other. The only available light came from the stars. The moon was still below the horizon and not due to rise for some time. Jimbo turned the headlights back on to add some light. Then the three of them got out of the car.

They walked around trying to check out the surroundings, but even with the headlights on, anything that wasn't illuminated by the high beams disappeared into darkness. They gathered around the trunk. Willie Bee touched the trunk and said, "It's been mighty quiet back..." He stopped talking to slap his neck, then his face and finished saying. "...here. I think he might already be dead, Jimbo." Willie Bee smacked at his face again. "Son of a bitch! That hurt."

There is no shortage of biting bugs on the Forgotten Coast during a warm, windless night back in the forest and around a swamp. The bugs were hungry and Willie Bee and Jimbo were fresh

184

meat. The other guy was fine. Lathering up with DEET was a normal part of his personal hygiene routine.

With both Jimbo and Willie Bee smacking bugs, the other guy asked, "What did you say?"

"I said it hurt, goddammit! You deaf?"

"No ... the other part. The part before that. Something about someone being dead."

"The guy in the trunk, dumbass. I think our business is done. I think he's already dead."

"Whoa! Whoa!" said the other guy. "Nobody ever said anything about killing. You're kidding, right?"

Neither Jimbo or Willie Bee said anything.

They were all silent for a beat or two before the other guy said, "Oh no! Hell no! They told me you guys needed someplace to scare the shit out of somebody. I don't want to be a part of any of this." He stared at Jimbo and Willie Bee. Back and forth he looked at them trying to decide what to do. He said, "Screw this!" And he started to walk away.

Jimbo was already uneasy with having another person involved, a third wheel. He was now even more unsettled. Jimbo knew too many guys like him. Not only could he talk, he would talk; anything to save his own ass. Jimbo didn't like it, not one bit. He grabbed the guy by the arm and said, "What do you think you're doing?"

"I'm getting the hell out of here. That's what I'm doing. You two do whatever you came here to do, but I'm not having any part of it."

Logan listened to voices outside. Nigel heard one of them mention his own demise, that he might already be dead. He figured that might be something he could use to his advantage. He could tell an argument had ensued between two of them, but he couldn't make out the details. Logan tilted his head in hopes of hearing more. It didn't help, but there was no mistaking the sound of the gun when it went off. It startled Nigel and he almost jumped out of his skin as he felt his heart and nerves run wild.

The other guy tried to argue his point. He just wanted to leave, that was all. Murder wasn't on his radar, and it wasn't about to be. He was being firm in explaining all this to Jimbo.

Jimbo listen as he swatted at the assault of mosquitoes, biting flies, and no-see-ums. Aggravated, Jimbo was getting pissed. This guy was wasting valuable time. Jimbo didn't even give the guy a chance to beg for his life. And, it was so dark; the guy never saw it coming. Jimbo reached into his pocket and pulled out a snub-nose .38 caliber revolver and shot the guy between the eyes. He fell in a heap where he once stood.

"Jimbo!" Willie Bee yelled. "What the hell did you do that for?"

"Shut up, Willie Bee. If I have to tell you, then maybe I need to shoot you too."

Willie Bee said nothing.

"Now get your ass over here and let's drag this son of a bitch over and throw him in the water."

The water was still like glass. Not a breath of air stirred the first little wave and the reflection of stars could be seen between the stand of cypress. It was a beautiful sight, ruined by the splash of a warm, dead body. The ripples rolled away from the body, broadcasting activity in the water and stimulating reptilian curiosity.

They stood by the water and watched the body as it floated away. Another fly ripped more flesh off Jimbo's neck and blood ran down behind his ear. "Shit!" he yelled as he slapped and missed.

"Jimbo," Willie Bee pleaded, "can we get this over with and get the hell out of here? We are going to be eaten alive."

For awhile things were quiet outside the trunk. Then Logan heard what he thought were the jingle of keys and the sound of the lock being penetrated. He closed his eyes and thought of Candice, her smell, her soft skin. He could see her face. Nigel whispered, "I love you," and kissed her in his mind. Then he opened his eyes to face what would come next. *Here we go*, he thought.

Willie Bee inserted the key and began to turn it. Jimbo stood next to him with his revolver at the ready. The lid popped open and the bright trunk light blinded both of them. They shook their heads and looked away before settling their eyes back on Logan. He was alive. He was on his side, facing the back of the car. His arms were still behind his back and his legs tucked up tight around his butt. He was panting, looking at them with the concern and fear the situation warranted.

Logan was getting a good look at his attackers for the first time. One was skinny, but firm looking. He had tight braids in his hair and a smart ass smile with big white teeth, except for the gold plated ones that shone in the dim light. He seemed the nervous type, a jittery sort.

The other guy, the one with the gun, the one that had ambushed him back at the house was bigger, much bigger. He looked to be as tall as Logan, which put him around six foot three, but had a few extra pounds. He had a shaved head, gold rings in each ear, and prison tattoos down his neck. No smile.

Logan got to study the big guy's face. Everything back at the house happened so fast he hadn't had time to pay attention. The light gave Logan a chance to see Tom's good work. The cat had worked the guy over in a special way. The guy's face and neck was an intricate network of deep scratches and teeth marks. Tom did everything he could to protect Nigel and the house. That was obvious. In the end, he suffered and died trying. Imagining how Tom's life had been taken from him lit a fire inside of Logan.

"Well, Jimbo," Willie Bee said. "What do we have here?" Then he looked up towards the sky and yelled, "Hey, T-Daddy! Look what we got."

That was when Logan spoke for the first time saying, "You're looking in the wrong direction, dickhead."

Willie Bee leaned in and said, "Dickhead, huh?" Then he punched Logan on the side of his head.

With caution, Logan observed the big guy as he spoke, the barrel of the gun still trained on him. "Knock it off, Willie Bee. Get the bastard out of my trunk."

Willie Bee was leaning in when something caught Jimbo's attention. "Wait! What the hell is that?"

Nigel tilted his head to see what they were looking at. It was something he forgot to hide. And as the meaning of the wadded-up duct tape began to sink into the minds of his abductors, the lug wrench swung out from behind Logan's back. He brought it across Jimbo's wrist, the one with the gun. The weapon discharged a round over Logan's head before it dropped to the ground. Jimbo spun away in agony yelling, "Son of a bitch! The gun. Get the gun!"

Willie Bee tried to re-contain Logan by slamming the trunk lid back down. But as he reached up, the tire tool was introduced into the side of his rib cage. Willie Bee doubled over in pain and Logan hit him again in almost the same spot dropping him to his knees.

From the edge of the darkness Logan saw Jimbo moving fast towards him. Logan swung for his head, and Jimbo put out his one good arm to block. And he did, but not enough to prevent a solid blow to his left ear. Jimbo fell forward into the trunk and Logan used the tire iron again to land a solid blow to the back of his head. Then he used his feet to kick Jimbo's head and body away as he scurried to escape the trunk. He landed on Willie Bee who was trying to get up off the ground while holding his side. Willie Bee moaned in pain and grabbed him, but Logan drove an elbow into his broken ribs and was set free. Logan rolled away towards the darkness, all the time thinking, *the gun, the gun, where is the damn gun?*

He made it to the tree line and hid in the tall brush to observe his enemies. Of all the crazy things to think about when two guys are trying to kill you, Logan thought to himself about how good it felt to lay there and stretch. Being taped up and stowed away in a trunk for hours was no fun, and twisting and contorting your body to get yourself released while bouncing down the road only added to the discomfort.

His wrists had been taped up pretty tight, but he was successful at getting his hands down and around his butt. It was difficult and painful for his shoulders. He even stopped once to laugh at himself. He found some comfort and confidence at the return of his sense of humor, vowing to do something about his Texas-sized ass when he got out of this mess.

He could see the back of the car. The trunk light showed the big guy named Jimbo still slumped over in the trunk. The skinny one was on his feet. He was walking, searching. His torso was bent over and his movements slow and deliberate. His busted ribs made it difficult to do anything, especially breathe. Logan also saw the gun in his left hand. His right was occupied with holding his left side.

A left handed shooter. What are the odds? Logan knew there was about a ten percent chance the skinny one might be left-handed. He didn't like those odds, so he concentrated on the fact that there was about a ninety percent chance he wasn't. He still had the tire tool in his hand. It was a lug bolt wrench and pry bar type, the kind that was also used to ratchet up an old school car jack. Logan was still and watched his opponent. He liked his odds, but he knew he would like them better if he could add some darkness and smash out those headlights.

Willie Bee had worked himself around to the front of the car so he could see. His eyes were searching, his head swinging from side to side as he yelled, "Hey, you mother... Come out. I know you're out there. Let's talk about this. I won't hurt you."

Of all the stupid things to say, Logan thought that had to be the dumbest. *Good. I'm dealing with an idiot.* Logan felt around and found a good sized rock to throw. When Willie Bee was looking away, Logan hopped on his knees and threw the rock hitting the car.

He watched as the skinny one swung around and fired into the darkness. Logan turned his head and spoke, "Hey, dipshit. You're not a very good shot are you? I'm over here."

Willie Bee swung around again and pointed the gun in what he thought was the direction of the voice. Logan found another rock and lobbed it several feet away along the side of the road. Willie Bee took another wild shot and started to walk in that direction.

"I see you," Willie Bee said, "and when I find you, I'm going to kill you. Just like you killed T-Daddy."

Logan rolled on his back and spoke straight up into the air, "Well, if you see me, why do you have to find me?"

Willie Bee made his way to the edge of the woods, looking and searching. He began to walk in the direction of Logan's voice when Logan spoke again, "You were there, weren't you? The night he raped the girl."

Willie Bee was moving quicker now along the side of the road. Logan turned his head and could see his dark mass coming.

"Yeah, I was there. She was a sweet thing. We all had a turn. Now come out where I can see you. You know you want to."

And he did. There was nothing Logan wanted more than to get up and confront this guy. But, patience was in order. While Logan was still in the dark weeds, he imagined what it must have been like for Grace. The words of the skinny one resonated through his mind. *She was a sweet thing. We all had a turn.* His heart was racing and breaking all over again. It took everything he could muster to keep from getting up and charging the guy head on.

Willie Bee kept his careful approach down the side of the woods when Mother Nature decided to intervene. It was one of her rattlesnakes that brought Willie Bee to a halt. The warning was loud and crisp. It filled the air and seemed to come from every direction. It was a sound that roared through and bounced off the trees. Willie

Bee looked around, but could see nothing. It could be coming from anywhere.

"That's a rattler, shithead," Logan said. "A huge one. A six or seven-footer by the sound of it. I wouldn't move if I were you."

Willie Bee stood frozen for several beats, but the sound of the big rattler was too much and the longer he stood there, the louder it seemed to get. He gritted his teeth as he moved his right foot one step back. Nothing. Then he went to move his left and that was when the fangs pierced through his jeans and into his lower calf. He screamed with pain and jumped back, but not before the rattler hit him again. Willie Bee pointed the revolver at the ground and started to pull the trigger missing with every shot. Pow! Pow! Pow! Click. Click. Click. Click.

Having done its job, in silence and with grace, the snake moved back into the forest. As the big rattler slipped away, Logan tightened his grip on the tire tool and got to his feet. "Here I am."

Through the darkness, Logan made his slow and deliberate way towards the skinny one. Visibility was still poor, but Logan's eyes were adjusting to the light shared by the canopy of stars and the moon that was beginning to make its appearance through the tree line.

Willie Bee appeared as a shadow moving in the night, but Logan could see him well enough. He was rolling and moaning in the dusty road. The broken ribs hurt, but they were a walk in the park compared to the powerful venom burning through his bloodstream. Logan looked over at the car. The big one was where he last saw him, already dead perhaps. Then he turned to focus his full attention on the skinny one, he was shaking with adrenaline, his mind full of thoughts about Grace Matthews and the way she had suffered. "Now," Logan said as he walked, "you're going to suffer. I promise. And I keep promises."

Willie Bee said nothing.

Logan stood over the skinny one. He saw the gun on the ground and kicked it to the edge of the weeds. "Get up!" Logan demanded. "Get on your feet!"

"My leg! My leg! It bit me."

"I don't care. Stand up."

Willie Bee was on all fours as he gasped and screamed, "I can't. It goddamn hurts too bad."

Logan drew back his right foot and kicked, driving his size thirteen shoe into Willie Bee's ribs, the good side. The skinny one groaned in pain as he rolled over on his back. Logan stepped closer and connected again, this time to the tender side.

"I said, get up, dickhead! And the name is Chief."

He was slow to move, but when Logan drew his foot back for another kick, he raised his hands and said, "Okay! Okay! Don't kick!"

Logan watched as the skinny one got to his feet. He crouched over holding his broken ribs and favored the bitten leg, now swelling beyond belief. With a tilted head, he looked up at Logan.

"What's your name?" Logan demanded.

Willie Bee told him and Logan started walking, getting closer. "Good," said Logan. "Welcome to Tate's Hell, Willie Bee."

Willie Bee was limping backwards step for step. They moved into the high beams of the Buick and they were blinding to Willie Bee, but Logan could see just fine. Willie Bee took a quick look behind him and saw the black, calm waters of the swamp. He stopped and said, "What do you want?"

"You said you were there," said Logan in a cold, calm voice, tapping the tire tool in the palm of his left hand. "You said, 'We all had a turn.' That's what you said."

"You weren't there, man. You don't understand."

In the same cold, emotionless voice Logan said, "Here's your chance to explain. Help me to understand."

Willie Bee was having a difficult time thinking of something to say. He mumbled and stumbled through some unintelligible nonsense and said, "She wanted it, man. Don't you see? She was asking for it. We didn't do anything wrong, man. I promise."

Logan didn't say anything. He was still and stoic, unaffected by the ridiculous notion that Grace Matthews had asked to be beaten and raped. Those words, *She wanted it,* sparked a quiet rage inside. A rage Willie Bee couldn't see.

"What you going to do?" asked Willie Bee. "My leg is killing me. I need help."

"Your leg isn't going to kill you," said Logan. "I am."

They stood looking at each other for a few seconds before Willie Bee made a futile effort to escape. He dashed away alongside the water, but Logan was there to stop him with the tire tool. Another hard shot to the ribs sent him to the ground.

191

Logan demanded again, but in his cool and collected tone, "Get up. Now."

As Willie Bee was getting to his feet, he pleaded nonstop for mercy and his life. He stood there in tears as he begged, but there was no sympathy in Logan's heart or eyes. Willie Bee's voice travelled past deaf ears and disappeared into the forest. Logan was about to finish the task with the tire iron, but he became distracted.

Out over the water, two lights shone back towards them like beacons. They were big, bright, and moving slow towards them. Nigel smiled.

The curious gator used its stealth to swim and crawl along the bottom. The instant its eyes breached the black water of the swamp, the headlights of the Buick brought them to life. Logan watched with patience as it cased itself along, moving closer without leaving a wake. It was stalking.

Willie Bee was still talking, trying to think of anything that might get him out of this mess.

"Shut up." Logan said.

Willie Bee kept talking and Logan pulled the tire iron back as a warning and said, raising his voice, "I said, shut up!"

Willie Bee winced and cowered as he went silent.

"Maybe I will give you a chance to live," Logan lied. Willie Bee was going to die. It was only a matter of how.

Willie Bee said nothing.

"Can you swim?" Logan asked.

"Swim? Oh shit! Hell no I can't swim."

"Doesn't matter. Turn around. See all those trees?"

Willie Bee took a quick look, then another. The headlights lit up the network of cypress that was scattered across the swamp. "The water here is waste-deep. Tops," Logan said. "Start walking. Stay in the headlights where I can see you. The other shore is just beyond the reach of the headlights."

Willie Bee looked back over his shoulder for another look before saying, "Man, you fucking crazy. My damn leg. I can't walk that far."

"Then you will die here. It's your only option and when you get out of here, don't ever come back. You hear me. Now, get!"

Willie Bee hesitated, but, when he saw Logan load up the lug wrench for another strike, he put up his hand and said, "Okay! Okay, dammit," and hobbled his way to the water's edge. He stopped and looked back at Logan again before taking the first couple of baby steps.

Logan looked at the water. The eyes were gone. *Had the gator gotten bored and moved on?* He watched Willie Bee take a couple more steps. *Where are you, dammit?* He watched for a couple more steps before deciding to take matters into his own hands. He tightened his grip on the lug wrench and slipped into the water. He was slow and quiet in his movement, but he was faster than Willie Bee. Willie Bee's slow, terrible limp caused a great splash as he plowed as fast as he could go through the water. Battling the bugs off his face, he never heard or realized Logan was right behind him.

Logan was on his target. He thought about spinning him around so he could see it coming, but he didn't. He was tired and wanted to get home. He picked a spot on his right temple and pulled back the tire tool.

Even though they came on like yellow flood lights, Willie Bee never noticed the eyes when they reappeared. But Logan saw them and froze. *Damn! Don't move*, he told himself. He was close enough to see the slit pupils; they looked to be the size of footballs.

The largest alligator on record with the Florida Wildlife Commission was fourteen feet, three and a half inches long. The head alone was two feet long. It was a male weighing in at six hundred fifty-four pounds and was taken from Lake Washington on November 1, 2010. The gator in the water with Logan and Willie Bee had to rival that, if not exceed it.

Logan was nervous and scared too. He had every right to be. The gator could pick either one of them, have his choice for breakfast. Even though he had the heavy tire iron, he knew it wasn't enough to ward off any attack. He tightened his grip nonetheless. Then he watched in both horror and satisfaction as Willie Bee took his last step and breath.

The explosive movements of a creature so huge when taking down its prey, especially one the size of a human is terrifying. The sudden attack took only a few seconds, and, at first, Logan thought he was done. The gator's thrashing tail knocked Logan to his ass. But, as he sat there in water up to his chest, he saw Willie Bee bitten at the waist and being dragged to places unknown.

Logan was quiet and amazed at what he just witnessed. Calmness came over him and he remained still, long enough to observe the thick black water return to its normal slickness. Then it occurred to him, *he was still in the water.* His thoughts returned to the gator, and sounding almost comical, he yelled, "Oh, shit," as he scrambled to his feet and high stepped his way back to shore.

The excitement and adrenaline rush had Logan out of breath. He dropped the tire tool and bent over with his hands on his knees. He took a couple deep breaths looking at the ground. Then he stood and walked towards the car. He opened the driver's side door and looked around. He saw his safe laying in the back seat. *Bastards,* he thought. *What else did they take?* He leaned in and opened the glove box. *Nothing.*

Logan was backing out of the car when he was grabbed around the chest, a tight bear hug. It was the big one, the one called Jimbo. Logan was pulled from the car, hitting his head on the way out. It was sudden, unexpected and caught Logan between breaths. He found himself struggling for air. He knew, if he didn't get free soon, he would pass out and it would be all over.

Jimbo had him lifted off the ground, and, as Logan would exhale, Jimbo squeezed even harder. Jimbo dodged all Logan's attempts to get him with an elbow. He bounced Logan in the air and knew the struggling would cause him to lose his air supply sooner. It was just a matter of time, and he could already sense Logan succumbing to the pressure. Patience was all he needed.

Nigel realized it was true; one does see their entire life flash before their eyes as they approach eternal darkness on earth. He saw everything, and, even as it rushed by, the images were vivid. He saw himself as a kid and his own struggles of being a meek target. He saw his own transformation when he took the social studies book off the desk and drove it into the nose of Stan Hornbuckle. He saw himself in uniform on the bridge of his last ship, his old friend Captain Charley Matthews at his side. He was at the con, leading his team in navigating a treacherous approach into an unfamiliar harbor. He felt a slap on his back as the captain said, "Who needs a harbor pilot anyway." He saw the eyes and face of Terrance Lundsford. He saw himself drop anchor in St. Joe Bay. There in front of him were the faces of all his new friends: Red, Trixie, Joe Crow, Brian Bowen, and the rest of the gang, even Tom the cat. *He would miss them all,* he thought. Then he saw Candice. He loves her so, and realized he hadn't told her enough. She was the one thing worth living for. He tried one last time to free himself, but he was too weak.

He was fading fast. He closed his eyes and as everything was going dark he heard a faint high-pitched moan in the distance. The wailing moan became a shrilling scream. It got louder and louder, closer and closer. Then Nigel felt himself go limp and he hit the ground as everything went black.

He had no idea how long he had been out, but he remained on the ground and let his eyes get reacquainted with the darkness. He must have been out for quite awhile. The headlights of the Buick had faded, just illuminating the edge of the water. The near full moon was now bright above the trees. He sat up and looked around. The pain in his head had returned, and he rubbed his eyes. He saw nothing but scraps of torn clothing and blood. *What had happened here?*

Nigel stood up and held his head. It was killing him, but he didn't hesitate. He had no time to lose. It was time to get the hell out of there. He scrambled to the car to collect his things. He grabbed his safe and saw a cell phone on the floorboard. He grabbed it and powered it up. *Good,* he thought. *No security.* But there wasn't a signal either. He put both the safe and the cell phone on top of the car and started to look around.

Nigel never saw them, but from the edge of the water a set of eyes was looking his way. They watched as Nigel stood up and went through the car pulling things out. They watched as he found a piece of torn shirt and wiped down the car and threw it off to the side. Then the eyes started to move in closer.

Nigel was confident he had taken care of all the prints he may have left behind. He stood by the car and collected his stuff. He slipped the phone into his pocket and held fast to his safe. Then he caught a whiff of an awful, hideous smell. Then he heard movement. He turned around and froze.

Both were quiet as they looked at each other, no more than three feet separating the two. Nigel looked up at the face and studied it. The smell was terrible, and he noticed it was holding the lug wrench. Nigel could feel its hot, moist breath bear down on him. It was disgusting.

Then Nigel turned around with great care and started to walk away. He walked twenty-five yards or so down the road before stopping to turn around for another look. It was gone.

Nigel walked for more than an hour. He didn't know exactly where he was, but the moon was high in the night sky. That told him enough to know which direction to walk. Sooner or later he would find a paved road and then a highway. From there, it would be easy.

Ten minutes later, he stepped out on some pavement. He glanced at the moon and headed south towards the coast. Then the cell phone started to vibrate in his pocket. He set the safe down and pulled it out to look at the name on the screen: Mansfield Lundsford. He answered it grunting, "Yea."

"Where the hell have you been, Jimbo? I've been calling for hours."

Logan said nothing.

"So tell me. Is it done? Have you taken care of everything?"

Logan was quiet at first then Mansfield spoke again, "Jimbo, goddammit, talk to me. Is it done?"

"Not exactly, Mr. Lundsford."

Mansfield heard the change in the voice and realized that neither Jimbo nor Willie Bee had answered. There was silence on the line then Big Man asked, "Who is this?"

Logan didn't answer the question but said, "They're dead. They're all dead."

Mansfield said nothing and ended the call the instant he heard the voice say, "And you're next."

When the phone rang, it woke up both Red and Trixie. Red didn't recognize the number on the caller ID but answered it anyway. About an hour and a half later, Red found Nigel walking down the shoulder of Highway 98. He got in the car and Red looked him over. He looked like hell. Red knew better than to say anything, and there was but one spoken word the entire trip home. And it was in the form of a question. Nigel asked, "Whiskey?"

As he drove, Red reached behind the passenger seat and produced a handle of seven-year-old Jim Beam and handed it to him. Nigel held the bottle tight in his lap for several miles before taking a swig, but his visits to the bottle became more frequent.

When Nigel got out of the car, he was drunk.

Red got out too and spoke over the hood. "You gonna be okay?"

Nigel nodded and said, "Yeah, thanks."

Red watched as Nigel turned and walked towards the back door. Then he called after Nigel and said, "We'll talk about this in a few days, okay?"

Nigel kept walking but nodded his head.

Red got back in the car and drove away.

Nigel stopped when he noticed the back door was cracked open. He didn't care. If there was someone still inside, then come what may. He'd had enough and was exhausted. He stepped inside the small kitchen and stopped to listen. The place was screaming with quiet. He was tired but too worked up to sleep. He fixed himself a long pour of Four Roses Small Batch and went back outside to sit on the steps. He didn't want to face what was waiting for him inside.

He took a deep pull on the bourbon and began to think about the entire day. It had been a long one, and, in a couple more hours, the sun would begin yet another. He sat and went over everything in his head, from the time he got back from the boat to now. He had almost lost everything, and the thought of that was too much. Overcome with emotion, his humanity surfaced and he began to sob. He put the bourbon down and started an uncontrollable bout of crying. He put his face in his hands and cried for several minutes, often gasping for breath. He couldn't stop. But he did, the second he received a nudge on the leg.

He sniffled and rubbed his eyes dry and looked. He couldn't believe what he was seeing. The tears returned, but this time in a shift of emotion as laughter was added. He looked to the heavens as his cat, Tom, jumped up in his lap and headbutted the bottom of Nigel's chin. He grabbed the cat, hugged him tight, and rocked back and forth as he laughed and enjoyed the tears that were streaming down his face.

It started to rain. Hard. The forecast map was an abstract painting of greens, yellows, and various shades of red. It stretched well into the gulf, as far west as the Mississippi River and north, upwards towards Chattanooga. It was a wall of water moving east and expected to drop for the next couple of days, maybe more if it stalled. It kept a solid lid on most activities and even caused several scheduled outdoor events to either cancel or postpone. It was a hunker-down type of rain.

The first sprinkles started before morning light and marked the second day since Nigel's return from Tate's Hell. The Buick had yet to be found, and, given the weather, it wouldn't be for several more days. The park rangers had no reason to venture into the messy, muddy interior. There hadn't been any suspicious activity reported and no visitors had come up missing. The risk of fire with this much rain was nonexistent. Any ignition from cloud-to-ground lightning would get extinguished by Mother Nature.

No ... It was best to keep the vehicles off the mud and on the pavement. Park personnel are expected to keep their assigned vehicles clean and shinny. All washings occurred after their shift, not an unreasonable expectation since they drive their vehicle to and from work each day. There is a standing joke in the park service. *What do you call a ranger patrolling in the mud? -- A rookie.*

After three days of solid rain, the weather system pushed through. The difference was like night and day. The rain didn't just fade away to make room for sunshine. It just stopped. The rain was still pouring off to the east, but right behind the slow-moving system there was nothing but clear skies and a hot sun. The pavement started to cook and the wetness surrendered itself as steam.

Both Nigel and Red suffered from a critical case of cabin fever. They'd had enough of the rain and welcomed the opportunity to escape. They ended up at the Raw Bar and occupied a corner table. Red played the part of serious listener as Nigel told his whole story. Well, almost.

Absent an admission of guilt, he would leave that up to Red to decide, he put most everything out there. Nigel spoke of his dear friend Charles Matthews, their bond, both professional and personal. He spoke of the kids, especially Grace. For Red, he painted a picture of her sweetness, her beautiful face, and her incredible strength. He told Red about the brutal beating and rape, how it affected him. How it still affects him.

Red stopped Nigel by holding up a hand. He got up and said, "More beer. We need more beer."

Nigel laughed as Red strolled over to the draft station and pulled another pitcher of Coors Light. Red sat back down and said, "Sorry to stop you like that, but I could tell your throat was getting a little dry."

"Just like you Red, to be thinking of others."

Red chuckled and said, "Well, my ears were getting a little dusty too." Red topped off their cups, took a sip and motioned for Nigel to continue as he said, "Go ahead. I'm all ears."

"Okay, Ross Perot."

Nigel told Red about the rapper Terrance "T-Daddy" Lundsford. He explained his thug and gang reputation. Red watched Nigel become irritable as he spoke of how the prosecution screwed up the DNA evidence, how they screwed up everything, which led to the dropping of charges and T-Daddy's release. Red leaned in to interrupt, "Take a sip, brother. It's okay. He can't hurt anybody anymore."

Nigel spoke of the unsolved murder of T-Daddy, how his weapon had been found at the murder scene, how he expected to be formally charged with the murder, how he was ready for that. But the Grand Jury changed everything, despite what many legal experts considered an adequate preponderance of evidence; they refused to hand down an indictment.

As Nigel told his story, he was a little surprised at how easy his friend was taking the news. It made him wonder, so he stopped to ask, "How much of this do you already know?"

"Plenty, I guess."

Nigel said nothing.

"I found it odd when that sexy little news girl came snooping around."

"Sherry Stone?" Nigel asked.

"Was there another?"

Nigel felt stupid.

"I saw how you two interacted, in a cloak of secrecy," said Red. "I figured there was more to the story. So, what can I say? I got nosey and Googled your name. I'm sorry. I probably shouldn't have done that."

Most would have gotten offended, considered it an invasion of privacy, but Nigel didn't care. A simple Google search of any person's name will reveal all their little details, if they're newsworthy. So, unless you have a double common name like Bob Smith or Jim Jones, you can forget any reasonable expectation of privacy. With a name such as Nigel Logan, it means you're a pretty unique commodity.

Red had gone through and studied everything available on Nigel. There wasn't much online except the murder investigation. He discovered a few Navy-related issues, but those were few and far between. He read every report and news clipping. He watched every broadcast video feed on YouTube. Based on what was out there, Red had become quite an expert on the Nigel Logan-Terrance Lundsford affair. What he didn't know was the whole truth, the exact details of what happened. The more he listened to Nigel, the more he was sure he didn't want to know.

"Are you mad at me?" asked Red.

"Naw. A bit relieved actually. It's tough having this stuff bottled up inside."

Red asked, "Have you told Candice?"

Nigel shook his head and said, "I need to. Before she finds out from someone else." Then he looked up at Red and asked, "Trixie?"

"No. She doesn't know anything."

"Good. For now anyway."

Then Red said, "The other night. What was that all about?"

Nigel did his best to recall the entire night. Many of the details remained foggy. The repeated blows to the head didn't help his memory. He could recall all the important details, including the strange roaring screams he heard right before he passed out. And later, his encounter with the creature, the creature Nigel believed intervened to save his life. Nigel said, "You're not going to believe this. Hell, I still don't believe it."

Nigel described the creature's size, its awful smell, and hot, moist breath as it stood before him. He described the strange and awkward feeling as they stood toe-to-toe studying one another. Then the eerie sensation when it disappeared without a sound. "I've tried many times to chalk it up as a hallucination, but I can't," said Nigel. "It was too real and I can still smell it today."

Red said nothing but the look on his face said, *I told you so.*

"So," Nigel said, "I have a little something for you. I bought one for each of us."

Nigel reached into a bag and pulled out two new matching T-shirts. They were black with white lettering. Nigel thought he saw

Red get a little misty-eyed when he said, "Really? This is great. I don't have a black one."

Red held his up so he could look at it. Beaming with pride he said, "Let's put 'em on!"

And they did.

Moments later Trixie came in to find them beaming with pride and hand pressing the front of their new shirts. She stopped in the middle of the room and said, "Nigel. You have to be kidding? You too?"

Nigel smiled and said, "What?", and looked down at his shirt. It had a white silhouette of a Yeti in the middle, the words **I Believe** underneath.

While Nigel and Red were sporting their new T-shirts, two young guys on four wheelers were ripping down the old logging roads of Tate's Hell, sliding and slinging mud to the heavens. Wide open was the only speed and they were both covered in mud; no less than an inch covered their bodies. They could barely see through their goggles, but there was no missing the big, purple Buick when they rolled up on it.

The guys sat on their vehicles looking at the car. It looked as if it had been there a few days. There were no tire tracks and the driver side door and the trunk were wide open. They looked at each other, shut down their four wheelers and took off their helmets.

While one of them was looking around the entire area, the other said, "Jimmy, that is one ugly car."

The one called Jimmy didn't say anything, but he got off his four wheeler to look around. The other guy followed. They peeked inside the car which was soaked; the trunk had standing water. They looked inside the trunk and noticed the bullet hole. The other guy reached in to touch it, but Jimmy smacked his hand away. "Don't touch that, you idiot." Jimmy stood tall and looked all around and said, "What the hell happened here?"

They started to search the area. Jimmy was walking along the side of the road when he came across the gun. *Shit.* He called out, "Hey, Bobby! Stop what you are doing and get over here."

Jimmy showed Bobby the gun in the grass. Jimmy said, "Keep looking, but don't touch anything."

They split up to search. Bobby found the tattered and torn clothing that was scattered about the car. There was nothing in plain view inside the car. It looked to be emptied out. Then he saw something in the road that caught his eye. He moved in for a better look and leaned over to get closer. He looked around and found another, then another. "Hey Jimmy! Come look at this."

Bobby looked at Jimmy as he approached and said pointing, "Tell me ... What do you think?"

Jimmy spent a minute looking and studying. Then he took his right foot and stepped inside.

"That's what I was thinking too," said Bobby, "footprints."

"Yeah ... But look at the damn size!" They looked at each other thinking the same thing. Then Jimmy said, "They seem to go in that direction. Let's see where they lead." They followed the tracks best they could. Some were near washed out, but they could see where they once had been. The trail led them up into the woods where the leaves and brush began to disguise which way the creature had gone. They continued to look for clues. After a few minutes, Bobby called out. When Jimmy ran up, Bobby was bent over throwing up. That's when Jimmy saw the shirt sleeve, torn at the shoulder with the swollen arm still inside, its yellow and purple fingers draped into the leaves at the cuff.

Jimmy didn't throw up, but he did say, "Come on. We've got to call the Sheriff."

Bobby didn't protest.

The area was roped off with yellow crime scene tape and there was a buzz of activity. Things were becoming more bizarre and grotesque. The Franklin County deputies were scouring the woods searching for additional evidence and had already produced the other hand and part of a lower right leg, the foot still attached. Sheriff Lamar Williamson was on scene and running the show. When the additional body parts were discovered, he called off further searching until the dogs could be brought in. The deputies wasted no time coming out of the woods and never offered a complaint.

Jimmy and Bobby were separated and provided statements to a couple of county detectives. Sheriff Williamson was in the middle of the road looking around and taking in the entire scene. In 29 plus years of law enforcement, never had he seen such a sight. "Eight.

Eight damn more months left to retirement and now this," he said to himself. "Why in hell did you have to come to Franklin County?"

The deputy searching the car called out, "Sheriff! ... Come here please. Let me show you something." The deputy was standing at the trunk and pointed. "Except for the spare and jack, it's really the only thing in there."

The sheriff leaned in to study it. On another subject he asked, "What about the lug wrench? Did you find that?"

"No, sir. Not yet."

"Well," Sheriff Williamson said, "keep looking. I'm guessing it's around here somewhere. But first, bring me an evidence bag."

The Sheriff reached in his back pocket and brought out a big pair of tweezers. He reached down towards the back corner of the trunk and squeezed the corner of a big wad of duct tape. He brought it up to the light and studied it. He noticed the strands of hair stuck in the tape's adhesive. He looked at the hairs and said, "Why, hello there. Now, who are you and what were you doing in the trunk?"

The sheriff placed the duct tape into the clear bag and told the deputy, "Tag this for the lab."

Epilogue

Candice escorted the last patrons to the door and told them to drive safe as they walked out onto the sidewalk. She locked the door behind them and watched through the window as they made it to their car. Then she pulled a chain and the flashing neon "Open" sign went dark. The Reid Avenue Bar and Bottle Shop was closed.

She stood at the door and turned to look at Nigel. It was just the two of them left. He was sitting at the end of the bar, deep in thought, staring at a neat stack of bar napkins. She saw the worry on his face. That's how he'd been all night, present but absent at the same time. She walked back over behind the bar and pulled him a pint of draft beer, a Coors Light with a squeeze of lime. She placed it in front of him and reached over and kissed him on the cheek. They smiled at each other. Hers was genuine. He tried to fake a smile, but it didn't work. She saw right through him and noticed his hands. He was holding something, rubbing it between his fingers.

She looked up at him and their eyes locked. They stared at each other in silence for a spell. Her sweet smile had little effect on whatever was troubling him. He looked deep into her eyes, searching for something. He watched the starburst of her eye color move in and out as her pupils opened and closed with the light. When he blinked, she dropped her eyes to his hands and asked, "What do you have there, baby?"

He answered with a question, "Do you love me, Candice? I mean, really love me."

She liked the question and grinned, a small puddle of tears worked into the corner of her eyes. She tried to play it off, tried to think of something sassy and fun to say. But she saw the serious look on his face, and the question began to worry her. She sniffled and wiped her eyes. Then she reached out and touched the side of his face with her fingertips and said, "With all my heart. Yes ... I do love you."

He said nothing, stood up, leaned across the bar and kissed her. Then he sat back down and changed the subject. He opened his palm and said, "Here ... I want to show you something."

Candice looked down and saw an old weathered brass plaque in his hand. She picked it up. The surface was polished and worn. It wasn't flat but curved for mounting on a like contour. There were holes on each end for the fasteners, and just readable on the surface was the word *Seventeen*, engraved in cursive lettering.

"I don't understand." She handed it back to him.

He frowned, unsure of himself and how things were about to go. He said, "It's a token. A small but significant token of my life. Some might call it a silly and meaningless artifact," he stopped to express a genuine smile and continued, "and in many ways I guess it is. But it means a lot to me."

"Nigel," Candice said, "you're starting to scare me. What does this have to do with us?"

Nigel held the plaque up in the air and asked, "This?" Then he placed it on the bar and slid it between them where it rocked back and forth on its curved side. "This has nothing to do with us. Not really. But the places it has been and the things it has been a part of, well ... that could be a different story. Those things could have a profound effect on us, you more so than me."

"What do you mean?"

"I'm at ease with the stories this little brass plaque might tell, if it could talk. You on the other hand..."

"Nigel," Candice demanded. "Dammit! What is this all about?"

Neither one of them knew they were being watched. It darted about the rafters in the form of a nervous Carolina Wren. Earlier in the day, during a beer delivery, it flew in through a propped opened door. Unable to manage an escape, it took refuge above and watched the proceedings of the day.

With the bar cleared of customers, the bird became more active. It never sat still for more than three or four seconds. Its exceptional flight skills allowed it to move undetected through the building, but it never let the two humans out of its sight for long. Scattered broken peanut shells and other bar food still littered the floor. The bird noticed the bounty and decided the rewards were well worth the risk.

It glided to the floor and began to feast on the crumbs as it hopped about the bar stool legs.

Nigel saw the bird swoop down to the floor in a singular motion. He tilted his head and watched the wren peck at crushed particles about the deck. Then he looked up and said, "Candice ... if you love me. If I'm going to allow you to love me, there are some things you need to know. Things that wouldn't be fair for me to hide from you."

Candice said nothing. She grabbed a stool that was behind the bar and sat opposite him as he began to tell his entire life story. He told her most everything. She enjoyed his tales about the Navy and his connection with the brass plaque and stool seventeen. As he began to speak of his retirement and departure from service, his deportment changed. She saw a sadness overcome him. Then, almost as quick, he smiled as he told the story of how he decided to make landfall in St. Joe Bay. They both smiled when he said, "I sailed into town and my life flipped upside down. I met you."

Nigel looked at the floor and saw the wren eating about his feet. Remaining cautious, the wren kept checking his surrounding and caught Nigel looking at him. Their eyes met and Nigel remained calm and still. When Nigel returned his attention to Candice, the wren went about eating again.

"You loved the Navy, didn't you?" asked Candice.

"I still do," replied Nigel. "I love almost everything about the Navy, especially the older days. It was my entire life. I'd still be in today had ...," he stopped himself.

He had come there to tell her everything, but he still hadn't gotten to the tough part. He knew he had to tell her. He just wasn't sure how he would do it, but he came prepared with options. He continued to talk of the Navy.

"The Navy has changed since I first joined. Its leadership has become soft and replete with political correctness. They have forced the chief's community into becoming what I call, 'the corporate CPO.' They have stripped the meaning out of *Tested, Selected, and Initiated.* Hell, they don't even have an initiation anymore. Now they *transition* them. What a bunch of shit. It won't be long before junior sailors have no idea what it means to work for a *real chief.* There will only be E-7s running around wearing anchors. It pisses me off."

He was upset. And she felt bad because she had nothing to offer. The things he spoke of meant nothing to her. With no naval background, she couldn't appreciate any of the things he was talking about. Yet, the one thing she knew was, if Nigel Logan was talking about it, she could believe every word. Candice let him talk.

"Luke ... Luke McKenzie. Now that guy is for real, an old school Navy Chief Petty Officer. I worked for many just like him when I was young."

Candice smiled and said, "Luke? My sweet Luke, really?"

"Yes, really." Nigel grinned and continued, "Luke is sweet to you because you're damn pretty. Don't let him fool you. Beneath the feigned sweet disposition of his is a crusty old chief. I can promise you, if one of his sailors made a serious mistake, he'd rip his head off and shit down his windpipe. Then, ten minutes later, he'd take the same young sailor under his wing and show him the error of his ways. He'd teach him good and, rest assured, the same mistake wouldn't repeat itself."

"Were you that kind of chief?" asked Candice.

"I'd like to think so. Lord knows, I served under some of the best and toughest chiefs the navy had to offer." Nigel paused and thought for a moment then said, "Those were the good old days. The *Navy Chief* is a dying breed. Now it's all about self-esteem, not hurting feelings, creating a positive work culture, and touchy-feely corporate bullshit like that. I'm sorry. The Navy is not a civilian work environment. It's a goddamn war machine. Somewhere along the way, top leadership forgot that simple fact. Makes me sick to think about it."

Nigel looked past Candice. The wren had landed on top of the bar just a few stools down. It hopped towards them where a mix of pretzels, peanuts and an assortment of crackers sat in a bowl. Candice turned to see what he was looking at. The wren took a couple hops back and they studied each other. Then it moved in closer. "Aren't you a brave little soul?" Candice said.

She turned back to Nigel and they were both smiling. "So is that why you left the Navy? Did you just get sick of the bullshit?"

His smile was gone now. Nigel looked at the bird which was now perched on the lip of the bowl. Nigel thought, *Brave. Sometimes he hated having to be brave.*

Neither of them said anything. There was an awkward silence and Nigel took a deep breath. He pulled a folded page of newspaper out from his back pocket and handed it to Candice. She opened it to the wrong side and looked at Nigel, "What is this?"

"Flip it over to the other side," he said.

She did and he pointed to the article. It was Sherry Stone's piece she had sent him. Candice read the title out loud, "Who really killed Terrance Lundsford?" She looked up confused and said, "Nigel, baby. What is this?"

"It's the truth about me. Read it."

He leaned over and they kissed. He said, "I'm going to the house. If you're still interested, that's where I'll be. If not, well ... I'll understand."

"Baby, you're scaring me. What's going on?"

"Just read it."

He pushed the stool back from the bar and stood up. The wren got startled and took flight. Nigel headed for the door. The wren again took refuge in the rafters. Nigel unlocked the door, cracked it open, and turned to see Candice watching him. He said, "Just remember. I do love you."

Before she could say anything, he flung the door open wide and left.

The door sat open for a suspended period of time before beginning to close. The wren saw its opportunity for escape and took flight. It slipped through the crack of the door right before it latched shut.

Candice was shaking. She looked down at the paper and began to read. It didn't take long before she was reading through tears, one hand over her gaping mouth as she cried.

###

Stay tuned! Nigel, Red, and the rest of the gang will be back as we conclude the series in the third and final volume of *Tales from Stool 17*.

Thank You!

Kirk Jockell would like to thank you for purchasing and reading Stool 17. A book means nothing without a reader. You have helped to make this work a whole and meaningful piece. He so hopes you liked it. If you did, please help him by spreading the word. Tell a friend. There is nothing better than word of mouth endorsements. They are the most meaningful. He would also appreciate it if you took the time to leave a review at your favorite online retailer. Those are so important too.

And he would love to hear from you. Tell him what you thought, about what you liked, what you didn't like. He's pretty thick skinned, and it will only make him a better, stronger writer. Connect with Kirk via one of the options below and say, Howdy!

Email: mail@kirkjockell.com
Facebook: www.facebook.com/Kirk.Jockell

www.kirkjockell.com

About the Author

Kirk Jockell loves a good story. Growing up with ADD--
nobody knew what it was way back then--his imagination ran
wild. Little stories constantly danced through his head. His
Mom would say, "He lives in his own little world." Over
fifty years later, he still does. The only exception is now he
puts his little world on paper. He wishes he had done so
sooner.

Kirk sleeps most nights in Flowery Branch, Georgia but
considers Port St. Joe, Florida home. He is a sailor, avid
photographer and a lover of small batch bourbon. He lives
with his wife Joy, Dixie, the smartest dumb dog in the
world, and a black cat named Stormy that pukes a lot.

Kirk Jockell's Other Work

Tales from Stool 17; Finding Port St. Joe

Made in the USA
Columbia, SC
07 August 2017